THE
NANNY

BOOKS BY RUTH HEALD

THE NANNY

RUTH HEALD

Bookouture

Published by Bookouture in 2022

An imprint of Storyfire Ltd.
Carmelite House
50 Victoria Embankment
London EC4Y 0DZ

www.bookouture.com

ISBN: 978-1-80314-509-9
eBook ISBN: 978-1-80314-508-2

THE BANGKOK OBSERVER

THE BANGKOK OBSERVER
5TH MAY 1999

BANGKOK'S KILLER NANNY?

The disappearance of a young baby has shocked the expat community in Bangkok. Julie and David McFarlane, who live in the Sukhumvit area, reported the baby missing yesterday morning. The police have arrested Hayley Taylor, who was employed as a nanny by the family. A child witness came forward and told police she saw Ms Taylor carrying the baby out of the McFarlanes' apartment. Julie McFarlane informed reporters about the nanny's neglectful behaviour and her late nights out drinking. She had been looking for her replacement before the tragedy happened.

Hayley Taylor, from London, England had been working for the McFarlanes for three months. She had no previous nannying experience. It is believed that she may have harmed the child and could face a life behind bars. There are concerns that the baby may no longer be alive.

The Bangkok Observer
10th June 1999

Case of Missing Baby Goes Cold

Julie and David McFarlane are still anxiously searching for their baby daughter, Chloe. The baby is just four months old and her devoted parents, a doctor and an engineer, are determined to find out what has happened to her.

It is now over a month since her disappearance and police believe it is most likely she is dead or has been moved out of the country, although they continue their investigations. The McFarlanes' nanny, Hayley Taylor, who was arrested early in the investigation, has now been released. It is believed that until a body is found, there is not enough evidence against her. The parents are understandably distraught and have once again appealed for more information.

PROLOGUE

Hayley stood at the bus station, the sun blazing down on her face, her back a pool of sweat. She was leaving, running away from everything that had happened in Bangkok. Her dad's old hiking rucksack was heavy on her back, stuffed full with everything she'd brought with her on what was supposed to be the trip of a lifetime: clothes, make-up, suntan lotion, a copy of the *Lonely Planet* guide, with destination after destination circled in pencil. She was going to one of those places now. Chiang Mai. But she felt nothing of the excitement she had when she'd first circled it in the guidebook.

Chloe's red blanket was at the bottom of the rucksack, protected by a plastic bag. Hayley couldn't stop thinking about her. She'd been to David and Julie's apartment block that morning and had stood outside looking up at it, her mind crowded with memories of her time there, tears streaming down her face, David's words echoing in her head, telling her to get out and never come back. They hated her and she understood why. She'd hate her if she was them. All she could do now was get away to Chiang Mai, find a job, a new life and try to escape this nightmare.

The bus pulled in and she pushed forward with the crowd to show her ticket and put her rucksack in the hold. Only a few days before she had been in a police cell and now she was free. Would they come for her again? Ask her more questions that she didn't know how to answer? They'd told her to stay in Thailand, just in case. She swallowed as she climbed onto the bus, waiting anxiously for the other passengers to get into their seats, so that it could move away.

She stared out of the dirty window at the small street stalls and the high-rise shopping malls, remembering how excited she'd been when she'd first arrived in Thailand. She thought of how much she'd loved the children she'd cared for, how much she'd loved Chloe. Tears slid down her face, blurring her vision, as the bus pulled out of the station and transported her away.

ONE

NOW

Hayley rushed out of her office at the university, saying a hurried goodbye to her colleagues in the student support team. The rain had started earlier than the weather forecast had predicted and she quickly zipped up her coat, put up her umbrella and then ran awkwardly in her heels to the bus stop, catching it just in time. As the bus trundled slowly through the Ealing traffic, Hayley could feel the clock ticking. She jumped off as soon as the doors opened at the stop for the school and raced to the entrance, dodging the puddles created by the downpour. A stream of parents passed her in the opposite direction, carrying their small children's rucksacks as they clutched their hands, exclaiming over artwork and chivvying them along. She smiled hello at the ones who glanced up, although she didn't know many names. She envied the mums who knew the names of all the children, and who seemed to have easily become friends, lingering after morning drop-off to chat. Sometimes she felt like an outsider, a part-time mum, always rushing to pick up Alice from the after-school club before it closed at 6 p.m. She tried to give a hundred per cent to her job and a hundred per cent to being a mother. But she ended up feeling she was failing at both, and completely exhausted.

She arrived at the door to the club, breathless. The group leader was waiting, with three children wrapped up in their coats behind him.

'I'm here for Alice,' she said, forcing a smile.

Alice frowned and walked slowly over. 'I was nearly the last, Mummy,' she said, accusingly. 'I thought you'd never come.'

'Well, I'm here now,' Hayley said, not intending to sound as brusque as she did. She softened her voice. 'How was school?'

'Fine,' Alice mumbled. She hurried ahead of Hayley, trying to catch up with one of her friends.

'Stay close to me, Alice,' Hayley called out after her. She jogged a little to catch up and reached for her daughter's hand. They were coming up to the main road, where the cars sped along without a thought for the school or the zebra crossing. A toddler on a scooter suddenly whizzed past them, his face scrunched in concentration as he raced towards the main road. Hayley glanced behind her and saw his mother a good way back, typing something into her phone. The boy was approaching the junction at speed and Hayley broke into a run, letting go of Alice's hand. She grabbed him just as the scooter reached the road, tucking her arms under his and pulling him back onto the pavement as the scooter clattered into the traffic. A car coming round the corner braked sharply, then swerved, honking his horn at them both.

Hayley shook as the boy screamed in her arms, lashing out and hitting her. An alternative scene flashed through her mind. The boy and his scooter under the wheel of a car, blood on the tarmac. That had been too close.

The boy's mother appeared beside her.

'What happened?' she said breathlessly. She reached out and took her son back.

Hayley glanced behind her to check Alice was still safe. 'He was about to scoot into the road,' she said. 'I got him just in time.'

'He knows when to stop,' the mother said, frowning. 'He would have stopped at the edge of the pavement. He's never gone into the road.'

Hayley tensed. 'It looked like he was going to go into the traffic.' She'd been so sure of what was going to happen. But could she have misjudged the situation? She'd always been a nervous parent, worried about the worst happening to Alice.

'You shouldn't have grabbed him,' the mother said, stony-faced, as she reached for the scooter in the road.

'I—'

'Come on, Mummy, let's go,' Alice interrupted, pulling at her arm.

'I was just trying to help,' Hayley said, taking Alice's hand as they walked away. 'Let's get home,' she said.

When they reached their house, Hayley put her key in the lock and shouted out 'Hello.'

'Hello,' a voice called back croakily. Hayley smiled. Although her mother still hadn't got over her cold, acknowledging her daughter at all meant that she was having a good day. A few months before, the doctor had diagnosed her with dementia. It had soon become clear that she hadn't been managing as well living on her own as Hayley had thought, and shortly after Hayley had moved her in with her.

Michelle, her mother's part-time carer, was in the kitchen, unpacking the shopping. They must have been to the supermarket together. Even though Hayley did the family shop online, there were still things her mother liked to buy herself. Mainly sweet things: Bourbons, Haribo, Flake bars. Her mother delighted in them all. After years of always eating healthily and often too busy on her shifts as a nurse to find time to eat, as an older adult she had developed a sweet tooth. Hayley had learnt to stop repeating her mother's own words about healthy eating back to her; she didn't want to begrudge her any pleasure as her health deteriorated.

When Hayley's husband Lars arrived home from work, Alice squealed and ran to him, wrapping her arms around him. They'd always been so close, and Hayley sometimes felt envious. She was the worrier, seeing risks and threats everywhere, whereas Lars was calm and relaxed. Hayley waited until Alice reluctantly detached herself from her dad, and then leant in to kiss him herself. He wrapped her in an embrace, his lips briefly brushing hers, before he bent to take off his shoes.

'How was your day?' she asked. 'Have you heard back about the new project?'

He shook his head, looking down at the carpet. 'No news,' he said glumly. For the last ten years the consultancy he'd set up had provided him with a very comfortable income. But three months ago he'd lost a major client, and for the last couple of months he'd barely brought enough in to cover his staff bill. Lars had reduced his own salary, not wanting to let any of his staff go. He thought things would pick up. 'We're going to have to cut back some more,' he said.

Hayley looked at Alice, listening intently beside her. 'Alice – go to the living room and play. Daddy will come in and see you in a minute.'

'I don't know where else we can save money,' Hayley said, once Alice had gone. They'd already cut their spending back. Hayley had left the gym she'd been a member of for the last five years, they'd stopped eating out at restaurants and they'd cancelled their annual family holiday to Spain. Their only spending now was food, household bills, and care for her mother and Alice.

Lars shook his head. 'Nor do I. We're on the edge, Hayley.

We really are. I mean, the only cost we could cut is Michelle. But we need her. Unless your brothers can help with your mother?'

Hayley shook her head. 'They do what they can, but they're struggling themselves and they live too far away to take her in. Mum would hate to move out of Ealing.'

'We might have to cut back on childcare then.'

'I don't see how we can do that,' Hayley said. 'If Alice isn't in after-school club then I can't work.'

Lars ran his hands through his hair. 'But if we don't cut down, we can't pay the mortgage.'

Hayley swallowed. 'Maybe we should get a lodger,' she said reluctantly. It was something that Lars had suggested before, but Hayley had always resisted. They'd had a lodger when they were first married and he'd kept himself to himself, but since they'd had Alice Hayley hadn't wanted a stranger sharing their house.

Lars kissed her on the forehead. 'Maybe,' he said. 'Unless we can come up with a better solution quickly, then we might have to.'

That night, it took Hayley a long time to drift off to sleep. She and Lars had moved up to the loft room when her mother had moved in, and she'd always felt a bit uncomfortable being on a different floor to Alice. Since Hayley had become a mother, anxiety had surrounded her like a fog. During her pregnancy she'd worried about what she ate and what it might do to the baby. When Alice was a toddler she'd worried about Alice choking, Alice falling off the climbing frame, Alice pushing forks into electric sockets. Her mind still whirred constantly with worries, even though Alice was older. She couldn't trust herself to look after a child without being in a constant state of high alert.

Outside, the rain had returned, lashing against the windows, and the wind whistled through the trees. Beside her Lars slept peacefully, undisturbed by the noise.

They needed another solution to their money troubles. The more she thought about it, the more it seemed like the only option was to get a lodger. She rolled over in bed, and watched Lars, his chest rising and falling. She closed her eyes and tried to let herself drift.

Out of nowhere, she heard a crash.

Hayley bolted up in the bed, her breathing quickening. *Alice!*

As she hurried to the door of the bedroom, her daughter's screams pierced the air.

'Alice!' Hayley shouted, her heart pounding as fear shot through her. She ran down the wooden stairs, her feet stomping noisily, wishing Lars would wake. Horrific scenarios flashed through her mind: a stranger in Alice's room attacking her; Alice kidnapped, nowhere to be found; Alice dead in bed from an unknown heart condition. She felt a sudden sense of inevitability, as if whatever horrible thing had happened was always supposed to happen, as if it was only what she deserved, as if this moment was the one she'd been holding her breath for, waiting for, ever since she'd become a mother.

She burst into Alice's room, heart pounding, her muscles tensed, ready to take on whatever greeted her.

She could see immediately that the bed was empty and for a second she thought Alice was gone.

But the screams were coming from the corner of the room, where Alice cowered in a ball. 'Mummy!' she cried out.

A figure stood over the bed, and Hayley swallowed her own scream.

She flicked on the light, adrenalin pumping through her veins, and stepped towards the bed, prepared to take on whoever had come for Alice.

Then she stopped in her tracks.

The figure by the bed screamed too.

It wasn't a stranger in her bedroom. It was her mother.

Hayley hesitated for a second, then ran to her daughter, crouched down on the floor and wrapped her arms around her. Alice's shaking eventually subsided, as Hayley kissed her over and over again, squeezing her tightly.

'It's OK,' Hayley said. She pointed to the bed, where her mother was now sitting facing away from them. 'Look, it's only Granny.' Behind her mother, Alice's bedside lamp had been swept onto the floor.

Lars appeared at the door and came over to them, kneeling on the floor and putting his arms round both of them.

'What happened?' he asked softly.

'It's Mum,' Hayley said softly. 'She came into the room and scared Alice.' She got up and walked round the bed to her mother, who was staring blankly into space, tears of confusion running down her cheeks.

'Mum?' Hayley said gently.

'Yes?'

'This isn't your room.'

'Oh, right, dear.'

Hayley took her hand and led her back to her room, watching as she got into bed.

'Night night, Mum,' she said, kissing her gently on the forehead.

Then Hayley went back into Alice's room and repeated the same routine. 'Night night, Alice. I love you.'

As she went back upstairs, she thought of their money problems, her mother, Alice. She'd do anything to keep her family safe and happy. But sometimes it felt impossible.

TWO

ONE WEEK LATER

Hayley took a sip of her coffee, holding it carefully in one hand as she continued to type up her notes from her last appointment. Being at work felt like respite from being at home, even though she'd been busy this morning with a steady stream of students. At home she was always looking after someone else, trying to navigate Alice's and her mother's needs.

Alice hadn't been sleeping well since her grandmother had come into her room in the middle of the night. Hayley would stay with her until she dropped off and then return several times in the night to calm her when she woke from her nightmares. She'd spoken to her mother about which room was hers, but she didn't seem aware that she'd done anything wrong. At the moment Hayley and Lars were just about coping with her at home, mainly because Michelle came four times during the week to make her lunch and take her out, and the occasional Saturday. On the weekday Michelle wasn't there, Lars would help Susan with lunch and periodically come down from his home office to check on her. They needed Michelle, but Hayley wasn't sure how much longer they'd be able to afford to pay her.

She looked in her calendar to see who she had for her next

appointment. Ryan Davies. She smiled. He was one of the student volunteers who worked as part of the student support team, helping other students to settle in, providing a listening ear for them. He was a sweet guy, in his early twenties, studying for a creative writing MA.

'Hi, Ryan,' Hayley said with a smile as he sat down. 'How's it going?'

'OK. A bit better. Not thinking of dropping out for the moment.' He smiled sheepishly. At their last meeting he was ready to quit. He'd told her that his writing wasn't up to scratch and that he was never going to get anywhere. They'd looked at his work together and Hayley had been impressed by how good it was. She'd persuaded him to stick with the course.

'I'm sure I'll see your name on a book cover in a shop one day,' Hayley said.

'Sooner rather than later, hopefully. I don't know if I can hack it as a chef much longer.' Ryan worked in a high street restaurant in the evenings and at weekends to fund his MA. 'Last night's shift was a total nightmare,' he continued. 'No staff, customers sending back food... I'm exhausted today.'

'That sounds stressful,' Hayley said gently. 'Now, what can I do for you today?'

Ryan smiled at her and ran his hands through his dark hair. 'You mentioned you'd be able to help me with my character study,' he said.

'Yes, of course, I'm happy to.' She'd agreed to help him last time they'd met. His class had all been asked to find an ordinary person they didn't know well to interview and he'd thought of her.

'Great,' he said. 'First I need to ask you general questions about your likes and dislikes, that kind of thing. Then a bit about your background, what drives you, all of that.'

'Sure,' Hayley said, beginning to relax.

·   ·   ·

When Ryan had finished his questions, he went back through his pages of notes. 'That's great,' he said. 'I think I have more than enough.'

'I'm glad I could help,' Hayley said. 'And I'm pleased you're enjoying your course a bit more.'

'Yeah, me too. It's just my living situation and money I've got to sort out now.' He ran his hand through his hair nervously and pulled out a scrap of paper from his bag. Hayley recognised it. It was from one of the 'lodger wanted' adverts she'd pinned up all over the university. She'd left her name, number and email address on pull-off slips. 'I saw your ad,' he said. 'I could really do with moving out of my place. I wondered if I could view the room?'

'I already have someone viewing tonight, and she sounds keen,' Hayley said. She'd been worried that she wouldn't get that many replies to her advert in the middle of the academic year, so she'd put it on all the local Facebook groups, as well as in physical locations around the university. A few people had contacted her with questions, but only one had wanted a viewing: Johanna, an international student who'd seen the ad online.

'Well, let me know if that doesn't work out,' Ryan said, smiling tensely at her, his eyes hidden by his overgrown fringe.

Hayley nodded. Ryan would make a great lodger. She'd seen how he behaved with the students he supported. He was kind and conscientious, and very trustworthy. But it didn't seem appropriate to have one of the students she worked with as her lodger.

'I'm sure there are other rooms available in Ealing, if you want to move out,' Hayley said.

'No, it's OK,' Ryan said. 'I'll stick with what I know. My housemates are noisy but I can cope. Better them than moving in with someone I don't know at all.'

Hayley shivered, thinking about how she was going to let a stranger move into her home.

She looked at her watch; her next student would be in in a minute. If they finished up now, she'd have enough time to make herself a cup of coffee before they came in. 'Well,' she said. 'Time's up for today, but if you need anything else, you know you can come back anytime.'

Five minutes later, she was in the kitchen in the open-plan office, waiting for the kettle to boil. Her colleague Kim walked past and grabbed a glass from the cupboard.

'Who was that in your office?' she asked.

'One of the student volunteers,' Hayley replied. 'Why?'

'That's the second time I've seen him with you,' she said. 'He's good-looking, isn't he?'

Hayley shrugged. 'I hadn't noticed.'

'You hadn't noticed? Seriously, are you blind?'

'Kim!'

'I think he's interested in you. He's just asked me what your favourite flowers are.'

'Really?' Hayley frowned. That was odd. She'd never got the impression he was interested in her. But maybe she needed to tread carefully. She didn't want him to get the wrong idea.

That evening, Hayley pushed the Hoover haphazardly round the hallway. Johanna was due to come and see the room any minute, and she'd been frantically tidying and cleaning since she got home. The lodger's room was ready, completely clear of clutter. The other day, she'd fitted a new bolt on the door, just in case her mother wandered in the night again.

She hoped Johanna turned out to be nice and wanted to take the room. Hayley didn't know much about her. She thought for a moment of Ryan, a known entity. Johanna's Facebook profile picture was a cat, which didn't tell Hayley much but had immediately endeared her to her. She was studying in central London and wanted to live a bit out of town where she could get more room for her money.

At 8 p.m. the doorbell rang and Hayley switched the Hoover off and pushed it out of the way, looking at her watch. Johanna was exactly on time, to the minute.

She moved a stray umbrella out of the hallway, put on a smile and opened the door.

The woman was standing a bit back from the path, in the dark, neither the light from the house nor the street lamp reaching her. She was a shadow in a black coat, her head tilted upwards, staring at the house. Hayley felt a prickle of concern. There was something odd about this woman who hadn't acknowledged the open door.

'Hello?' she said, peering out into the night. 'Are you Johanna?'

'Yes,' the woman replied. 'I'm Johanna,' Her accent was Scandinavian, so similar to Lars'.

She stepped into the light of the porch and Hayley's heart leapt in her throat. Johanna was tall and angular with neat dark hair in a bob. Her gaze was intense, and her expression serious. Hayley looked into Johanna's piercing blue eyes, set a little far apart. She saw her roman nose, the collection of freckles spotting her cheeks, her high cheekbones and wide forehead. Her features were strikingly familiar. Hayley reached out to the wall to steady herself. There had been moments in the past when she'd seen women like her and she'd been convinced she recognised them. She'd always been wrong.

Johanna was reaching out her hand to shake Hayley's. It couldn't be. She was imagining things. Again.

Hayley had to stop herself from taking a step back. But then she composed herself. 'Hayley,' she said, with a forced smile, her heart thudding in her chest. 'Welcome to our home.'

THREE

BANGKOK, THAILAND, 1999

Hayley sat in the back of the taxi, squeezed between her friends Sunita and Lyndsey, her back sticky with sweat, breathing in the traffic fumes through the open window. She'd been in Bangkok two weeks and was loving every moment. The 'land of smiles' was fulfilling all its promises and everywhere they went there was something going on, from the stalls selling pirated CDs, to the vendors making fried noodles on the street, to the crowds streaming into the huge shiny shopping malls in the upmarket part of town. Cars, tuk-tuks, motorbikes and people were all crammed in together in the heat of the city.

Today, they were touring some local temples on a trip Sunita had negotiated with a local taxi driver. Sunita and Lyndsey had already been travelling round Asia for three months while Hayley had been at home working in the fish and chip shop to save up, so her friends were showing her the sights. The driver was taking them to the less popular temples, and Hayley loved the relative quiet, the squares full of pigeons that scattered when they walked through and empty stone steps that led to the entrances. Inside, away from the glare of the sun, it was cooler and the huge gold Buddhas watched them from their platforms.

The third temple was right next to the river, and Hayley decided not to go in, choosing to explore the riverside instead.

'I'll sit this one out,' she said to her friends, watching as they climbed the temple steps in their bright sarongs. She wandered along the side of the building until she reached the river, grateful for the breeze through the hot air. There was some shade at the river taxi stop and a trader selling water. She went onto the platform and basked in the coolness for a moment, watching as the water taxi arrived and people poured off with huge bags of shopping. Hayley reached for the camera strung round her neck and took a photo, lining up her shot carefully, not wanting to waste the film.

Once the crowd had left, she sat down on a small bench and took out her *Lonely Planet* guide, reading about all the places she wanted to visit. Her friends were talking about travelling on to Australia, but there was no way her budget would stretch to that. She was getting through her funds quicker than she'd anticipated, but if she ran out of money she could always find some part-time work here, cleaning hostels or teaching English.

She needed to know how much money she had left. She had all her cash with her; it wasn't safe to leave it at the hostel. The money reserved for the flight home was strapped to her body in her money belt and her spending money was in her small back-pack. It was better to count it now when no one was about, rather than under the prying eyes of some of the others in the dorm.

She glanced round again and then took her purse out of her backpack and counted the money, note by note. Aside from the flight money, she had £150. If she budgeted £30 a week then it would last her five weeks. Then she'd need to get a job, or fly home.

She put her money back carefully, and then went back to the taxi to wait for the others. They were already there, fanning themselves with their hands in the heat.

'Where have you been?' Lyndsey chided. 'I was thinking we could have a break soon, find somewhere to grab a drink. I'm so thirsty.'

On the Khao San Road in the centre of the backpacker district, the three of them mingled with locals and tourists as they wove through the stalls, heading towards their hostel. They stopped for a drink at one of the makeshift bars, sitting on tiny stools. Lyndsey and Sunita drank alcohol from a bucket, while Hayley sipped her mineral water, watching tourists approach the stall selling fried insects opposite.

After their drink, they went to their hostel and lay back on their bunk beds, letting the air from the fan circulate around them.

'What shall we do for dinner?' Sunita said.

'Curry?' Lyndsey said. 'Back at one of the street food places?'

Sunita was rifling around in her handbag. 'Guys, have you seen my purse?'

'What?'

She looked panicked now. 'It's not here. I have £300 in it. It's gone.'

'Look properly, you must have misplaced it,' Lyndsey said casually.

Sunita kept looking. 'It's not here.'

'Not in a pocket? Or did you put it on your bunk when you got in?'

Hayley felt a sinking feeling. She reached into her own day rucksack.

She felt around into all its nooks and crannies and then emptied out every pocket.

Her purse was gone too.

FOUR

NOW

Hayley took Johanna's outstretched hand and shook it. There was a pause as the two women stared at each other. Hayley was taking in all of Johanna's features, trying to work out if she was mistaken, or if she really had recognised Johanna after all these years. When Hayley came back to the present, she knew the handshake had been longer than usual, that it had been awkward.

'Nice to meet you,' she said into the silence, tripping over her words. She couldn't think of anything to say. 'Johanna's a lovely name.' It was the first thing that came into her head.

Johanna blinked.

'Do you want to come in?' Hayley said quickly. 'Oh, of course you do. You're here to see the room.'

'Yes, please.'

Hayley took her through the hallway, trying to get her head straight, to focus on the house, the room, on showing Johanna round. She couldn't be who Hayley had thought she was. After so long, it seemed impossible. Johanna was a stranger, a student. Hayley had to stop her brain whirring and concentrate. After all, apart from Ryan, Johanna had been the only person interested in the room, and she needed to impress her.

'So there's four of us living here,' Hayley rambled. 'I think I said that in the ad. There's me, obviously.' She laughed nervously. 'And my husband Lars, he's from Sweden too.' She blushed. 'Is that where you're from?'

'Yeah, how did you know?'

'Oh, I recognised the accent. From Lars and his family. And I've been there a few times as a tourist.'

'Oh, have you? It's not usually on the tourist map.'

'No, but I love the peace there. And Lars' family gives me the excuse to visit.' Hayley reddened. 'So, there's me, Lars, our daughter Alice, who's five, and my mother, Susan. She'll be in the room next to you. That is, if you take it. She...'

They were at the top of the stairs now, and there was her mother, opening the door to her room and staring blankly at them.

'Hello, Mum,' Hayley said, wondering if she should have kept her out of the way. But she couldn't do that to her, and besides, whoever lived here needed to know about her mother before they moved in.

'Hello,' her mother said absent-mindedly.

'This is Johanna, I'm showing her the room.'

'Hello, Susan, it's lovely to meet you,' Johanna said, and Hayley was impressed by her manners.

Her mother reached out and clutched both Johanna's hands. 'Hello, my child,' she said.

Johanna smiled back at her.

'Well, here's the room,' Hayley said, opening the door. Suddenly she saw it with fresh eyes: the slight scuffs on the wall, the old-fashioned curtains that she'd moved from the main bedroom when she'd updated it, a cobweb in the top corner by the window that she'd somehow missed. 'It's lovely and bright when the sun shines,' she added cheerfully, trying to sell the room to Johanna. 'And it's got a view of the garden.' She indicated out the window, drawing back the curtain a bit to expose the dark sky.

Johanna put her hand on the windowsill and peered out. Then she glanced round the room. Hayley held her breath. She was staring at Johanna, mapping her face. When she looked at her head-on her features aligned and Hayley was certain for a second that she'd been right, she'd recognised her. But from the side, her profile looked all wrong. She just couldn't be sure. She'd made this mistake so many times before, convinced that a stranger was *her*.

'So what do you think about the room?' she asked cautiously.

'It's lovely,' Johanna said. 'So spacious. And great to have the desk too, so I can work.'

'You're at University College London, aren't you?' Hayley said.

'Yes,' Johanna said. 'How did you know?'

'Just Facebook.' It had been the only piece of information about her that had been available on her public profile.

'Oh, of course. I forgot I put it on there. I'm studying for a master's in biochemistry.'

'Wow.' Hayley didn't know what to say to that.

'This is perfect,' Johanna said, running her fingers over the wooden desktop. 'So much nicer than my current place.'

'Your current place?'

'Yeah, I found somewhere quickly when I first arrived. But the others are hard to live with. Messy, noisy. Typical students, maybe. But I like things a bit quieter. That's why I want to move out.'

Hayley nodded. 'Well, I'm sure you'll love it here. We keep everything clean and tidy. Although it isn't always completely quiet.' She swallowed, worried she might put Johanna off. 'My mother, who you just met, she has dementia. She sometimes gets confused.'

'Oh, I don't mind that,' Johanna said. 'I miss my own family back in Sweden. It will be nice to feel part of one here.'

'Hello?' Lars knocked on the door. 'How's it going?'

'Good, thank you,' Johanna said. 'Your wife told me that you're from Sweden too?'

'Yes, that's right. Whereabouts are you from?'

'Stockholm.'

'Me too.'

They both grinned, and Hayley let their conversation about the relative merits of Stockholm versus London wash over her as she thought about the reality of letting out the spare room. There'd be another person in her house, in her kitchen, in her space. Another person interacting with Alice and her mother. Johanna had said she wanted to feel part of the family. Her family. Hayley knew she was lucky that Johanna felt like that, but at the same time, it made her feel nervous.

They all went downstairs and sat in the living room together. Lars asked Johanna about the degree she was studying for and about her life in Sweden. Hayley listened intently, but Johanna didn't give much away about her family. No mention of her parents or any brothers or sisters.

'It's £600 a month, isn't it?' she asked, when Lars had finally finished his questioning. He had a broad smile on his face.

'Yeah, that's right. Including bills.'

'I'll take it,' Johanna said. She smiled, nervously. 'If it's still available, that is.'

'Of course it is!' Lars said. 'We'd be delighted to have you living with us.' Hayley shot him a frown. They'd agreed to discuss it first before they accepted anyone. But there had been nothing wrong with Johanna. In fact, she'd been lovely, an ideal lodger. She was polite and a non-smoker. She'd even said she wanted to help out with the cooking and could help with child-care if they needed her. There was nothing not to like.

'Oh, great,' Johanna said, glancing over at Hayley. Hayley smiled back at her. She really had to get this idea that she recognised her out of her head and see Johanna for who she was: a stranger who wanted to rent their spare room.

'Brilliant. Well, I can send you the contract paperwork tonight and get that sorted,' Lars said.

When they shut the door behind Johanna, Lars turned to Hayley and beamed at her. 'That worked out well!'

Hayley nodded. 'I suppose it did.'

He looked at her. 'Are you still worried about a stranger sleeping so close to Alice?'

'A little.'

Lars squeezed her arm. 'You're right to worry, but I'll run all the appropriate checks on her. Speak to the university and get a reference from there. But I really think we can trust her.'

'You're probably right,' Hayley said. 'I just...'

'What is it?' Lars' forehead wrinkled with concern.

She sighed, then confessed what she'd thought. 'I just thought I recognised her, that's all. When she first came in.'

'Oh. From where?'

Hayley couldn't tell him the truth. 'I'm not sure.'

Lars frowned. 'We're both from Stockholm, but I don't think I've met her before. We're not connected through me.'

'I'm probably imagining it.'

'Probably.' He put his arm round her shoulder. 'Remember what you were like when your stepdad died?'

Hayley nodded. In the months after he'd died she'd been so sure she'd spotted him in the supermarket, in the park, walking down the street. The realisation that it wasn't him had jolted her back into grief each time.

'Johanna can move in next week,' Lars said. 'Thank good-ness. Without her rent we'd be in real financial trouble.' He squeezed her shoulders. 'Thanks so much for finding someone so quickly. You've fixed everything. Just like you always do.'

Hayley nodded, but her stomach clenched with anxiety. This had all seemed such a good idea. But now the thought of Johanna living with her, in her home, filled her with nerves. She just hoped her feelings were misplaced.

FIVE

1999

Hayley's taxi pulled up in front of the concrete apartment block on Sukhumvit Road, narrowly missing a motorbike taxi that had chosen that moment to undertake. She was clutching the job advert from *The Bangkok Observer* which she'd torn out of the newspaper:

NANNY REQUIRED, FEMALE, 18–25, MUST BE NATIVE
ENGLISH SPEAKER

British expat family looking for a caring and enthusiastic live-in au pair/nanny. Duties include looking after children aged 4 and 5 and occasional help with baby. Accommodation and meals provided. Driver available. Salary £150 per week (8,000 Thai Baht). Contact Julie and David McFarlane

This job was her only hope. Otherwise she'd be packing her bag and getting on the plane home. Since her purse had been stolen, she'd been having to borrow money from her friends. Sunita had been lucky; her parents had bailed her out, transferring the extra funds to her bank account. But Hayley hadn't asked her family for help. She knew they couldn't afford it.

She'd looked for other work, enquiring about cleaning or cooking at the hostel and asking about teaching English at the language school, but there'd been no vacancies. The closest she'd come to finding work was when another backpacker had offered her the opportunity to become part of his 'international delivery business'. She'd turned it down as soon as she'd realised he was offering her work as a drugs mule.

When she'd seen the ad for a nanny she'd thought it was worth a shot, even though she didn't have much experience of looking after children, beyond helping her mother with her three younger brothers. She'd rung the number on the ad yesterday and had got on well with the mother. Even so, she'd been surprised to be invited to an interview at the family's apartment today.

Hayley got out of the taxi nervously, smoothing down the only smart skirt she'd brought with her. She'd paired it with a flowery top she'd bought from the market and white sandals, and put on silver earrings, but despite her efforts, when she'd looked in the mirror that morning, she'd still seen a backpacker, not a nanny. As she went into the building, a security guard opened the door and a blast of air-conditioning hit her. At the reception desk she said she was here to see Mr and Mrs McFarlane at Flat 37 and the receptionist rang them.

'They're coming down,' she said.

They were there within a few minutes, and Hayley was comforted by the familiarity of their English accents.

'Hello, I'm David,' the man said, holding out his hand and smiling at her warmly. He was older than the woman, in his early forties, and his blue eyes sparkled. He was wearing branded gym gear, and she could see he was in good shape. 'Nice to meet you.'

'Hayley,' she said, shaking his hand.

'I'm Dr Julie McFarlane,' the woman said. She was small and petite, but heavily pregnant. Her eyes had huge bags underneath them. Hayley thought she must be in her early thirties. 'I work at the hospital in expat relations.'

'And I'm an engineer,' David said. 'So you've come about the nanny position?'

'Yes.'

'Where's your accent from? Is it London somewhere?' Julie asked quickly.

'Ealing, it's part of greater London.'

'Good. We want someone British. Who speaks proper English.'

'Sure,' she said. 'Well, I've lived there all my life.'

'Excellent,' Julie said. 'I moved to Thailand five years ago. With my husband at the time. But then we split up and I met David.' She smiled at her husband and leant over to kiss him. 'It was love at first sight. We've never looked back.'

David smiled at her adoringly.

'When are you due?' Hayley asked Julie.

'I'm having the baby in two weeks' time.' She stroked her bump affectionately. 'I've booked a caesarean. And then after that I'll be on maternity leave for ten weeks.'

'OK,' Hayley said. 'The advert mentioned you have two other children.'

'Yes, we do. Well, at the moment. They're leaving us soon. And they're not mine. They're David's. Your main role will be with them, picking them up from school, looking after them, serving their dinner.'

'OK, great, I can do that,' Hayley said brightly. It sounded manageable.

'The role is short-term, while the kids are with us. You

understand that, don't you?' Julie was looking her up and down, taking in her clothes, and Hayley knew that she was thinking she was just a tourist, that she probably wouldn't want to stick around for long.

'Of course,' Hayley said. 'And it's live-in, isn't it?' If she had to spend all her wages on hostels then there wouldn't be much point taking the job.

'Yes, it is,' Julie said. She turned towards her suddenly. 'Do you like babies?'

'Yeah, I do. I have three brothers. All a lot younger than me. I helped my mother with them when they were babies.' She'd been nine when her mother had remarried and Freddie had been born. She'd felt so important when she'd helped change his nappies and give him baths. Then Kieran and Christopher had come along and the novelty had worn off a bit.

'Oh, that's good,' Julie said. 'Three is good. There will be three little ones here. Although, of course, I'll be with the baby. We just need you to look after Emily and Eva, until their mother takes them back to England.'

'When's that?' Hayley asked.

'We don't know at the moment. But at least a month, I expect. She's not ready yet. She's been unwell. I'll take you up to the apartment to meet the children in a minute. But first, we wanted to show you the facilities here. If you got the job, you'd have use of them all, of course.' She clasped David's hand and they led Hayley through the lobby area to the lift, which they took to the top floor of the building.

When they stepped out, back into the searing heat, Hayley drank in the view. She could see for miles, although a few nearby buildings towered above, looking down on them. The swimming pool at the top of the apartment block shimmered in the sunlight and the water looked cool and inviting. A lone towel hung on the back of a sunlounger, but otherwise it was deserted. A tiny bird flew down and drank from the pool.

'This pool is open until late,' David said. 'And there's a terrace where you can have drinks. Sometimes we host parties here.'

Hayley smiled. This was the kind of life she should be living. Drinking cocktails and expensive wine at parties with rooftop pools, not downing buckets of spirits on Khao San Road.

'There's a sauna too,' Julie said, opening a door to the inside. 'And a gym.' She showed Hayley the running and cycling machines, and the cross trainer. 'And there's a squash court through here, and two tennis courts outside. You'd be welcome to use all of it on your days off.'

'It's amazing,' Hayley said.

David smiled. 'This is the standard of living you can expect round here. I'm so glad I moved here.'

'Now, let me take you down to show you the apartment and meet the children,' Julie said.

'I'll bow out here,' David said. 'I need to go to the gym.'

Hayley and Julie went down in the lift together, Julie quizzing Hayley about her childhood and education. When they reached the flat, Julie opened the door and Hayley took in the huge living room, covered in massive rugs, and sparse furniture that only made it seem bigger. The walls were lined with bookshelves, but the books looked unread, their spines smooth. This room alone was four times the size of her dorm at the hostel, and that slept twelve. The huge windows looked out on a breathtaking view of Bangkok.

Two young children were sitting on the floor, staring at a television screen.

'This is Emily,' Julie said. 'And Eva. Girls, please say hello.' Around them everything was tidy. There wasn't a single toy on display.

The children just grunted.

'I'm sorry, they're not so talkative. Sometimes I think they're not very keen on me. They prefer their real mum.'

Hayley heard the sadness in her voice and saw her fingers resting on the top of her bump, as if trying to protect the baby inside.

A Thai woman bustled in and handed each girl a glass of milk. 'That's the maid,' Julie said. 'Mae. She looks after us.'

She didn't introduce them and Mae left again, filling a bucket and taking a mop onto the balcony.

'Let me show you the baby's room,' Julie said quickly. She took Hayley to a room at the end of the corridor, decorated in a pale pink. There was a chest of drawers of baby clothes and nappies, which Julie proudly showed off. Hayley was sure there were more clothes than one baby could ever wear. In the centre of the room was a cot with an animal mobile. A stuffed elephant sat on a rocking chair.

'I think she'll be happy here,' Julie said.

'Of course she will. It's beautiful.'

Julie put her hand to her stomach. 'She's kicking at the moment. She likes the sound of your voice. She's excited.'

Julie led her out of the room and to the back of the apartment.

'These are the rooms where you'll be saying. She briefly opened the door to a dark room, but Hayley couldn't see inside.

'Rooms?' Hayley said faintly, thinking of the dorm she was sharing. Her own private space sounded amazing.

'It's a bedroom and a shower room. You'll share the kitchen with us. I think you'll be comfortable here.'

Hayley shifted from one foot to the other, imagining the freedom of a guaranteed roof over her head, a place to come back to. A place to call home.

'It's lovely,' she said to Julie. 'Your whole flat is perfect.'

'Thank you,' Julie replied, with a smile. 'So when can you start?'

SIX

NOW

Hayley watched Alice as she concentrated on her colouring, carefully selecting a red pencil and then focusing on staying between the lines of the fire engine. Her long hair was tied neatly in a ponytail, fastened with a pink bow that she had insisted on. Beside her, she had lined up her family of toy squirrels. She'd brought them down from her bedroom, where she kept her collection of Sylvanian families on her dressing table. She had three sets: squirrels, pandas and rabbits. Each family was a self-contained unit with a mother, father and one or two children.

'You know that our lodger is moving in tomorrow?' Hayley said to Alice. She'd spoken to her about Johanna a lot, trying to prepare her for having someone else living in her home. Hayley still felt uncomfortable about it, the ball of dread in her stomach growing with each passing day, even after Lars had checked Johanna's references. She'd tried to find out more about her, but all Johanna's social media profiles were private. She couldn't find any information at all.

'Yeah, Mum. You already told me,' Alice said impatiently, sounding more like a teenager than a five-year-old.

'OK,' Hayley said, kissing the top of her head. She needed to give Johanna's room a quick dust and then she'd take Alice to the park, make the most of the sunny weather. Alice had been stuck indoors all day while Hayley had been cleaning and tidying.

The doorbell rang and she went to answer it. It was probably the new lamp she'd ordered from Amazon for Johanna's room. Alice ran past her and opened it first, still holding her red colouring pencil.

Alice stared up at the man there without speaking. Hayley stepped round her and saw it was Ryan.

She smiled, pleasantly surprised to see him. 'Hi. What are you doing here?' He hadn't been to her house before, but they'd talked about where she lived in her character interview the other day, and she'd mentioned that one day she wanted to have all the student volunteers round for drinks to say thank you for the work they'd done.

'I was just in the area,' he said. 'I hope you don't mind me knocking. I was walking by, and I thought I'd just double-check whether or not you'd rented your room out? Things haven't got any better with my housemates.'

Hayley felt a flash of regret. 'I've found a lodger already, I'm afraid. She's moving in tomorrow.' It was such a shame it couldn't be him, but she was certain the university rules wouldn't allow it.

'Ah, no worries,' he said, sweeping his long fringe out of his eyes. 'I thought it was worth asking. Just in case. The pictures in the ad looked lovely.'

'Of course,' she said. 'I'm sorry I can't be more help. But I'm sure you'll find something.'

'I'm sure I will,' he said. 'And I had some other questions to ask you. Following up on the character study.'

'Oh,' she said, surprised he had come to her house for this. 'Now's not a good time, I'm afraid. I'm just finishing getting everything ready for the new lodger. And once I'm done with that, I said I'd take this one to the playground.' She smiled as she stroked her daughter's hair.

'The one at the end of the next road?'

'Yeah. Over the bridge.'

'Ah. I know it well. My niece lives nearby. I take her there sometimes.'

Hayley nodded. She hadn't realised he had a niece.

'I can talk to you another time then,' he said. 'Important for you to spend quality time with your daughter, while it's sunny.' Hayley felt a flash of guilt about Alice's morning cooped up inside the house.

She nodded. 'You can pop into my office anytime to talk about character.'

'Thanks. I'm really enjoying this part of the course. We've just started studying non-fiction. We're looking at how to create stories out of real-life experiences.'

'Oh?'

'And that's what I wanted to talk to you about. As part of the character study, I did a bit of research. And I think... well, I'm hoping you can help me with this next module.'

Hayley blushed. 'What do you mean?'

Ryan frowned. 'It's a bit sensitive. I wanted to discuss it. I have a brilliant idea for a book and I want to know what you think.'

'An idea? Well, that's great! I know how long you've been trying to come up with something.'

'It came from my research into you, actually.'

'Did it?' Hayley glanced back into the house. She really needed to get Alice to the playground before the weather turned. 'What sparked it off?'

'Well, we were encouraged to find out everything we could about our subjects. I found your marriage record online, saw your maiden name. When I looked you up under that name, I saw that the marriage wasn't the first time you'd changed your name. You'd changed it before, when you were twenty.'

'I changed it to my stepdad's name,' Hayley said quickly. 'He brought me up.'

Ryan nodded thoughtfully. 'That makes sense. Anyway, I googled your original name, Hayley Taylor...'

Hayley's blood ran cold. She felt Alice's small hands pulling at her arm, wanting her to play with her. 'Go and watch TV,' she said to her.

Alice looked up at her, her eyes wide with surprise. Hayley had been telling her not to turn the TV on the whole morning. 'Go on then,' Hayley said, giving her a little push. 'Before I change my mind.'

She turned back to Ryan. 'I'm sure there are lots of Hayley Taylors.'

'There are a lot. But not so many exactly the same age as you. Did you live in Bangkok when you were younger?'

Hayley stared at him. She couldn't speak.

'*The Bangkok Observer* has digitised all their old papers now. And your name came up. I'm sure it was you. There was even a photo. You look the same, you haven't aged a bit.' He smiled at her.

She wanted to say that he must be getting her confused with someone else. Someone with the same name that had a similar appearance. But when she looked at him, she could see that she wouldn't get away with that. She knew exactly what the article had said. She could remember it word for word. *Bangkok's Killer Nanny.*

'OK,' she said, braced for his next words.

'Chloe's story was so tragic,' he said. 'I bet you always wondered where she went.'

Hayley didn't know what to say, or how to react. 'The police never solved the case,' she said.

'Exactly,' Ryan said, unable to hide his excitement. 'It's a complete mystery. It's the perfect subject for a true-crime book, or a podcast. It has all the right ingredients. So many unanswered questions. And I really don't think the Thai police did a good job of solving it. The trail went cold.'

'No one knows what happened to her.' Hayley thought of Lars upstairs. She couldn't risk him overhearing their conversation.

'All this time I've been wondering what to write,' Ryan said, 'having false start after false start. But they say write what you'd want to read yourself. This could be my book. I could investigate the case and write about it. With your help I can get the inside story. I think that together we can find out what really happened to Chloe McFarlane.'

SEVEN

1999

A waitress held out a tray of canapés towards Hayley and she took a selection, holding them carefully in a napkin in one hand, her other hand clutching her glass of champagne. The evening breeze ruffled her shawl as she looked out over the sparkling lights of the Bangkok skyline.

'We're on top of the world,' a voice said beside her, and she smiled at the woman who'd appeared.

'I love it here,' Hayley said. It seemed a world away from the heat and noise of Khao San Road. She thought of her friends back there. She had said she'd go back and meet them for a drink, but she hadn't had time, and on the one occasion she'd managed to work out how to ring their hostel, they'd already gone out for the day. She'd left them the phone number of the McFarlanes' apartment to call her back, but they hadn't yet.

She was enjoying her job. The children were at a local English-speaking school most of the day and her job was to get them up, make their breakfast and go with the driver to take them to and from school. After she'd collected the girls, she'd play with them and read to them. Mae made their dinner and kept the place tidy. Compared to the chaos at home in England with her three younger brothers, it was easy.

She heard the sound of a child's wail and reached for the baby monitor, which was perched on a glass table, surrounded by cocktails.

'Excuse me,' she said to the man beside her. 'I have to go down and check they're all right.'

'You're very attentive, aren't you?' he said.

'Well, you have to be. They're only little.'

'I'm sure they'll get back to sleep.'

'Maybe,' she said, as she went towards the lift, taking her canapés and champagne with her.

She hadn't been sure about leaving the children with only the baby monitor, but David and Julie insisted that she enjoy the party with them. Mae would be in and out of the flat preparing food and bringing it up, so the children wouldn't be alone. And besides, they were in a secure apartment block.

The cries on the baby monitor got louder and Hayley wondered why the maid wasn't going to the children's aid now. She was probably too busy.

When Hayley got to the apartment the door was propped open, and the flat was hot. Mae was cooking, and had wanted to let some air in. In the children's room, Emily was sitting up in bed, crying.

'What's wrong?' asked Hayley, stroking her hair. 'Did you have a bad dream?'

She nodded tearfully, wiping her eyes, and Hayley put her arms around her. 'Yeah, about my mummy.'

'Your mummy's upstairs with her friends.'

'Not that mummy. My real mummy.' Of course. She meant the mother who was supposed to be taking them back to England soon, who Hayley hadn't met.

'What happened in your dream?'

'She was hurt and I couldn't help her.'

Hayley kissed the top of her head. 'Don't worry about that.' She remembered Julie telling her that the girls' mother had been unwell. When she'd tried to ask her more about it, Julie had changed the subject. Now Hayley didn't know what to say to Emily. She could only repeat what she'd been told. 'Your mummy's taking you to England soon.'

'I just want her to hug me.'

Hayley stroked Emily's hair. 'I'm sure she'll see you soon. She must miss you.'

The child nodded tearfully, then rested her head on the pillow. Soon she was asleep.

Hayley went to her room at the back of the apartment and checked her make-up in the small, cracked mirror. Whereas the rest of the house was painted, her room was a grey concrete block. A previous occupant had put up pictures on the wall. There was one of the Thai king and queen, and some posters of Thai pop stars. Hayley hadn't had the heart to take them down. No one had mentioned a previous nanny, so she didn't know whose space she was invading or how long they had been gone.

Despite the room's limitations, it was so much better than the hostel. She had a small shower and toilet in a tiny en suite, and the space was all hers. She was sick of sharing. Here she had a bedside table, a lamp plugged into the only socket in the room and her own wardrobe. She didn't need anything more.

She looked at herself in the mirror in the green dress and shawl she'd borrowed from Julie. She was wearing a necklace and earrings she'd bought at the market, and an old perfume of Julie's – an unwanted present Julie had been given by David. Hayley smiled at herself in the mirror. She wasn't a child any more. She was an adult with a job, attending an upmarket party in Bangkok. It was like everything had finally fallen into place. After always feeling second place to the overwhelming needs of her younger brothers, her time had finally come.

· · ·

When Hayley arrived back at the party after checking on the children, the music was thumping. David put his hand on her shoulder and led her through the group to Julie. She was sitting on a bar stool at a small high table, her pregnant belly pushing her centre of gravity forward, which she compensated for with a perfectly straight back.

'Another drink?' David asked, taking a glass of champagne off the tray and handing it to Hayley. She noticed he hadn't asked how the kids were. He must know she'd gone to check on them.

She accepted the drink gratefully.

'So,' Julie said. 'How have you found your first week working for us?'

'It's been good. The children are lovely.' Hayley had had fun playing with them. The two girls were well behaved and sweet, and at the age where they were curious about everything. Hayley loved trying to answer their endless questions as best as she could.

Julie laughed. 'I think it's your influence making them well behaved. They're little tearaways with me.'

David nodded.

'I'm happy here,' Hayley said. 'And it's wonderful to come to a party like this.'

'Isn't it?' Julie said. 'I worked so hard for this. It took me ages to qualify as a doctor in the UK, and then it was a dream come true to find a job here. I feel like I've finally got the life I deserve.'

'Me too,' Hayley said, and laughed.

Julie looked at her discerningly. 'I hope everything's OK for you. Your room?'

'Oh, it's fine,' Hayley said.

'Good. Mae was in there before you.'

'Mae?' She swallowed. She hadn't known the maid had lived there. How had she felt about Hayley moving in?

'Yeah. We explained to her a while ago that we would need the room for a live-in nanny. We were always planning to find someone for the baby once my maternity leave finished, but it turned out we needed someone earlier than planned when Emily and Eva came to stay. We want a day maid, really, and so Mae's staying on to do that for us for the moment.'

Hayley nodded, thinking of the posters in her room. She felt bad that Mae had been forced out because of her.

'Do you feel ready for the baby?' she asked.

Julie laughed. 'Of course. I'm a doctor. I know all about the mechanics.'

Hayley nodded. 'I love babies.' She loved their tiny feet, their chubby faces, their curious eyes. When her brothers had been younger she'd been one of the few people whose hugs had stopped them screaming.

'I do too,' David said. 'Mine were gorgeous when they were babies. I'll always remember those days.'

'I thought you said you were working too hard back then to be involved much?' Julie said.

'I remember the important bits,' David said with a smile. 'I wish they were more like that now. All cute and cuddly and easy. They're harder when they're older.'

Hayley's brow crinkled. She remembered her brothers screaming all the time when they were babies, her mother saying it got easier when they were older. It must depend on the child. But David's girls were lovely.

Julie smiled. 'I've always wanted my own child. A child just like me. Successful, determined. I can't wait until she can talk and we can have a proper conversation.' She touched her stomach. 'I just felt her kick! My little girl's clearly ready to get out!'

'Another girl. That will be lovely. I had three brothers,' Hayley said.

'Not just another girl,' Julie said quickly, taking David's hand and putting it over her bump. 'Our girl.'

They smiled at each other, and then one of Julie's friends came over to talk to her.

'I'll take you over to meet some people,' David said to Hayley. She grabbed the baby monitor from the table and brought it with her, following him as he approached a couple in their late thirties.

'This is Hans,' he said, as the man smiled and reached out to shake her hand. David gestured towards the woman. 'And Karolina. They're from Sweden. In Bangkok for business. He works in pharmaceuticals, exporting medicine to Thailand.'

The woman smiled and gripped Hayley's hands in hers. 'So lovely to meet you,' she said, as David wandered off to speak to another guest.

'How do you know Julie and David?' Hayley asked.

The couple looked at each other. 'I met Julie at pregnancy yoga,' Karolina said.

'Oh,' Hayley said. She couldn't help looking at Karolina's stomach. It was pancake thin. She must have already had the baby and worked out at the gym to get her body back.

'We lost the baby,' Karolina said softly.

'I'm so sorry to hear that.'

'We'd been trying for so long. It had been a real struggle. But we're so pleased for Julie and David. They waited a long time for their baby too. We're so excited that the baby will be here soon.' Karolina had tears in her eyes.

Hans squeezed her hands. 'It will be our turn eventually.'

'Yeah, I think so. Life has a way of working out. Look at David and his children. Those poor girls – with what happened to their mother. And now they'll be blessed with a sister. A whole new family.'

'What happened to their mother?' Hayley asked, surprised. 'I thought she was taking them to England.'

'That's what she was planning to do. But she was in an accident about a month ago. She was knocked off the back of a motorbike taxi. It was touch and go for a while, but I've heard she's on the mend now, although we don't know how much longer she's going to stay in hospital, or if she'll ever completely recover.'

EIGHT

NOW

Hayley held Alice's hand as they walked back from school. When they got to their road, Alice picked up her pace, speeding towards the house. Hayley smiled. She knew she was looking forward to seeing Johanna.

When they went through the door, Alice ran upstairs.

'Don't disturb her,' Hayley shouted after her, 'she might be working.' Johanna studied late into the night most evenings after spending her mornings at the university lab. But she always had time for Alice. Ever since Johanna had asked Alice to help her take her belongings from her car to the house when she'd moved in two weeks before, they had been close. She always included Alice, and made her feel grown up.

'It's OK,' Hayley heard Johanna say, as she came out of her room. 'I need a break.' Alice followed her back downstairs, chatting happily about her friend Nila's new cat, and then they went to the living room together. 'I want you to colour with me,' Alice said. 'I have two more pictures to do in my book, so we can do one each.'

'Sure,' Johanna said, and Hayley marvelled at her patience. She sometimes thought it was easier before you had children, before you were ground down by the relentlessness of childcare. She'd been the same in Thailand; enthusiastic and energetic.

'I'll put your tea on,' she shouted out to Alice. Michelle was in the kitchen with her mother, packing up her things for the day.

'How was Mum today?' Hayley asked, aware that Michelle was staying later more often these days. The cost would be adding up. Her mother paid for most of her care out of her pension, but until she sold her flat, Hayley and Lars were paying for any extra hours. And lately her mother was needing more and more help.

'She was fine,' Michelle said. 'We took the bus to the river and went for a walk. She had a good day.'

'Oh, I'm glad.'

'I've met your new lodger. She introduced herself.'

'Ah, that's good.'

'She seems nice. Is she a friend of yours?'

'No,' Hayley said, surprised. 'Why do you ask?'

'She seems to have settled in well. I thought you must have already known her.'

'No,' Hayley said. 'We've just been lucky.'

Michelle nodded. 'It seems that way. I've heard some horror stories before. A friend of mine had a lodger move in who nicked her bank card and ran up huge bills. Even then, she found it hard to get rid of him.'

'Gosh, that's awful,' Hayley said.

'Well, I'd better be off,' Michelle said. 'Your mum's upstairs. See you soon.'

'Bye, Michelle.'

Hayley hummed to herself as she placed the chicken for Alice's dinner in the oven. Things were working out so well with Johanna. She was polite and tidy and fitted in easily with the family. All Hayley's concerns had proved unfounded. And she hadn't recognised her. Of course she hadn't. She'd been imagining things.

Her phone beeped. *Ryan.*

She sighed. Another text message asking her to get involved in his book project. This time suggesting he came round with wine to talk to her. She decided to ignore it. She'd already told him she couldn't help.

When Alice's food was ready, she dished the meal up onto the plate and called her through to the kitchen. There was no answer, so she went into the living room, where she'd left her with Johanna.

Johanna was putting the colouring pencils back into the packet.

'Where's Alice?' Hayley asked. 'Her dinner's ready.'

'Oh.' Johanna looked flustered. 'She went upstairs to get a toy a few minutes ago.'

'Right, I'll go and see what she's doing.' For some inexplicable reason Hayley's heart started to beat faster as she went up the stairs. Since she'd woken up to Alice screaming in the night a few weeks earlier, she'd become more on edge.

'Alice!' she called out. No answer. Her pace quickened as she went up the stairs and pushed open the door to her daughter's room.

She saw her on the bed, curled up, fast asleep.

Leaning over, she kissed her daughter's cheek and stroked her hair back from where it had fallen over her face. 'Wake up, sweetheart, it's dinner time.'

Her daughter stirred and half-opened her eyes, then dropped back to sleep. Hayley had seen her like this before. She was too tired to eat. Gently, she pulled off her clothes and eased her limbs into her pyjamas. She cleaned her teeth while she was half asleep and then pulled the covers over her and turned the light out.

As she tiptoed out of Alice's room, she heard the door open and Lars calling out hello. Hayley went down the stairs to greet him, and kissed him passionately. 'What did I do to deserve that?' he said with a smile.

'Nothing,' she said. 'I don't do it often enough.' With so much on her mind, keeping the flame of her marriage alive with Lars was one of the last things she thought about, she was so preoccupied with Alice's schoolwork and activities, her mother's care and her work.

'Alice has gone to bed early,' she said. 'I thought we could relax tonight, maybe have a glass of wine together and then dinner.'

Lars nodded. 'That would be great. I've got some work to do for tomorrow. Big presentation for a new client. I need to finish it off, then I'll come down. Is Johanna joining us?'

'Not tonight. She's meeting a friend. It will be just the two of us. Plus Mum, of course.'

Hayley pulled a casserole out of the freezer and started to defrost it in the microwave. She tidied up the living room and went upstairs to check on her mother. When she told her about the casserole, she wrinkled her nose and said she'd have a cheese and ham sandwich instead. Usually Hayley would have objected, but Alice was asleep and Johanna was out, and the idea of having a meal alone with Lars was so appealing that she agreed to her mother's request and brought the sandwich up for her to eat in her room.

When Lars finished work and came into the kitchen, she poured them each a glass of wine.

'So, how's work?' Hayley hated asking this question now. It was so loaded, with their whole future depending on it.

'Actually, it was good today,' Lars said. 'We ran a workshop with this new client in the drinks business, and everyone loved it. We're meeting them again tomorrow to talk about a multimillion-pound project.'

'Wow,' Hayley said. 'Congratulations, that's brilliant.'

'I've just finished the presentation,' Lars said. 'But I mustn't drink too much tonight. I need to be fresh for the morning.'

Hayley dished up the casserole and they sat opposite each other at the dinner table. Lars reached for her hand. 'It's great to have an evening together,' he said. 'Just the two of us. It reminds me of when we first met. Before we had Alice it felt like we had all the time in the world.'

'Thank goodness you offered to give me a guided tour of the city,' Hayley said, smiling. They'd met in Stockholm, when he'd come over to speak to her while she was reading her *Lonely Planet* guide at a coffee shop in the afternoon sun. She'd come to Stockholm on a whim, prompted by seeing Lyndsey's baby photos on Facebook. She'd felt a pang of envy and had decided to take advantage of her single status to go away for a weekend. The flights to Sweden had been cheap, but she hadn't planned anything in particular for when she was there and she'd spent the day wandering around the residential streets near her out-of-town hotel, shivering despite her thick jacket. She'd seen ordinary life: people putting bins out and mowing lawns, balloons pinned to a door for a child's birthday.

When she'd told him about her aimless morning, Lars had offered to show her the sights, and he'd hardly left her side the whole weekend. He lived in the UK, but often went on business trips to Sweden and to see family. Within months she had moved into his flat in London.

'You've gone quiet,' he said now, reaching across the table for her hand. 'You know things will be all right? I'm really hopeful about this new client.'

She nodded. 'I know,' she said. She looked at him, saw the tension in his shoulders, the pressure he was putting himself under. 'Michelle's been doing a few more hours,' she added.

'Yeah, but we need her, don't we? To be honest, I just need to win the work from this new client. If we get the project it will be enough to jump-start the business. If we don't, then... well, I don't know what will happen. Johanna's rent helps, but it only goes so far.'

Lars' eyes were bloodshot from all his long hours working.

'But we can manage, whatever happens.' Hayley tried to reassure him, to stop him putting himself under too much pressure. 'All that matters is that we're together.'

'We worked so hard for everything we've got,' he said.

'You're right.' She squeezed his hand, and gestured at the house around her, the house they'd spent so long doing up in the years before Alice was born. She thought about what would happen if they ran out of money, if they couldn't pay the mortgage. 'I love this house,' she said, 'but if we had to, we could downsize. The most important things in the world to me are you, Alice and my mother. As long as we have each other, we'll be all right.'

Lars smiled at her. 'Thank you,' he said. He leant across the table and kissed her. 'But it won't come to that,' he said. 'I promise our financial situation will get better.'

She squeezed his hand. 'Whatever happens, I love you.'

'I love you too,' he replied. 'And for now, things are OK. Thank goodness for Johanna.'

Hayley nodded, relaxing as she sipped her wine. Who knew where they'd be without Johanna? She felt a sudden surge of gratitude and contentment. All things considered, her family were weathering the storm. She and Lars were a team. They always had been. Nothing would come between them.

NINE

1999

Hayley lay back on the sunlounger by the pool, reading a book she'd borrowed from the shelves that lined the walls of Julie and David's living room. It was a thriller, set in the UK, and it made her think of her family back home, her mother, stepfather and little brothers. It would be early morning back in England, and she imagined her mother hurrying her brothers along to get them ready for school.

She'd sent her mum an email the other day, from David's computer in his study, and had told her all about the job and how kind David and Julie had been to her. Life was easy here, and in her first week she'd spent the time while the girls were at school wandering round the local area, buying spicy food from the street vendors outside or else swimming on the rooftop of the apartment building.

Julie was swimming slowly back and forth in the pool now. She had taken this week off to prepare for the baby's arrival, before her caesarean next week. Hayley had enjoyed getting to know her better, and while the girls had been at school they'd been for coffee and shopped for baby clothes and toys to add to the already bulging cupboards in the nursery.

Julie swam over to the ladder, climbed out and sat down on the lounger beside Hayley, stretching out on her towel, her bump neatly displayed over the top of her bikini.

'How are you feeling?' Hayley asked. 'Are you ready for the baby's arrival?' She couldn't imagine what it might feel like to be pregnant, to have another being growing inside you.

Julie smiled. 'I think so. I'm so excited. I really can't wait to meet my little Chloe.'

'Chloe?' Hayley said, rolling the name over her tongue. 'That's a beautiful name.'

'Thank you. It took me and David a while to agree. He wanted another name beginning with E, so it matched his daughters, Emily and Eva. Enid, he suggested, after his grandmother.'

'That's a bit old-fashioned.'

'I know. That's why I vetoed it. Anyway, he's come round to Chloe.'

Hayley smiled back at her. 'I can't wait to meet her,' she said. She'd always liked babies, and she loved the feel of them snuggling into her, their soft skin and fresh milky smell.

Julie looked out over the swimming pool. 'You know, when I was growing up, nobody expected me to amount to much. But I studied hard, became a doctor. Then I moved here to Thailand. I always wanted a child of my own.' She stroked her bump affectionately. 'And now it's finally happening. Everything I worked so hard for.'

Hayley lay back on the lounger, recoiling slightly as the sun-heated cushion touched her skin.

'You've done so well for yourself,' she said. 'I'm so glad I found the job with you and David.'

'I'm glad you did too,' Julie said. 'You fit right in with our little family.'

TEN

NOW

'Come on, Alice,' Hayley said, as she finished applying her make-up in the mirror. 'Please put your shoes on.' She could hear the frustration in her voice, anticipating the rush to get to school in time, followed by her own rush to work. Johanna appeared in the hallway, sat down next to Alice at the bottom of the stairs and helped her with the shoe buckle.

The school was on the way to the Tube station, and on the days when Johanna needed to work in the lab at her university, she'd walk Alice to school with Hayley before she travelled in to the city centre. The first time it happened was just a coincidence; the three of them had been leaving around the same time. But now Johanna would try and join them when she could, and Hayley enjoyed her company.

Johanna and Alice were chatting happily about Alice's school science project. 'I have to make a model out of recycling, that will protect an egg when it's dropped from the top floor of the school,' Alice explained excitedly.

'We can work on that together,' Johanna said. 'I'm sure you'll come up with loads of ideas.'

Hayley smiled, feeling a stab of guilt that she hadn't remembered to talk to Alice about the science project. There'd been a letter about it sent home, with an emphasis on parent participation, but she'd completely forgotten, distracted by worries about her mother and the family's finances.

She and Johanna waved goodbye to Alice at the school gate and then Johanna headed off to catch the Tube, while Hayley walked to the bus stop.

Her morning at work passed in a blur of meetings. It was always the same on Mondays. She caught sight of Ryan in the office once or twice between meetings and nodded hello at him. She knew he wanted to talk to her. She still hadn't replied to his latest text message about his book.

At lunchtime, the sun was shining so she grabbed her home-made sandwich from her bag to make the most of it in the nearby park.

As she was walking out of the office, Ryan fell into step beside her.

'Where are you off to?' he asked.

'Just for a walk,' she said vaguely.

'In the park?' He glanced down and saw she was carrying her sandwich box. He held up his own box. 'Snap. I brought sandwiches today too. I'll join you.'

'I don't have long,' Hayley said weakly.

'No worries. But I did want to talk to you. Are you sure I can't change your mind about helping with my book?'

Hayley sighed. 'You're still going ahead with it?'

'Yes,' he said firmly. 'We're looking at research methods at the moment in class, so it really is the best time for it. I've trawled the internet for all the information available publicly on the case, and I've made a list of people to speak to.'

'You're planning to interview people?'

He nodded. 'I need as much information as I can get my hands on. An interview from you would be ideal, of course, but I can probably get round that if I speak to lots of other people who were involved. I'd need to do that anyway, to build up a complete picture.'

Hayley's heart rate quickened. 'I really don't think this is a good idea, Ryan.'

Ryan stopped at a bench, facing the sun, opposite a small pond. 'Why don't we sit here and eat our lunch?'

Hayley sighed. She couldn't let him go off and research the case without speaking to him first. She needed to understand what he planned to do. 'Sure,' she said.

They took out their sandwiches and a pigeon waddled under the bench, looking for crumbs.

'Look,' she said to Ryan, hoping to appeal to his kind nature. 'I find talking about Thailand painful. That time is something I'd rather forget.'

'But why?'

Hayley chose her words carefully. 'Because of Chloe's disappearance. It was devastating for me. For everyone who loved her.' She tried to stop the images of Chloe coming uninvited into her head, reminding her of the grief that was buried deep inside her.

Ryan nodded thoughtfully. 'I understand. But isn't this an opportunity to process what happened? It could be cathartic.'

She shook her head. 'No, Ryan.'

'Do you blame yourself for what happened?'

'What?' Hayley's breath caught in her throat.

'Because some people do, don't they? Especially when they're young. They go through all the things they could have done to make things turn out differently. But this is your chance, Hayley. To come to terms with the past.'

She looked up and saw he was smiling. 'I don't need a therapist, Ryan. I just need to not think about it.'

He nodded. 'OK, then. I'll see how I get on without you.' She knew he hoped she'd give in and agree to help him. But she wasn't going to.

They chewed their sandwiches in silence for a while, at a stalemate. Then Ryan opened his backpack and pulled out some papers. Copies of *The Bangkok Observer* articles.

'I've seen all of those,' Hayley said quickly. 'I saw them all at the time. I don't want to see them again. There were some articles in the British press, too, although not many. I'm sure you've found them. I don't want to see those either.'

Ryan nodded. He pulled something out from the bottom of his folder. 'Have you seen this?' he said. It was a printout of an obscure crime blog. Hayley remembered it. About six months ago, she'd found it online. It was a long and rambling article, questioning what had happened to Chloe. After she'd seen it she had been worried that the author might write more posts, but that had been it. Nothing more.

'Yes,' Hayley said. She suddenly remembered that blog post had included a computer-generated image of what Chloe might look like today. Dark hair, intense blue eyes. The image had looked so like David. Hayley took the page from Ryan and turned it over, saw the computer-generated photo on the other side. He'd printed it out in colour.

She studied it, realisation sinking in. It hadn't been her imagination. Johanna looked exactly like the photo on the page.

ELEVEN

1999

David was pacing up and down the apartment, while Hayley did a simple jigsaw puzzle with Emily and Eva, lining the colourful pieces up for them so they could slot them into place.

'She'll be all right,' Hayley said quietly to David. Julie was at the hospital, having her caesarean section, giving birth to baby Chloe. She hadn't wanted David with her, hadn't wanted him to see her cut open. He'd been told to make sure the house was in order for her return and only come to see her when the hospital called.

He had thought about playing golf with his friends while he waited, but he needed to be in the apartment to be close to the phone.

'Things can go wrong,' David said. 'You never know. Just look at Karolina.'

Hayley remembered what Karolina had said about Julie and David's struggle to have a child and wondered if they'd lost babies before. 'I'm sure Julie will be fine. And Chloe.'

He nodded. 'I wish I could do more to help. She said I should get the house ready, and I'm supposed to talk to Emily and Eva about the new rules when the baby is here.'

'What are the rules?' Hayley asked, curious.

'Just not to go near the baby, not to touch the baby, not to try to play with the baby. She wants to protect her.'

Hayley swallowed. 'But you'll want them to have a strong bond with their sister? I have half-brothers, and I think of them as my real brothers. They might feel left out if you tell them to stay away entirely.'

David sighed. 'It's Julie,' he said. 'She's a perfectionist. She just wants to keep her baby safe. You know, when we were trying for a baby we didn't expect to be looking after my other children. Marion was going to take them back to England. It's hard having them with us now. Julie's tried to make things work, but it's difficult when she's not their mother.'

Hayley frowned. She didn't like the way he was talking about his children, as if he didn't want them there. 'What's happened to their mother?' she asked, remembering what Karolina had said about the accident.

'She fell off the back of a motorbike taxi. Her own fault, I think. She was seriously injured.'

'Have you spoken to the children about it?' They were always asking after their mother, and Hayley never knew what to tell them.

'Not much. They're too young. I've just told them she's in hospital and that she'll come and collect them soon when she's better.'

'I see. Have they visited her?'

'No, I think... it would be too upsetting. She has lots of scars. She doesn't look the same.'

'Maybe they need to see her. I could take them.'

'I don't know if that's a good idea. Once the baby comes, we'll all be busy.'

Hayley nodded. 'Maybe another time then. Or one week-end, when you want them out of your hair.'

'Maybe,' he said, sighing. He looked at his watch. 'God, I hate waiting. Do you want a drink?'

'No, thanks,' she said.

He went to the fridge, pulled out a bottle of white wine and poured himself a large glass. 'Are you sure?' he asked. 'This is Italian wine. Only the best.'

'Oh, OK then,' she said. 'Why not?'

He poured a second glass and she took a sip. It was so much better than the cheap alcohol they sold at the hostel.

'You've settled in so well,' he said. 'Julie's so pleased.'

'Hayley! Hayley!' Eva called out. 'Come and play!'

'I'm needed,' Hayley said to David, smiling. 'Why don't you do the jigsaws with us?'

He shook his head. 'Oh, I have work to do.' She nodded. He'd spread his work over the kitchen table that morning. Endless detailed technical drawings of the new Skytrain that would carry passengers over Bangkok. David was one of the engineers. He sat down now and pored over the drawings, sipping his wine and making notes in a notebook.

Hayley went back to the jigsaw puzzles with the girls.

After a few minutes, Eva got bored and ran over to her father. 'Daddy, Daddy, what are you doing?'

'Just working,' he said, patting her head.

'Can I help?'

'I suppose so.' He pulled her up onto his knee and started to explain the plans to her and Hayley. 'This will completely ease the traffic in the city,' he told his daughter. 'You'll be able to glide through the sky, see all the little people below. Won't that be amazing?'

She nodded, smiling in awe.

Hayley studied the proposals, the maps of the foundations, the supporting pillars and the railway structure. She'd seen some of the holes that had already been made in the Sukhumvit road. Huge mounds of tarmac and earth dug up, ready for the foundations to be put in.

'When will it be operational?' she asked.

'Later this year, we hope. The work's going at a fast pace. That's why I'm always so busy.' He ruffled Eva's hair.

At that moment the phone rang and he rushed to pick it up. When he put it down again he was smiling broadly.

'That was Julie,' he said. 'She's had the baby.'

He picked up his wine glass and held it out, clinking it with Hayley's. 'Cheers,' he said, grinning at her. 'Here's to the baby.' Then he downed his wine, called his driver and went over to the hospital.

TWELVE

NOW

Hayley stared at the picture on Ryan's printout, blinking back her shock. This was why she recognised Johanna. Even so, she knew that these computer-generated images could be extremely inaccurate. Thousands of people all over the world would probably see a likeness to themselves in it. And yet... Hayley felt hope rising in her chest. Could it be possible? When Hayley had first met her, she'd seen her likeness to David, and felt that flicker of recognition. But she'd dismissed it, knowing how unlikely it was. But now, this image showed her she wasn't going mad.

'I'm going to contact the crime blogger,' Ryan said. 'It looks like he did a lot of research. Maybe he'll share it with me.'

'Maybe,' Hayley said. The article had contained nothing new, only what had been in the press and a lot of speculation about what might have happened to Chloe.

'Look, I've finished my lunch. I need to get back.' She got up and hurried away, unable to stop thinking about Johanna, how well she fitted in with the family. She looked so much like David. What if she was who Hayley thought she was?

. . .

All afternoon, Hayley's mind whirred as she thought of Ryan's research. What if he saw Johanna, or spoke to her? Or if he spoke to Lars? Lars knew nothing about her time in Thailand, other than the vague details she'd given him, about teaching in Chiang Mai and learning Thai. She hadn't told him she'd been a nanny in Bangkok. She hadn't lied, just omitted those months of her life. She'd lived in Chiang Mai far longer than Bangkok, and she'd felt safe and secure with the Thai couple who ran the hostel there. Her gap year had been extended and by the time she'd gone to university she was two years older than the other students. She'd taken her stepdad's surname and no one had associated her with Hayley Taylor, the nanny in Thailand who'd been accused of being involved in Chloe's disappearance. She'd lost contact with Sunita and Lyndsey, stopped replying to their emails, not wanting any connection to the past.

But she hadn't been able to disconnect completely. She kept her photos of Thailand in her old travel rucksack and had taken it with her every time she moved house. Now it was at the top of her cupboard in her bedroom. She kept a photo of Emily and Eva in her bedside drawer. She had loved those children so deeply. If Lars ever saw the photo, she'd always planned to say they were one of her university friends' children. But he'd never mentioned it. Hayley took it out sometimes to look at as Alice got older, remembering the fun she'd had with Eva and Emily, trying to recapture something of the person she'd been back then, who could enjoy playing with the children without being consumed by worries of every possible thing that could go wrong.

That evening Hayley started cooking a Thai curry for Lars and Johanna and her mother. Thai cuisine was one of the few things she was good at. The couple at the hostel in Chiang Mai had taught her. As she cooked she could hear Johanna and Alice laughing in the living room, as Johanna helped Alice with her science project.

When Lars got home, he put Alice to bed, before coming to the kitchen to join Hayley, her mother and Johanna.

'How did the client meeting go?' Hayley asked Lars, remembering how hopeful he'd been about it the night before, how determined he was to get new business in.

'OK,' he said. 'They might want a project in a couple of months' time.' She heard the defeat in his voice. The company needed the money now.

'That would still be good,' Hayley said brightly, trying to sound cheerful and not let on to Johanna or her mother how bad things were. She squeezed his arm. 'We can talk about it later.'

'This smells delicious,' Lars said, breathing in the scent of the red curry. 'My favourite.' He saw Johanna standing in the kitchen, pouring water into glasses. 'Johanna – are you joining us? If so, you're in for a treat. My wife's chicken curry is divine.'

Hayley dished up the spicy version of the curry from one pan and a plain version for her mother from another.

'This is so tasty,' Johanna said, once they'd sat down to eat and she'd taken her first bite.

'I hope it's not too spicy.'

'No, not at all. Where did you learn to cook like this?'

'In Thailand,' Hayley said. 'When I was travelling.'

Johanna glanced at her. 'Were you there long? If you had time to learn to cook, I mean.'

'Over a year,' Hayley said.

'What did you do there?'

Hayley's body tensed. 'Just travelling, really. Bumming about. You know how students are.' She blushed, realising her comment could be misconstrued. 'Not you, of course.'

'It must have been really interesting.'

'It was. Always good to come home, though.' She glanced at

her mother, who was pushing the plain chicken curry round her plate.

'We were worried about you over there,' her mother said suddenly. 'Not a safe place, all sorts of things happen there. Awful.'

'How's your food, Mum?' Hayley asked, trying to change the subject.

'Too spicy.'

Hayley glanced at Lars and he smiled.

'Just eat the rice then.' Hayley didn't have as much patience with her mother as Michelle, who would respond to her mother's every whim, going to the supermarket with her to buy ingredients and cooking whatever she liked for lunch.

'It's so kind of you to make dinner for me,' Johanna said. 'I'll have to cook you Swedish food in return.'

'Oh,' Hayley said, 'that would be lovely. Lars used to cook that occasionally, but he's been busy.'

'I'll have to correct that,' Lars said, jumping in quickly. 'It's been too long since I cooked.'

Hayley smiled. 'Well, that would be good.' She was tired of cooking every night, but Lars usually worked in the evenings and it always fell to her.

She settled down and started to enjoy the food, the spice lighting up her taste buds. They almost felt like a proper family sitting here. It felt natural.

'Pass the salt, Hayley,' her mother said suddenly.

'Mum, it's at the other end of the table. And it doesn't need salt.' The salt and pepper shakers were closest to Johanna.

'Pass the salt, Hayley,' her mother said again, looking directly at Johanna. 'And hurry up about it. I haven't brought you up to be rude.'

'Here you go,' Johanna said nervously, as Hayley realised what had happened.

'I'm so sorry, Johanna,' Hayley said. 'She's just confused.'

Her mother turned to her. 'Shut up,' she said, her voice angry. 'I can speak to my own daughter however I like.'

After dinner, Hayley went to check on Alice. She was relieved to find her in a deep sleep and she kissed her lightly on the cheek and whispered, 'Good night.'

She heard a noise from Lars' office upstairs. He must have gone back to work. It was late, and she wished he would allow himself a break sometimes.

She climbed the stairs slowly. 'Lars?' she called out, as she pushed open the door of his office.

But it wasn't Lars in there. It was Johanna. She was bent over, rifling through one of the drawers in the desk.

'What are you doing?' Hayley asked, sharply.

'Oh,' Johanna said, jolting upright. She turned to Hayley, blushing. 'I was just looking for some bits and pieces for Alice's science project. Scissors, Sellotape. Alice said everything was upstairs. I thought I'd get them while I remembered.'

Hayley looked suspiciously at the pile of papers Johanna had put on the desk. It was their personal paperwork: bank statements, marriage and birth certificates.

'Actually, I think the scissors and Sellotape are in the drawer below,' she said. She went over to Johanna and pulled open the drawer, then felt around until she found them.

'Here you go,' she said.

Hayley looked at Johanna, wondering why she had really come up to Lars' study. Suddenly it struck her that it didn't make sense that Johanna wanted to live in Ealing, when her university was in central London. There were cheaper areas to commute into London from. And although she'd said she had connections here, she hadn't mentioned them at all once she'd moved in.

'Thanks. Sorry about that,' Johanna said, tucking her hair behind her ear. 'I should have asked before I came up here.'

'Yeah,' Hayley said. 'You should have.' She watched Johanna's retreating back as she went down the stairs. She was sure she was here for a reason. She just didn't know what it was.

THIRTEEN

1999

Hayley rocked Chloe back and forth in her arms, trying to calm her screams. It was a few days since Julie had returned from hospital and Hayley had offered to get up with the baby in the night, so she could get some rest. She watched Chloe's mobile of floating blue elephants flutter in the breeze from the fan, and stroked her dark hair. The time was 2.34 a.m. and the temperature on the yellow chick-shaped room thermometer read twenty-two degrees; the perfect temperature for a newborn, Julie had said. In another world, Sunita and Lyndsey were out drinking.

Chloe rooted for Hayley's nipple, getting increasingly angry. Hayley knew she wanted to suck on something, and she longed to give her a dummy, but Julie had forbidden it. Instead she had to wait for her bottle to heat up. It sat in a jug of boiling hot water, slowly heating through. Every few minutes Hayley lifted the bottle up and poured out a little onto her wrist to see if it was the right temperature. It was still too cold.

A face appeared at the doorway, then another behind it. Eva and Emily. They were rubbing their eyes, and Eva clutched her soft toy lion, that she'd told Hayley she'd got at the zoo when she'd gone with her mother before her accident.

'She woke us up,' Emily whined.

At the sound of her voice, Chloe seemed to calm.

'Do you want to come and see her?' Hayley whispered. She wondered how the children had been woken up by Chloe's screams, but not Julie and David. Then she remembered that Julie had told her she was going to sleep with earplugs.

The girls nodded, their eyes wide, as they came over to the baby. Eva held out her finger and Chloe clenched her hand around it. Eva beamed.

'Do you want to hold her?' Hayley asked Emily, the oldest.

Emily grinned from ear to ear. 'Yes, please.' Her brow furrowed. 'But won't Julie be cross?' Julie had hardly let her near Chloe since she'd been born.

Hayley put her finger to her lips. 'Shhh... she won't know.'

The girls got into the armchair together with Hayley's directions, and she placed baby Chloe in their arms. Her eyes looked from one girl to the other.

'She's so cute,' Emily whispered.

'I love her,' Eva said with a smile.

Hayley felt a pang of empathy for them. They were out on their own here with Julie and David, and since Chloe was born the couple had become even less interested in them. Yet the girls were the ones who were up in the night when she was screaming.

'I can't believe we have a sister,' Emily said. They grinned at each other and Hayley thought of their mother, how if all went to plan, she would take them to England. That was if she ever got better. Hayley hoped she did, for everyone's sake. But if their mother took them away, she doubted they'd see their sister again.

Chloe looked like she was almost asleep now. Hayley let a

drop of milk from the bottle fall on her wrist. It was finally the right temperature.

'Do you want to feed her?' she asked Emily.

Emily nodded and she showed her how to hold the bottle. Chloe took a few short sips and then fell asleep. Hayley took her out of the girls' arms and tried to rouse her. If she didn't drink now, she'd wake up again in half an hour. And if Chloe didn't finish the bottle, she'd have to throw it away as Julie didn't like the bottles being reused. Hayley was in an endless cycle of throwing away nearly full bottles of milk, washing up the bottles and preparing more.

As Hayley tried to feed her again, Chloe spat out the milk and let it dribble down her chin. Hayley sighed, gave up and let her fall back to sleep.

FOURTEEN

NOW

When Hayley got back home from work after collecting Alice from school, Michelle and her mother were still out at the hairdresser's. Hayley had wanted to talk to her about how her mother seemed to have deteriorated lately. It had worried her when she'd mistaken Johanna for Hayley at dinner.

While she was waiting for Michelle to come back, she went up to her mother's room to check she was remembering to take all her tablets. Michelle had helpfully sorted them into a container divided into the days of the week, which was kept on her mother's bedside table. Hayley hadn't been in her room for a few days and she was shocked by how untidy it was. There were clothes littering the floor, and open books resting on every surface. Hayley picked up the book from the bedside table, an old John Grisham novel. The container was underneath it. It looked like her mother had taken today's tablets. She breathed a sigh of relief.

She began to pick up her mother's clothes from the floor, thinking back to when she was a child and her mother had constantly nagged her to tidy her own room. When she put them in the cupboard, she saw a collection of Alice's toys at the bottom of it. They were ones that she didn't play with so often, ones that wouldn't be missed. Had her mother been collecting them from round the house, bringing them here?

When she looked at the chest of drawers, she saw her mother had hung jewellery from each of the handles. They were the necklaces she wore often. She must have forgotten where they went. Hayley took them off the handles and ran them through her fingers. The gold cross reminded her so much of her childhood. Her mother hadn't been particularly religious, but she'd worn the necklace every day. When Hayley had been arrested in Thailand, she'd told her that she'd gone to the local church for the first time in years and prayed for her. She'd been trying to borrow the money for a flight to Thailand from friends when Hayley had been released.

Now the tables had turned. Her mother needed her. Hayley opened the dressing table where she knew her mother had put her jewellery box when she first moved in. She saw a crumpled photo on top of the box, her own smiling face beaming out, her arms wrapped round Emily and Eva. She stared at it. It was the photo she kept in her bedside drawer. She felt a lump form in her throat as she wondered what had happened to those two beautiful girls. Her mother must have taken the photo from her bedroom. But why? She doubted Susan would have ever known who the girls in the photos were, let alone now when she was losing her memory. She must have hoarded it, along with Alice's toys.

Hayley heard the front door swing shut. She put the photo back and opened the jewellery box to put her mother's necklaces inside, then went downstairs.

She was expecting to see Michelle and her mother, but instead it was Johanna. She was bent over in the hallway, talking to Alice.

'Do you want me to help you put that away?' Hayley asked, noticing Johanna's heavy bags.

'Oh, no, you don't need to,' she said. 'It's for dinner tonight. Lars and I are going to cook you a special Swedish feast. Don't you remember?'

'Oh, yes.' It had completely slipped her mind.

'I'm going to help,' Alice said with a grin.

Hayley shook her head and she ruffled Alice's hair. 'I'm afraid not. I'm going to give you an early dinner. You've got school tomorrow.'

'No,' Alice said angrily, stamping her foot. 'I want to eat with you and Dad and Johanna.'

Johanna knelt down to Alice's level. 'I could teach you to cook it yourself. I could give you a lesson, maybe at the weekend or after school one day? How does that sound? Or we could even bake Swedish cakes?'

'Cake!' Alice squealed. 'Let's make cakes.'

'I promise we will,' Johanna said. She turned to Hayley. 'You know I'm happy to help you out if you need it. With looking after Alice, I mean. I've always loved children. And after-school club can be expensive.'

Hayley frowned. Johanna must have picked up on their money worries. She thought of the other day when she'd seen her going through the desk drawer. She wondered if she'd seen their bank statements, realised they were in financial trouble.

'Thanks,' Hayley said. 'But I don't want to disrupt Alice's routine.' Even though Johanna was great with Alice, it seemed like too much to ask her to keep Alice entertained after school. She watched Johanna's forehead crinkle into a lopsided frown, exactly the way David's used to. There was a clear resemblance. But it wasn't enough for her to be sure.

'OK, well, I'll just get started on tonight's dinner. Lars said he'd help when he's back.'

'He often works late.'

She laughed. 'Well, it's easy for me to do myself if he's not back.'

'You're showing him up,' Hayley said, half serious. She was struggling to remember the last time Lars had cooked for her.

The door opened again and this time it was Michelle, bringing Susan back. Hayley put the spaghetti on to boil for Alice's dinner and went to the front door. 'Hi,' she said, as her mother climbed slowly up the single step and over the threshold. It was always a shock to see her mother with her stick. She suddenly saw her through fresh eyes, how frail she'd become since her fall the year before. She was only seventy, but now she seemed far older, hobbling slowly towards her, Michelle supporting her arm patiently as she struggled to slip her shoes off. 'Your hair looks nice, Mum,' she added.

'Thank you, dear. They did a good job.'

Michelle smiled. 'They're always nice in that hairdresser. Always treat her kindly.'

'She's been going there for over thirty years,' Hayley said, wondering where the time had gone.

'A loyal customer then.'

'Yeah. Michelle – can I talk to you in private before you go? About Mum?'

'Of course. I'll just get her settled in the living room and then we can speak.'

Once Susan was comfortable, Michelle came into the kitchen. 'How's your work at the university?' she asked politely.

'Oh, OK, same as ever.'

'I always thought working in student support would be interesting.'

'It is,' Hayley said, realising how downbeat she'd sounded. 'I love it most days, I'm just a bit tired today.'

'I know what you mean,' Michelle said with a smile. 'But I love working with your mother. She's my favourite client. Although I always imagined I'd work with children. I studied child psychology at university.'

'That must have been fascinating,' Hayley said.

'It was. It made me think about how everything we say, every action we take, can have such a big effect on young minds.'

Hayley shivered, her anxiety rising up inside her. She hated to think of all the missteps she must have taken with Alice.

'We can only do our best,' she said.

'Oh, I know,' Michelle said. 'That's why I ended up working with older adults in the end. It felt like less potential for things to go wrong.'

Hayley nodded tensely, trying to stop the memories of her own nannying experience invading her mind.

'So, how's Mum getting on?' Hayley asked. 'I've been worried about her lately.'

'She's doing well. She does get confused, though. I've found her in different rooms in the house, looking for things. She was looking for bills to pay in Alice's room the other day. I think she thought it was her room. And I've found her in the loft rooms before, in Lars' study and in your bedroom, looking for her glasses. She's always looking for things she thinks she's misplaced. It's harmless.'

'I want to show you something,' Hayley said. She took Michelle up to her mother's room and showed her the row of Alice's toys in the bottom of her cupboard. 'I think she's getting more and more confused. She got me and Johanna mixed up the other day. And now this.'

Michelle sighed. 'I don't know. You could be right. She can't remember as much as she used to. And you can see from her room that she's struggling more and more with the basics – remembering where to put things back, what day it is, even the year.'

'Do you think I need to do more for her? Maybe get her assessed again? Perhaps she needs even more help.' There was only so much Michelle could do.

Michelle shook her head. 'I don't think we've got to that

point yet. I can keep an eye on her for now. And keep you updated with how things are going, of course. I haven't noticed anything too concerning.' She smiled affectionately. 'But then your mum and I mainly talk about the past. Her childhood and yours. We don't talk about the present so often. She doesn't like to remember she's older now.'

Hayley nodded. 'Thanks, Michelle.' She patted the younger woman on the arm. 'I don't know what we'd have done without you. Mum loves you.'

Michelle smiled. 'I love her too,' she said.

They heard the sound of male laughter coming from downstairs. Lars must be home. Hayley hadn't heard him come in. A female voice joined him, laughing uproariously.

'I'd better be off,' Michelle said. 'I need to get back.'

'OK,' Hayley said. 'Thanks again.'

They walked down the stairs together, past the kitchen where Lars and Johanna were talking rapidly in Swedish together. Hayley felt a tinge of jealousy, wondering what they were talking about. At least they were getting on. Johanna had slotted in perfectly to their family, instantly bonding with Alice and Lars.

When Michelle opened the door to leave, Hayley thought she saw movement at the bottom of the drive, the flash of a black coat. She was about to close the door when she saw Michelle being approached by a man at the end of the road, before disappearing round the corner. She couldn't be certain, but she was sure from his height and his way of walking that it was Ryan.

FIFTEEN

1999

As Hayley prepared Chloe's bottle, Julie paced up and down the living room, looking at the tiny dresses she'd laid out in a line on the sofa. She seemed stressed and exhausted, the way she'd been ever since she'd had Chloe two weeks before. Hayley had tried to reassure her that this was a normal part of motherhood, but she'd snapped at her. 'What would you know?'

She'd had a point, and Hayley hadn't commented further. But she could see Julie was struggling and she tried to help with Chloe as best she could, while the older girls were at school. Hayley would hold and rock her when she cried, feed her bottles and change her nappies when Julie didn't feel up to it. Increasingly, Julie was spending more and more time in the study, saying she had to keep across her work while she was on maternity leave.

Hayley didn't mind. She liked spending time with Chloe. And it was great to have Julie around in the daytime for company. One day they spent the afternoon watching *Men in Black* on DVD with Chloe sleeping on Hayley's chest. Hayley hadn't had the chance to see it at the cinema, but Julie had copies of all the latest films.

'Which dress do you think is the prettiest?' Julie asked now, surveying the choice.

'What for?' Hayley said.

'Karolina's coming round.' Julie held up a pink dress with red polka dots.

'Oh, that's great.' Hayley thought of Karolina and how upset she had been about her own baby loss. It must be difficult for her to see Chloe.

Chloe started to cry, and Hayley felt the bottle to see if it was ready. Nearly. She picked her up gently and held her against her body.

'I think this one,' Julie said, pointing to a royal-blue chiffon dress. 'I think it will bring out her eyes.'

'That's a beautiful colour,' Hayley said.

'Let's get her into it now. Karolina will be here in half an hour,' Julie said. 'And I need to go and get changed, put some make-up on, look less of a disaster.'

'You look fine,' Hayley said. 'She won't be expecting you to look perfect. You only had Chloe two weeks ago.'

Julie smiled wanly. 'But I *want* to look perfect,' she said. 'Show her how I'm coping.'

Hayley nodded, although she wasn't sure Julie was coping that well. 'Sure,' she said. 'We'll need to give Chloe a bottle before we put on the new dress so she doesn't spit up all over it. Why don't you get changed and I'll feed her, then put her into her dress.'

'Great,' Julie said. She glanced at her daughter. 'Do you think they ever stop screaming?'

Hayley held Chloe closer, trying to calm her down. 'I hope so,' she said. She put her face towards the baby's, breathing in the floral scent of her baby bath gel. Chloe's arms gripped her jumper and she kept rooting, as Hayley waited for the bottle to cool.

'Almost ready,' she said softly, as Julie left the room to get changed.

When Karolina came into the apartment half an hour later, she was full of smiles as she wrapped Julie in a huge hug.

'You're looking lovely,' she said.

'Thank you,' Julie said, ushering her inside.

'I can't wait to meet little Chloe.' Karolina was laden down with bags of gifts, which she started pulling out as soon as she'd taken her shoes off.

'Could you wash your hands first, please?' Julie said tightly. 'We're trying to keep a germ-free household.' Karolina nodded and obediently went to the bathroom to do so.

'Beautiful dress,' she said, when she came back in. She stroked the fabric. 'She looks gorgeous.'

Julie nodded. 'Thank you.' Then she paused as if she didn't quite know what to say next. 'Do you want to hold her?' she asked eventually.

Hayley watched as Karolina carefully took the baby from Julie, holding her as if she was the most fragile thing in the world. She lowered her into her arms and gazed into her eyes, rocking her gently back and forth. Chloe's eyes fixated on her face, and Hayley could see Karolina was completely entranced, unable to take her eyes off her. Karolina put her face to the little girl and breathed her in. Hayley thought of how much she had wanted a baby; she could see the love and pain in her eyes as she held the little girl. It made her heart break.

'She is just so lovely,' Karolina said to Julie.

'Thank you.'

'You're so lucky.' She pulled her eyes away from Chloe's for a moment. 'So how are you finding motherhood?'

'Oh, you know. It's hard work. But not as hard as working at the hospital, of course.'

'Very different, I imagine.'

'It is. It's all nappies and wiping up sick.' Julie just about managed a laugh.

'It's supposed to get easier, though, isn't it?'

'It's not difficult,' Julie said. 'Just tedious sometimes, and repetitive. I can't wait for her to grow up, to be able to chat to me.'

'Yeah, that will be nice. She's so lovely though, isn't she? Gorgeous eyes. How long do you get to stay at home with her?'

'I have ten weeks of maternity leave technically, but I might need to cut it short.'

Hayley looked up in surprise. Julie hadn't mentioned that.

'Oh really?'

'It can't be helped. The hospital needs me back.' Hayley wondered if this was true. She didn't think Julie had received any calls from the hospital since she'd been at home, but perhaps they had emailed her.

'I bet you'll miss her when you're back at work.'

Julie nodded unconvincingly.

'How's it all going for you?' Hayley asked, moving the subject away from Julie.

'With what?' Karolina said blankly.

Hayley wondered if she'd been too direct, if she'd put her foot in it. 'You mentioned you'd been trying for a baby?'

'Yeah,' she said. 'We still are. It's not happening. Not yet.' She looked deep into Chloe's eyes. 'I guess I'll just have to make do with cuddles from this one, for the moment.'

SIXTEEN

NOW

Hayley and Lars sat on the plastic seats at the soft play centre together, sipping tepid coffee. Hayley used to bring Alice here on her own when she was a toddler, but today they'd come as a family. Hayley had a voucher she'd won in the school raffle and Lars had needed a break from work. Now they were in a warehouse off the A406 filled floor-to-ceiling with a huge colourful play structure.

'How's the business going?' Hayley asked Lars.

Lars sighed. 'I'm still pinning my hopes on that new project I told you about. Not much else has come in. In the meantime we're still haemorrhaging money.'

'That doesn't sound good.'

'It isn't.' He frowned into his coffee. 'And I've called everyone in my address book to try and drum up business. But nothing. I've signed up for every networking event too. I think I'm going to have to make redundancies. There's no alternative.' He put his head in his hands.

Hayley nodded. 'At least Johanna's here. Her rent helps with the bills.'

Lars shook his head. 'Well, a little. But it's only bought me time. And the redundancy process isn't cheap. I'll need to pay a few months' salary to each of them. I can't afford to do that without taking out a loan. But I'll have to do it, as I can't afford to keep them on either.'

'I'm sorry, Lars.' She put her hand over his. 'But it will be all right. I can support you however you need me to.'

'I was talking to Johanna the other day, when we cooked dinner. She was a good choice for a lodger.'

Hayley nodded. 'She was the only person to see the room.'

'And Swedish, too. It's nice to feel more connected to my home country.'

'It's just a coincidence,' Hayley said quickly.

'It's good to have her around,' Lars said. Hayley thought of them cooking dinner for her the other night, the laughter she'd heard drifting up the stairs, the conversations she sometimes overheard in Swedish between them. She felt her stomach knot.

'She fits in well,' she said.

'She mentioned that she could look after Alice sometimes after school. She said she'd be happy to do it in exchange for her meals. She doesn't like eating on her own, and it's expensive to cook just for one. She said if we bought the food, then we could share the cooking, all eat together.'

'I'm not sure,' Hayley said, hesitating.

'It sounds like a good arrangement, doesn't it? We'd be able to save some money on the after-school club. And Johanna would be happy. She loves Alice. And you.'

'What do you mean?'

'Well, she asks so many questions about you. She's just curious about who she's living with, I think.'

Hayley swallowed. Another person asking questions. She thought of Ryan, how she'd seen him talking to Michelle. She'd ended up sending Michelle a text message telling her that he was an odd man who she should ignore if he approached her. She'd felt guilty speaking about Ryan in that way, but it had been necessary. She didn't want him going anywhere near her family or friends in order to research his book. She'd messaged him and told him not to talk to anyone in her household without speaking to her first.

'Johanna can always talk to me if she wants to know anything,' she said to Lars.

Lars looked baffled, but then they were interrupted by Alice, who ran up to them from the soft play.

She pulled at Hayley's hand. 'Please can you come round with me?'

Hayley looked at Lars, and then nodded. 'Sure,' she said, 'where do you want to go?' She slipped off her shoes and followed Alice onto the soft play frame, climbing up the foam steps onto a rope bridge and balancing behind her.

'Look at this,' Alice said, when they got to a dark room at the top. 'This is the secret bit.'

'The secret bit?'

'Yeah, you can hide here.'

Hayley smiled and gripped Alice's hand. 'Who are you hiding from?' she asked Alice.

'The baddies.'

'And who are the baddies?' she said softly, hoping this was just a childish game.

'The older kids,' Alice said, shrugging. 'They run around shouting. I don't like it.'

Hayley wrapped her arms around her. 'I see.'

'Johanna says she'll always protect me from any baddies.'

'Johanna?' Hayley winced at the thought her daughter was turning to Johanna rather than to her. 'Is there anything bothering you?' she asked.

'No, don't be silly, Mummy! It's just a game. Johanna protects me from the baddies and I protect her too. We're friends. That's what friends do.'

Hayley nodded and squeezed her daughter's hand. 'Of course.'

'We play sometimes after school.' Alice twirled her hair round her fingers, smiling. 'I'm really glad she's come to live with us.'

Hayley stroked her daughter's hair. 'Me too,' she said.

When they got back from soft play, Hayley walked past Johanna's room to check on her mother. There was no light from under the door. She must be out. Curiosity overcame her and she knocked just in case Johanna was asleep and then opened the door. She'd resisted the temptation to go into her room so far, but since Ryan had shown her the aged picture of Chloe, and Hayley had caught her going through the desk drawers, she'd become suspicious. She had to know who Johanna was.

She flicked the light on. The room was excessively tidy and there was only a bottle of perfume and a hairbrush on the bedside table. The bed was neatly made and a line of photos sat on top of the chest of drawers, spaced exactly the same distance apart. A collection of smiling family and friends.

Hayley stepped closer and saw a familiar face in the centre of the row. Sitting on a mountainside, in hiking boots, grinning out at her. She was older and her hair had greyed but there was no mistaking her. It was Karolina.

SEVENTEEN

1999

Hayley was bleary-eyed as she made the kids' breakfast and put them in the car with the driver to take them to school. Julie had gone into the hospital today to discuss returning to work earlier than planned after her maternity leave. She had explained to Hayley that she needed more mental stimulation, and Hayley had understood. She could see the toll looking after Chloe was taking on her. Julie had offered Hayley an extra £100 a month to look after Chloe once she went back to work. In the meantime, she'd look for a professional nanny to take over.

Hayley sat in the front of the car with the driver. As they drove through the city, she glanced back at Chloe and saw her tiny eyes flicking back and forth, absorbing the details of the stifling city from their air-conditioned box. Once they got to the school, Hayley held Chloe as she helped Emily and Eva out of the car and then kissed them both goodbye, stroking their cheeks affectionately before they walked away.

'Have a good day,' she shouted after them.

On their way back home, Hayley got the driver to stop at the international supermarket, and she carried Chloe round, picking up more baby formula and stocking up on cereal and treats for the girls. Julie was strict about her own diet, but she didn't pay much attention to Emily and Eva, and Hayley liked to buy something sweet to give them when she collected them from school. As she wandered round the supermarket, local women exclaimed over Chloe, making faces and clutching her tiny fingers. Chloe made eye contact and delighted them. She was always so much easier when she was outside the apartment. Inside, she screamed and screamed, the sound bouncing off the walls until it became part of the room itself. Some days Hayley felt like she was going to lose her mind, she just wanted the noise to stop.

When she went to the till, Hayley realised she had picked up more than she had intended. She could afford to treat herself, especially with the extra pay around the corner, and she'd got some overpriced bread, cheese and ham. Hayley longed for something more substantial than the lettuce and rice cakes Julie insisted on buying to help her lose the baby weight.

As Hayley struggled to get her shopping onto the conveyor belt, Chloe started screaming. She was probably hungry, but they needed to get home before Hayley could feed her; there was nowhere to warm the bottle up in the supermarket. Hayley put her on her shoulder to burp her and a river of milky vomit ran down her bare shoulder and over her vest top. She reached into her bag for a cloth and wiped it ineffectively. At least Chloe had stopped crying.

The woman in front of her in the queue paid for her couple of items of shopping and then turned to Hayley with her arms out. Now Hayley's shopping was coming down the conveyor belt and she needed to pack it into bags, while holding Chloe. She smiled at the woman gratefully and handed Chloe to her while she packed up the shopping. Out of the corner of her eye she could see the woman pulling faces at Chloe and hear her making noises. It was true what everyone said about Thai people loving babies.

When Hayley had packed the bags, the cashier ran up the bill and she reached into her bag to find the new purse she'd bought from the market after her old one got stolen. At first she couldn't find it, and for a moment she panicked, but then her hand gripped around the leather and she opened it, took out a few notes and waited for her change.

She lifted up the bags, then looked up, ready to take Chloe back from the woman.

But there was no one in front of her. She glanced from left to right, scanning along the ends of the other tills.

But there was no sign of her. Chloe was gone.

EIGHTEEN

NOW

When Hayley turned her key in the lock she was greeted by the smell of fresh baking. She could hear the sound of voices in the kitchen; Alice's excited and high-pitched, and Johanna's cheery but quieter. A third lower voice joined them. Lars. He must have taken a break from his office upstairs. Hayley swallowed her sense of unease. She'd been feeling odd ever since she'd seen the picture of Karolina in Johanna's room. And there was something about the way Lars got on so well with Johanna that made her uncomfortable.

'Hello?' she called out. There was no answer. She knew she should be pleased to be coming home to a happy family, all laughing and joking together, but she felt like an outsider.

In the kitchen Alice was holding up a spoon of chocolate buttercream for Lars to taste.

'We've baked,' said Johanna, smiling. She was dressed in Hayley's apron, the one that had been a Christmas present from her mother-in-law three years ago and had sat unworn in the drawer ever since. Now it was coated in a homely dust of flour.

'It smells delicious,' Hayley said, breathing in the aroma.

'The cakes are in the oven, Mummy. We baked them for you after your day at work. And Daddy too.'

'Thank you, sweetheart.' She bent to kiss Alice on the top of her head, breathing in the scent of her strawberry shampoo.

'This is such a lovely surprise,' she said to Johanna. 'A real treat.' She tried to think of the last time she'd made cakes with Alice. She was always too busy. When she wasn't at work, she was cleaning, doing washing or tidying up. They never seemed to find the time to do this kind of thing together.

'I remember cooking with my mother,' Johanna said. 'It was a lovely part of my childhood.'

Hayley thought of Karolina and Hans, of the kind of child-hood they might have given Johanna. But Johanna only had a photo of Karolina. And she didn't use Hans' surname. What had happened?

'It sounds idyllic,' she said. 'Your childhood.'

Johanna frowned. 'Some of the time,' she said. Hayley felt like her heart was breaking. *Some of the time.* She'd always thought they'd be good parents.

'What do you mean?'

'Well, I don't know. My parents got divorced when I was nine. It wasn't pleasant. My mother moved us to the other side of Stockholm and we both changed our names to her maiden name. She tried to give me the perfect childhood. But looking back, there was always something underneath. Something not quite right.'

Hayley froze. 'Oh?'

'Mum was always so cagey about the time when I was a baby. We were in Thailand for a bit then, but neither of my parents ever talked about it. They'd lived in Thailand for years before I was born...'

The oven beeped then. 'Cakes! Cakes!' Alice shouted.

The two women turned towards the sound. 'I think they might be ready,' Johanna said with a wink. 'Let me check on them.' She turned the oven light on, and lifted Alice up to peer inside.

'They've risen!' Alice said.

'They certainly have.' Johanna put on oven gloves and pulled out the baking tray.

'Do you have a cooling rack?' she asked Lars, who looked blank.

'It's just here,' Hayley said, pulling it out of the drawer.

'Right, we just need to let them cool before we can ice them.'

Hayley felt like a spare part standing in the kitchen. She remembered that she needed to send a work email that she'd forgotten to send before she left the office. She went into the dining room and pulled her laptop off the bookshelf, where she stored it away from Alice.

There was a pile of papers on the dining table. Johanna's university work. Biochemistry. Row upon row of equations. Johanna was obviously clever, like her father. Hayley didn't have a mathematical brain. She had always preferred the arts. She'd done a history degree at Bristol after she'd got back from Thailand.

Karolina and Hans must be proud. She wondered how they felt about Johanna coming to England, whether it worried them. She wondered what they'd told Johanna about her background.

She flicked through Johanna's documents absent-mindedly, wanting to know more about who she was, what she was studying. At the bottom of the pile there was a blue folder with an opaque cover. Hayley could just about make out a familiar logo on the piece on paper underneath. *The Bangkok Observer*.

Hayley remembered Ryan saying that the paper had recently put its archive online. Hayley swallowed and opened the folder, nausea rising inside her as she read the familiar headline.

BANGKOK'S KILLER NANNY?

There was a black and white photo of Hayley beneath the picture, sitting on a sofa in David and Julie's apartment, holding a crying baby. Her face was partly obscured by her hair, but you could still see the tension in her shoulders, her slight frown. She'd never been able to remember the photo being taken or known how the journalist had got hold of it.

'Hayley?' Johanna called, coming towards her. 'We're just making the icing. Alice says you have some food dye in the cupboard but I can't find it.'

Hayley dropped the article, and it fluttered to the floor.

'Oh,' Johanna said, her face falling. 'I—'

'Where did you get this?' Hayley asked, her voice shaking. She felt tears welling in the corners of her eyes. She thought of Ryan's book. Had he approached Johanna as well as Michelle? Maybe he'd shown her the article.

Johanna hesitated. 'I've been meaning to talk to you about it. Since I moved in.'

Hayley took in her words. Johanna had known who Hayley was before she moved in. 'Is that why you're here? Is that why you wanted to be my lodger?' she whispered. 'Have you been looking for me?'

Johanna sat down heavily on one of the dining room chairs, the cakes forgotten. In the kitchen, Alice and Lars were laughing again.

'I needed to find you. I hope you don't mind. I have to understand what happened. The truth.' Johanna nervously folded and unfolded a napkin that had been left on the table, unaware of what she was doing.

Hayley hesitated. She felt sorry for her, the uncertainty in her eyes. But she couldn't tell her the truth. There was too much at stake. Too many people would get hurt.

'Why are you here, Johanna?' she asked. She had a sudden

desire to put her arms around her, to hold her and comfort her, to tell her everything would be all right.

'I'm here because I need you to tell me what happened in Bangkok. Because I know who I am. I'm Chloe. The baby who went missing.'

NINETEEN

1999

Hayley looked frantically from left to right, trying to see where the Thai woman from the supermarket had taken Chloe. She couldn't see them anywhere. For once she wished that Chloe was screaming, the noise echoing round the store so that Hayley could follow it and find her. But she couldn't hear screaming. She couldn't even hear any crying. Just the tinny music that the store was playing through the speaker system.

Hayley shivered. Chloe and the woman might not even be in the store any more.

How long had she taken her eye off her? Two minutes? Ten? She hadn't had that much shopping, but between packing it up and paying, she hadn't been taking much notice of her surroundings. There'd certainly been enough time for someone to leave the shop with her.

'Have you seen my baby?' she asked the woman behind her. But she just shook her head and Hayley could tell she didn't understand.

The woman who'd taken Chloe had been ahead of her in the queue. She wouldn't have gone back into the shop. She must have left. A million scenarios flashed through Hayley's mind. Chloe stolen and sold to a couple who desperately wanted a baby. Chloe sold to the sex trade or as a household maid. Chloe kidnapped by a depraved man. Chloe abandoned by the side of the street. She thought how easily she had handed her over to a stranger. Someone whose name she didn't even know. What had she been thinking?

The woman must still have her. They couldn't have gone far. She just needed to find her. Hayley scanned the aisle at the end of the checkouts. No sign of her.

She abandoned her shopping, ran towards the door and looked outside. People pushed trolleys through the car park and hung around in groups, chatting. Her eyes flicked from person to person in turn. No young children. No babies.

She was gone.

She needed to alert someone, let someone know. Should she call the police? She thought of Julie and David, how they'd blame her. For a second she glanced to the exit of the car park, considered running away from her mistake. But that wasn't an option. She had to find Chloe.

She realised she was standing beside her car. Her driver was folding up his paper and opening the door.

'Have you seen Chloe?' she asked him.

He shook his head quizzically.

'Chloe!' she repeated. 'The baby!' She pointed to her empty arms and she saw realisation dawn on his face.

He stared at her in panic. She realised she needed to alert the security staff in the supermarket, see if someone had seen her.

She rushed back into the shop, the driver behind her. He began speaking to one of the staff in rapid Thai.

And then she heard the cry, faint but recognisable. Chloe. She noticed a small circle of women standing at the far end of the checkouts and rushed over. As she arrived she saw Chloe being passed back to the woman Hayley had given her to. The woman quickly gave her to Hayley.

'Thank you,' Hayley said, shaking with relief. She held Chloe close to her, feeling the warmth of her tiny body. Then the anger came.

'Where were you?' she asked the woman. 'Where did you take her?'

But the woman only looked confused. She smiled at Hayley, gave a small bow with her hands held together in front of her and then turned back to her friends. Beside Hayley the driver seemed to be updating the security staff.

'OK now,' he said to Hayley, as they walked back to the car.

Hayley had tears in her eyes as she repeatedly kissed Chloe's head, breathing in the floral scent of baby shampoo.

'OK,' she replied, shakily.

TWENTY

NOW

Hayley stared at Johanna, the past rushing up to confront her. She had no idea what to say.

'You think you're Chloe?' she repeated.

'Yes, I'm Chloe, the baby that went missing. Look at this.' Johanna grabbed the folder, pulled out the computer-generated photograph from the blog post. There was no denying the woman looked like her.

Hayley's stomach knotted 'Those things are never accurate,' she said quickly. 'There are thousands of women who probably resemble this picture. It doesn't mean it's you.'

Johanna shook her head. 'I was hoping you could help me. I wondered... I wondered if you had something to do with the disappearance.'

'Like the papers said, you mean?'

'They suggested you might have taken her, that she might have been dead. But obviously I don't think that.' Johanna suddenly looked worried. 'I mean, I was that baby. I think that for some reason you kidnapped me, took me away from my birth parents. I wasn't sure why at first. I was nervous about moving in with you, wondering what kind of person might kidnap a baby. But I know you now. I know that you're a caring, kind person. Whatever your reasons were, they must have been good ones.'

'No—' Hayley said, but Johanna didn't let her finish. She was too caught up in what she was saying.

'I don't know what my biological parents were like. Maybe they weren't good parents. I think you must have taken me and given me to my parents, Karolina and Hans. You knew them, didn't you?'

Hayley nodded. She couldn't pull her thoughts into coherent words. Her mind was all over the place, trying to craft an explanation that made sense. She stuck to answering the question. 'I did know them in Thailand, yes. They were friends of my employers. But I didn't know them well.'

'You gave Chloe to them.' Johanna looked excited. 'I'm right, aren't I? All my life I've felt out of place, and now this. It all makes sense. I must be her.'

Hayley took a deep breath. Johanna was so convinced, but she was going to have to burst her bubble. 'You're wrong, Johanna.' She reached out to touch her arm. 'I'm sorry, but you are.' She had a lump in her throat as she swallowed. 'Look, I can see how you might think this.' She picked up the picture. 'You do look like her here. And your parents were in Thailand. But it just can't be.'

'Why not?'

Hayley sighed. 'Well, for one, I didn't take her. I don't know what happened to her. So I don't have any real answers for you.'

Johanna looked deflated, her shoulders sinking. 'You don't know anything?'

'I wasn't even there the morning she went missing. I left the night before.'

'But isn't that when she was taken? The night before?'

Hayley shook her head, trying to remain calm, to stop her body from shaking. She didn't like the accusatory tone in Johanna's voice. 'No, her parents would have put her to bed. They found her gone in the morning.'

'OK,' Johanna said, frowning. 'So maybe you had nothing to do with it. But don't you think it's possible?' Her voice wavered a bit, uncertainty creeping in. 'Don't you think it's possible that I'm Chloe? That someone else gave me to my parents?'

Hayley shrugged, wanting to appear casual. 'Anything's possible. But it doesn't seem likely. I left Bangkok soon after Chloe went missing. I didn't want to be a nanny any more. But Hans and Karolina stayed. The expat community was tight-knit. If they had suddenly had a baby just after Chloe disappeared, then people would have noticed, the police would have been informed.'

'Maybe my parents hid me?' Johanna said. 'Maybe Hans and Karolina hid me until it all died down. Then pretended I was theirs. My birth certificate says I was born several months after Chloe disappeared, but I don't think I believe it.'

Hayley reached out and touched Johanna's arm. 'That doesn't sound likely, does it?' she said gently. 'It would be hard to hide a baby.'

'Maybe,' Johanna admitted.

Hayley knew that it could be easy to hide things, to keep secrets. People didn't always ask the right questions. And, years later, the fear of everything coming out stayed with you, a burden you carried every day.

'You're not Chloe,' she said firmly.

Johanna frowned and pressed her hands to her temples. 'I was so sure I was her,' she whispered. 'We were both born in 1999. And we lived in Thailand. I look like the computer-generated picture. It all made sense.'

'I'm so sorry, Johanna. But it doesn't add up. Karolina and Hans are your parents. They care about you. They brought you up.'

Johanna slumped in her seat. 'I know that,' she said, dejectedly.

'Are you OK?' Hayley said, placing a hand on her shoulder. Her heart was thumping in her chest. She longed for this conversation to be over.

'I'm fine, just a bit disappointed. All these thoughts are whirring round in my head and I can't make sense of them. I've been working up the courage to talk to you about this for ages, thinking about it all the time. Ever since I moved in, I've been carrying that folder around with me, waiting for my chance to speak to you.'

'Why didn't you ask me earlier? I could have put your mind at rest.'

Johanna sighed. 'I'm sorry...' she said, looking forlorn. 'I feel like I've deliberately misled you. I took the room so I could get closer to you. For the last few months I've been obsessed with the idea that I'm Chloe. Ever since I saw that blog post with the picture. Once I started reading about the case, I knew you were the person I needed to speak to. But I didn't think you'd talk to me unless you trusted me.'

'So you applied to be my lodger,' Hayley said.

Johanna nodded. 'I've really overstepped, haven't I? I found out your married name and where you lived. I followed all the local groups on Facebook to see what you were doing. When you were selling that wardrobe a month ago, I even considered coming to look at it, just for an excuse to speak to you, to talk to you. So when you advertised the room it seemed perfect. And we got on so well. I thought I could build up a relationship with you, and then ask you about Thailand.'

Hayley nodded, thinking of all her visits to Sweden. How she'd found out where Karolina and Hans lived, how she'd sometimes watched their house, when Johanna had been small. The time she'd seen the balloons on the door, the children arriving for Johanna's birthday party. She'd caught a glimpse of her then, her dark hair so unlike her parents' blond looks. She'd never known her name.

'Don't worry,' she said. 'I understand.'

'You don't want me to move out, then?'

Hayley sighed. That was the last thing she wanted. Johanna was part of the family now. She reached for her hand and squeezed it. 'Of course not,' she said. 'But at least we've cleared everything up now. I'd like you to stay.'

'I think I'm going through some kind of identity crisis,' Johanna said, her face flushed. 'I'd just convinced myself I was Chloe. I feel so bad now. I don't know how I could have thought that my parents would do something like that. But they were always so cagey about their time in Thailand, and when I asked about it they always clammed up and changed the subject.'

'Did you tell them why you were asking?'

Johanna shook her head. 'No. It's such a big thing to think, a big thing to accuse them of. I couldn't say anything until I was sure.'

'And now what?' Hayley asked, looking sympathetically at her.

'I guess now I'm back to square one. I don't know what to think any more. But I'm sure there's something odd going on, that they're hiding something from me. It's just not what I thought it was. You said you knew my parents back then, didn't you? What were they like?'

Hayley nodded. 'They were lovely. Very kind people. And they desperately wanted a child. They wanted you.'

'Did they want me enough to take me from someone else?'

Hayley shook her head. 'No,' she said, resting a hand on Johanna's shoulder. 'They didn't. They'd never have done something like that.'

TWENTY-ONE

1999

Hayley sat on an old sagging sofa in the hostel in Khao San Road with Lyndsey and Sunita, drinking a can of Coke. It felt good to be back in the muggy warmth and the noise, the fan spinning to cool them. She was a world away from David and Julie's apartment.

Julie was back at work and Hayley was now in charge of the three children during the working day. Most of the time it was just her and Chloe, and Julie had typed up a list of rules and guidelines Hayley had to follow. Everything from what to do if Chloe cried, to how the house should look like when she returned from work; no toys out and the children's dinner cleared away.

Hayley had been worried that the sudden increase in rules was because Julie had found out that Hayley had lost Chloe in the supermarket. But Julie hadn't said anything about that, and Hayley thought she'd got away with her mistake. She'd never leave Chloe with a stranger again, but today she'd really needed to get out of the apartment for a bit, to see her friends. Dodging the motorbike traffic with Chloe in her arms made her feel nervous, but then she'd gone down the little alleyway to the hostel and seen Lyndsey and Sunita and it had all been worth it.

She bounced Chloe on her lap. She'd been screaming a lot lately and had seemed unsettled. Hayley thought that she must speak to Julie about whether or not she needed medicine. But now Chloe was calm, looking all around her, taking in all the brightly coloured embroidery hanging on the wall. The hostel was buzzing with backpackers arriving and leaving. Some had just stepped off the plane, with their new rucksacks and bright white trainers, whereas others carried dusty, faded bags.

'I can't believe you're looking after a baby,' Lyndsey exclaimed.

Hayley laughed. 'It's not that hard. And she's gorgeous, isn't she?' She stroked Chloe's hair. Her rucksack was filled with bottles of milk in cool bags. She didn't want her to get dehydrated. 'It's not just her,' she continued. 'She's got two sisters. They're four and five.'

Lyndsey peered round her. 'Where are they? Have you forgotten them?' she joked.

'No, they're at school.'

'I guess you were always looking after your brothers when they were growing up, so this should be easy for you,' Sunita said.

'Yeah, I love the kids.' Emily and Eva were hard work, but a lot of fun. She loved playing with them.

'And the flat, what's it like?'

'Oh, it's amazing. Huge windows. Views over Bangkok. Spacious, too. With wall-to-wall bookcases.' She glanced round the downtrodden hostel lounge. 'And it's very clean. They have a maid.'

'It sounds like the lap of luxury.'

'It is,' she said, not mentioning the concrete box that was her bedroom. It was still better than sharing a dorm at the hostel.

'Do they need any other employees?' Lyndsey said. 'I'm a bit sick of slumming it.'

'Lyndz and I were thinking of staying a night in a posh hotel, just to have sheets that aren't scratchy and a shower to ourselves,' Sunita said.

'You should come over one day, see the apartment.' Now Julie was back at work, Hayley was on her own with Mae for much of the day and although they got on fine, it was hard to communicate when Mae didn't speak much English and Hayley didn't speak Thai. It would be good to have company.

'Yeah,' Lyndsey smiled. 'Let's do that. And maybe I could have a bath while I'm there. I miss luxuriating in the bath.'

'Maybe,' Hayley said. One of Julie's rules was that Hayley wasn't allowed to use Julie and David's bathroom.

'Oh my god, that would be amazing,' Sunita said. 'Now, can I hold that lovely baby?'

Hayley handed Chloe carefully over to Sunita, and then spent a few moments enjoying the sensation of her empty arms.

'You'll have to come over here again for drinks. An evening or weekend,' Lyndsey said.

'I don't really get much time off,' Hayley said. 'Chloe always needs looking after.' She gazed at her in Sunita's lap. She looked so adorable.

'Don't the parents do it sometimes?'

'They do bits and pieces. But not much. I'm her main carer, I suppose.' Hayley quite liked it like that. She loved the feel of Chloe in her arms.

'So you don't get time off at weekends?'

'No. Julie and David like to do things, meet their friends at the weekend. And if they go out with the children, they like me to come with them. I have all the milk and nappies, et cetera, in the nappy bag. They need me.'

'It sounds like you're working too hard. You'll have to see us one evening.'

Hayley nodded, but the truth was Chloe was still too young to have settled into any sort of bedtime routine. Often Hayley was up past midnight trying to comfort her and control her screaming. But a part of her had bonded so strongly with the little ones that she didn't want to be anywhere else. It felt like the three girls were her family, almost like they were her own children.

TWENTY-TWO

NOW

Hayley paced round her office, unable to concentrate. She couldn't stop thinking about what Johanna had said to her. Hayley was sure she'd convinced her that she wasn't Chloe, but it made her feel anxious to think she was curious, that she'd been looking into it. It wouldn't take much for everything to fall into place. At least Johanna was living in her home, so she could keep an eye on her. Hayley liked having her around. She was so good with Alice, and she got on well with Lars. Hayley had longed to get to know her for so many years, to know that she was all right, that she was happy. And now she was here she didn't want to let her go. As long as she could keep the past buried.

She glanced up through the glass wall of the office and saw Ryan in the waiting room, staring at her.

This was the last thing she needed. No doubt he wanted to talk about his book. She looked in her diary and saw he hadn't booked an appointment with her. Another student was due in ten minutes.

She got up reluctantly and went to the door, stepping out into the waiting room.

'Hi,' Ryan said, rising up and smiling. 'I've come to see you.'

She nodded. 'Look, I can't talk to you now. I have another student with an appointment.'

'But there are things I need to talk to you about,' he said. 'For the book. I really need your input.'

Hayley swallowed. 'Come in then,' she said quickly, opening the door. She couldn't afford for this conversation to be overheard.

He sat down opposite her. 'Thanks for giving me a chance,' he said, smiling shyly. 'Honestly, I'm so excited about this book. This could be my big break. And I'm enjoying the research so much.'

'So how's it going?' Hayley was longing to know what he had found out. She was sure he wouldn't be able to find out any more than anyone else had done previously, but there was a niggle at the back of her mind. She'd heard of writers discovering new evidence in cold cases. Sometimes a new perspective could change the case entirely.

'Well, I'm still researching at the moment. I'm trying to track all the connections to Chloe.' He pulled out his notebook from his bag. 'There are the obvious ones: the parents – David and Julie – and of course you, working as a nanny there. Then Emily and Eva, the half-sisters. But there were also some other people around at the time. Marion, David's ex-wife. And a couple I'd love to know about, Hans and Karolina. Did you know them?'

Hayley tucked her hair back behind her ear. How did he know about Hans and Karolina?

'I didn't know them well,' she said quickly, trying to hide the alarm in her voice. 'I was just the nanny. Not a part of their social circle.' First Johanna, now this. She thought uneasily of Ryan hanging round the house and speaking to Michelle. The last thing she wanted was for him to speak to Johanna. But she'd told him not to speak to anyone else from her house and he'd agreed. 'But look, I can't talk now, I've got other appointments.'

'What about the end of the day then?'

'No, I have to rush back to pick up my daughter.'

'Oh, Alice,' he said. 'Of course.' Hayley jumped. She hadn't thought he knew her daughter's name, but she must have told him.

'So you'll talk to me another time, then?' He wasn't going to give up. She thought of Johanna, how close she was to finding out the truth. She needed to shut Ryan down, to stop him digging deeper. She was going to have to speak to him.

'Sure,' she said. 'I'll talk to you another time. I'll contact you.' She had to work out what she'd tell him before they spoke.

He pulled out a shiny business card from his pocket and handed it to her.

RYAN DAVIES, CRIME WRITER

He must have had them made recently. 'Just in case you lose my number,' he said with a smile. 'And it's got my email address on it too.'

'I'll call you,' she said. 'I promise.'

'Great,' he said. 'If I don't hear from you, then I'll give you a ring tonight. Then I can arrange a time to interview you properly.'

'Tonight?' She was taken aback, imagining her phone ringing when she was with her family, trying to talk to Ryan while they listened. 'You don't need to do that,' she said quickly. 'We can arrange a time now.' There was no avoiding this. She was going to have to speak to him. Maybe this would be a chance to share her side of the story. She shivered.

'When are you available?' Ryan said.

Hayley thought through her timetable. She was out of the office all next week on a training course, so there would be no time then. And she couldn't see him in the evening. She hardly ever went out, so Lars would be instantly suspicious. Especially as they were supposed to be saving money. But she couldn't leave Ryan to his own devices for much longer. She didn't know who he'd talk to or what he'd find out. She needed to take control of this, help direct his research down the right avenues.

'Would tomorrow morning work?' she asked. It was Saturday. Lars had said he'd take Alice swimming and Johanna was going out for the day. There was a short window in the morning when only her mother would be in the house.

'That would be perfect,' he said. 'Where shall we meet?'

'How about ten a.m. at my house?' Hayley said. If they met anywhere else then she couldn't be sure she'd be back in time. She was taking Alice to a birthday party at lunchtime.

'Brilliant, I'll see you then.' He grinned, and stood up to leave. 'Thank you, Hayley.'

Hayley watched him stand and walk out of her office without turning back. She felt a shiver of unease run down her spine. She hoped she was doing the right thing.

TWENTY-THREE

1999

Hayley woke in the morning to Chloe's screams and padded down the hall to put the kettle on and start warming up her bottle. It was 6 a.m. and the light was starting to peek through the blinds. She could hear Julie and David talking in the bedroom and then one of them rising and getting in the shower. After she'd got the milk, she picked Chloe up and comforted her, rocking her back and forth.

She heard Julie and David getting their breakfast things. The girls would be up soon and then the day would start properly. Mae would arrive and clear the table from Julie and David's breakfast, and then Hayley would prepare the children's breakfast. Chloe started to calm in her arms, and Hayley felt calmer too. She enjoyed her time with her when the girls were at school. She loved the way she was so soft and cuddly and the way she smelt, so fresh and clean. When Hayley held her something in her heart melted, and she felt complete.

When the girls woke up, she made sure they went to the toilet, and then took them through to the dining room to sit them down. The table wasn't cleared yet, and it occurred to Hayley that Mae hadn't turned up. There had been some animosity between Julie and Mae and Hayley wondered if it had come to a head. Mae had never wanted to move out of her room in the apartment and Hayley had felt guilty when Mae had come in one day and taken her posters down from the wall and packed her picture of the Thai king and queen carefully into a little rucksack.

'Where's Mae today?' Hayley asked Julie, who was putting her plate in the dishwasher. 'Oh, she quit. I'm not quite sure why. I didn't feel she was doing such a good job any more. I'm afraid we'll all have to take on a bit more of the housework.' Hayley's heart sank. What did that mean?

'I'm here to look after the children,' she said weakly.

'Sure, but a nanny is usually expected to do some household tasks. Most of the ones we know do washing and ironing, and also some cooking and cleaning. You've been lucky so far that we had a maid as well. But now Chloe's more settled, you'll have time to do a bit more.'

'I can't do everything,' Hayley said. She thought of Sunita and Lyndsey at the hostel, thought how she would be having more fun if she'd stayed with them. Not that she could afford to. Even though she'd saved up the money from her job, it wouldn't stretch that far if she left now.

'Oh, you won't have to do everything. David and I are planning to be out most nights, at events or dinners. And if we host anyone here, we'll hire a cook. So most of the time you'll only be cooking for yourself. You'll just need to keep the place clean and tidy.'

'Let's discuss this later,' David said calmly. 'I think we all need to talk about it together, come to a solution.' He started clearing the table, and Hayley poured the kids' cereal into bowls.

'Can I have some water?' Eva whined. Hayley realised she'd forgotten to serve the girls their drinks. She went to get them, but Eva was impatient. She got up from her seat and went to

Julie, who was packing things into her briefcase. Eva patted her leg. 'Can I have some water please, Mummy?'

Julie jumped at the child's touch and knocked her coffee off the table and down her suit.

'Look what you've made me do,' she shouted angrily at Eva. 'And I'm not your mum.' She shooed her away and tears filled Eva's eyes. Hayley picked her up and hugged her.

'Your mother should be looking after you,' Julie snapped, 'not me. But she can't even do that.' She looked down at her suit. 'Now I'm going to have to get changed.'

Eva was in floods of tears, and Hayley rocked her, glaring at Julie's retreating back. She wished David would come over and comfort his daughter, but he didn't. Hayley knew how desperately both girls missed their mother. She'd sat with Eva at night as she'd cried into her pillow asking when her mummy was coming back.

'Julie's very stressed at the moment,' said David, as he loaded the dishwasher. 'I know that losing the maid isn't ideal, but I can talk to her about it.'

'She really upset Eva,' Hayley said. Hearing Julie reject Eva when she'd called her 'Mum' really hurt. Eva hadn't seen her mum once since Hayley had moved in, and no one ever seemed to talk about her.

'When will their mother pick them up?' Hayley asked.

David sighed. 'I don't know. She's due out of hospital soon. Julie thinks she'll take them to England as soon as she gets out. But I'm not so sure. She still struggles to walk. She'll need some time to recover.'

'The children need their mother,' Hayley said. She thought about how attached Eva and Emily had grown to her, how they told her they loved her each night. She always said she loved them too and then gave them a kiss at bedtime. But it tugged on her heart. She knew she wouldn't be with them forever. 'Maybe I could take them to the hospital to see her?' she said.

'Maybe. I haven't spoken to her for ages. We're not on good terms. She can't stand Julie. I'll speak to the doctors to find out how she is.'

'I'm sure she'd love to see the girls.'

David frowned, as if this hadn't occurred to him. 'Of course, you're right,' he said. 'It would be good for them. I'll give you the details of the hospital and the ward.' He wrote it down on a scrap of paper and handed it to her.

Julie came out of the bedroom in a fresh suit. 'I'm off now,' she said curtly. She kissed David briefly, and then leant down to kiss Chloe's head.

'Have a good day,' David said as the door shut behind her.

'Are you off too?' Hayley asked. She felt more relaxed when it was just her and David. She found him easier-going and more thoughtful than Julie.

'In a minute,' he said. 'I wanted to talk to you about something first.' For a moment Hayley's heart fluttered. David was good-looking and rugged, and occasionally she felt a glimmer of attraction towards him, despite the fact that he was old enough to be her father. She pushed the feeling back down.

'What is it?' she asked.

'I've been speaking to Panit.'

The driver. Hayley felt her heart sink. 'Oh?' she said.

'He's told me what you've been doing.'

'What?' Hayley said, squeezing her hands together nervously.

'He said you lost Chloe in the supermarket. And that you took her out drinking with your friends.'

'It wasn't like that,' Hayley said quickly. They hadn't been drinking.

David sighed. 'Look, I haven't told Julie yet. You're still young. And naive. I don't think she'd go easy on you.'

'OK.'

'But these things – they're serious, Hayley. You're only still here because you get on so well with my kids. They've bonded with you in a way they just haven't with Julie.'

'The kids are wonderful,' Hayley said. The children were the reason she enjoyed her work.

He reached out and touched her arm. 'You love the children. And I can't tell you how much I appreciate that. But Hayley, you really mustn't mess up again. No more trips to dodgy areas of Bangkok with Chloe. Watch them carefully.' He leant over her, a bit too close for comfort. 'I'll be keeping an eye on you,' he said softly.

TWENTY-FOUR

NOW

On Saturday morning, Lars and Alice were running late for their swim. Alice couldn't find her costume. She'd already searched everywhere in her room and had now come downstairs to look in the living room.

'I can't find it. We can't go swimming!' she said, sinking down onto the sofa and reaching for the television control. 'I'll watch TV instead.'

'No, you won't,' Hayley said, snatching it out of her hand. She looked at her watch. Ryan would be here in fifteen minutes. She needed to get them out of the house.

'Why don't you take Alice to the big playground off the ring road instead?' Hayley suggested to Lars, wracking her brains for activities that would keep them out of the house for at least an hour.

'It looks like rain,' Lars said, doubtfully. 'Maybe we should stay here.'

'No, Alice needs to get out. Besides, I've got the cleaning to do, and it's easier with you both out.'

'I've remembered where it is!' Alice shouted suddenly. She

ran up the stairs, then came down with a cuddly panda that was wearing the swimming costume. 'Here you go.'

'Well done, Alice,' Hayley said, aware of the minutes ticking by. 'Let's put it in your bag and I'll help you get your shoes on.'

Ten minutes later, Hayley was watching Lars and Alice drive off in the car. Ryan would be here any minute. She felt slightly nauseous. She'd spent the whole of last night planning what to say to him.

She checked on her mother, who was watching television in her room, and then started tidying up in the living room, only too aware that she'd committed to cleaning the house while Alice and Lars were out. The doorbell rang as she was straightening a cushion and she hurried to open it.

Ryan came over the threshold, clutching a box of chocolates, which he handed to her clumsily. She put them away in the cupboard, out of Lars' sight. She'd never normally buy them, so he'd wonder where they came from. She'd have to say her mother had bought them when she was out with Michelle.

'Thanks for agreeing to do this interview,' Ryan said, running his hand through his dark hair. She led him through to the kitchen and put the kettle on. He sat at the table as she made tea. 'I really appreciate your time,' he added earnestly. 'I know you weren't sure about speaking about Chloe, but I promise I'll be respectful.'

She nodded, passing him his cup of tea. 'No problem. You said you were trying to get hold of everyone involved in the case?' She wanted to find out what he already knew before she told him any more.

'Yeah, I'm just starting. The mother, Julie, still lives in Thailand, but she's moved out of the apartment. I haven't been able to get in contact with her yet. The father is dead.'

'David's dead?' Hayley said, startled. She'd never attempted to contact him after she'd left Bangkok, but a part of her had thought that, in some distant future, she'd see him again, that they'd have the chance to talk about what happened.

'Yeah, died of alcohol poisoning a few years ago. He was an alcoholic.'

'Oh?' David had liked a glass of wine when she'd known him, but he hadn't been addicted.

'They think the stress of everything that happened killed him.'

'That's awful,' Hayley said, pinching the bridge of her nose.

'It's all the more reason to find out what really happened,' Ryan said. 'To get justice for Chloe. And for David. Her disappearance will have had so many repercussions. For you too, I'm sure.'

'I've tried to forget about it,' Hayley said. 'To put it behind me.' She swallowed back her tears. 'Although you can never truly forget, can you?'

Ryan looked at her kindly. 'I wouldn't have thought so. But if we find out what really happened, then everyone can start to heal.'

'Maybe,' she said, thinking of David. She couldn't believe he was gone. 'I'd really prefer it if my name was kept out of all this, though.'

'The focus will be on Chloe, not you. I'm determined to find out what happened.'

'No one could ever find Chloe. No one had a clue where she was. I don't think that will change now.'

'Maybe,' he said. 'But maybe not. I guess it depends what new information I can find.'

'What do you want to ask me?' Hayley said. 'I don't have long. My family will be back soon.'

'Tell me about the job first. What was it like? What were the parents like?'

'David was nice. Julie could be up and down. She was kind

to me at first, but not so much towards the end. It was difficult for them having a small baby. And looking after David's older children too.'

'And Chloe? Was she a good baby?'

Hayley frowned, and it crossed her mind that he might be trying to trick her into admitting something unseemly. 'She seemed good. She cried quite a bit. But I didn't really know enough about babies then to judge either way.'

'You were inexperienced?'

'I was nineteen. I didn't have much life experience.'

'Did you feel out of your depth?' She frowned. She didn't like this line of questioning.

'Not really. I liked looking after the children.'

'Tell me about the night before Chloe went missing. Everything you can remember.'

Hayley tried to recall what she had told the police at the time. 'I'd been looking after Emily and Eva and Chloe all day,' she said. 'And that night I went out, just for one drink. I came back later. The children were all in bed. Julie and David asked me to leave, and I went. When they checked on Chloe in the morning she was gone.'

'And why did you leave that night? Why did they ask you to go?'

Hayley tried not to let the memories crowd into her mind, tried to block out the pictures in her head.

'We weren't getting on. Emily and Eva were due to go back to England soon after, and they didn't need me as a nanny for just Chloe.'

'So they asked you to leave permanently? Did that make you cross?'

'A little. I wanted to stay with Emily and Eva for their last few days in Thailand.'

'But not Chloe?'

'Chloe too.' Hayley wiped a tear from her eye, thinking of the poor baby.

'Had you argued with David and Julie that night?'

'Not really. Well, kind of.' Hayley stumbled over her words. 'But things had been building for a long time. It didn't come out of nowhere.'

'So you'd argued with them, and then the next morning you found out Chloe was missing.'

'Yes,' Hayley said, trying to stop her tears falling.

'And how did you feel?'

'Awful... Sad, confused... I didn't understand how it had happened. And I was worried, too. About how the family would cope. Particularly Emily and Eva.'

She pictured them, thought of how much they'd loved their sister. She felt her stomach clench. They didn't deserve what had happened, to lose their sister.

'And how did you find out?'

'Find out what?'

'That Chloe was missing.'

'Oh...' The question threw her for a moment, but she recovered. 'I was staying in a hotel that day. I didn't have a phone that worked. I only really knew when the police came round and took me in for questioning.'

Ryan looked at her. 'They thought you might be responsible for taking her? Any idea why that was?'

'I was never completely sure,' Hayley said. 'But I think Julie must have suggested it.' She remembered how crushed she'd felt when she'd seen Julie's comments about her in the newspaper.

'And why would she do that?'

'I don't know.'

'I think you do know. There was a witness to you taking her.'

'A witness?' Hayley said faintly.

'Yes, a child.'

Of course. 'That was a misunderstanding.'

'Eva said she saw you taking Chloe out of the apartment. It was in the paper, *The Bangkok Observer*.'

'That was a mistake. Eva was only four.' She thought of how close she'd been to Eva, how awful it had been that she'd been dragged into it. Hayley had only been in the cells for one night before they let her go. She remembered the stench of excrement, the screaming from the other women. When they'd let her out she'd got out of Bangkok as fast as she could, escaping to Chiang Mai.

Ryan looked at her. 'OK, sure,' he said. 'I'm just trying to get to the bottom of what happened.' He tipped the remainder of his tea into his mouth and looked down at his notebook. 'I have a few more questions.'

Hayley looked behind him at the untidy kitchen and the clock on the wall. She needed to clean before Lars and Alice got home.

'I don't have time. You have to go. My husband will be back soon.'

'Sure,' Ryan said. 'Maybe we can pick up again another time.'

'Maybe, but I'm in training at work all next week.'

'Right. Well, I'll see how I get on in the meantime. I still have a few people to contact. I mentioned Hans and Karolina the other day. I've sent them letters, and I'm waiting for a response. I only found a postal address for them. You don't have any other contact details, do you?'

Hayley looked down at the floor. 'No, I don't. I never knew them well, and we lost touch years ago.' She stood up from the table, and he took the hint and stood too.

'Could I quickly use your toilet before I go?' he asked.

'Yeah, sure. It's in the bathroom upstairs.'

Hayley looked at her watch and started to spray the kitchen surfaces, wiping them quickly with a cloth. If she could at least get the kitchen and the bathroom cleaned, then Lars would be happy.

'Working hard at the housework?' Ryan asked when he came down from the toilet.

'Yeah, I said I'd do it while my husband was out.'

'You didn't want him to see me here, did you?' She frowned, not quite catching his tone. She remembered what her colleagues had said about him being interested in her.

'No,' she said. 'He doesn't know what happened in Thailand. It was a hard time in my life and I don't talk about it.'

'Understood,' Ryan said. 'I won't mention it, if you don't.'

'Good,' she said, leading him towards the door. 'Please don't talk to anyone in my family.' She thought of Michelle. 'Or anyone from my household.'

'If I need anything else, I'll come straight back to you.'

'Thanks,' Hayley said. She felt slightly faint at the thought of more questions. How was she going to make sure the story she told Ryan aligned with everything she'd told Johanna? She felt the weight of the past on her shoulders, starting to crush her. She wasn't sure how much longer she could carry her secrets.

TWENTY-FIVE

1999

Hayley woke up with a pounding headache. She had had too much to drink the previous night and she felt queasy. She could hear Chloe screaming in her nursery and she knew it was her job to go to her, but she couldn't quite bring herself to get up. She thought of Julie, and tried to work up the energy to get out of bed. But then she remembered – Julie wasn't here. She was at a medical conference in Phuket. For the last few days it had just been her and David, and he'd promised he'd get the kids up this morning. She wrapped the blanket tighter around her and turned the pillow over to the cold side. She heard David pad out of the bedroom and go to Chloe. She smiled and thought back to the night before.

He'd made her feel better about things, better about the way Julie was treating her. He'd told her that he could see how much Hayley loved the children and appreciated how good she was at the job. He spoke about his children affectionately when Julie wasn't there, and it was the first time he'd ever asked how they were doing at school and how their mother was. Hayley had taken the girls to visit their mother, Marion, in hospital last week. She was leaving the hospital soon. When Hayley described the joy in the children's eyes at seeing their mother, she could see it made him happy and she wished he showed more of an interest in them when they were there.

She'd felt closer to him last night, but she cringed with embarrassment when she thought of the blur of the rest of the evening. She'd had too much to drink, and she remembered slurring her words, confiding in him about how difficult she found Julie. She just hoped he'd been as drunk as her, and he could forgive her for her actions. She winced as an image of her leaning in and whispering in his ear crept into her mind. She put those thoughts firmly to one side. Today was a new day. And at least he'd promised lots of things to make her work better. He was going to employ someone to clean a couple of times a week, and he said that he would get up in the night more with the baby. Now she could hear him with Chloe, singing softly to her. Her screams were quietening. It didn't matter what stupid things Hayley had said or done last night; the most important thing was that they'd spoken and her work would get easier now.

Hayley rolled over, listening to the sounds of the apartment. David had left Chloe's room now and she could hear him chatting to Emily and Eva. Their voices were excited and she was thrilled for them to have something as basic as the opportunity to talk to their own father. He was going to get them ready for school this morning before he left for work.

Half an hour before David was due to leave, Hayley got out of bed, showered and went to join him in the kitchen. Her face reddened when she saw him, suddenly embarrassed by her behaviour last night and by staying in bed so long.

'Feeling better this morning?' he said with a wink.

'Yeah, thanks,' she croaked. 'I'm sorry if I was a bit drunk last night...'

He laughed. 'Don't worry about it. I don't know about you, but I had a brilliant time.'

She blushed. 'Yes, me too,' she said. It had been fun, but she wasn't going to make the same mistake twice.

'Good,' he said. He met her eyes. 'Got anything planned today?'

She hesitated. She'd invited the children's mother round after school, but she hadn't told David, despite their heart-to-heart last night. She wasn't sure how he'd feel about her being in his home. And she didn't want anything to stop Emily and Eva from seeing their mother.

'Not really, just looking after Chloe while Emily and Eva are at school.'

'Well, have a good day,' he said, whistling as he walked out the door.

When the reception desk rang her to say Marion had arrived, Hayley had just got the girls back from school. She took the girls down in the lift to meet her, with Chloe in her arms.

As soon as she saw her mother in the waiting room, Emily ran straight over and hugged her. Eva clung to Hayley and she felt sorry for the little girl. Aside from the trip to the hospital last week, she hadn't seen her mother since the accident, and she seemed to have developed a fear of her. It was as if she was a stranger.

Marion had her eyes closed as she hugged Emily. She looked as if she'd never let her go. But Hayley could also see that she was shaky on her feet and that her body was thin, emaciated. She was only just out of hospital.

Eva looked up at Hayley. 'Go and give your mother a hug,' Hayley said softly, giving her a gentle push. Eva shook her head and stayed with her, wrapping herself around her body like a leech.

'She's a bit shy,' Hayley said, as Marion looked longingly at her daughter.

'She shouldn't be shy around her own mother.'

'It's a big change for her. You being out of hospital. It might take a while to get used to.' Hayley said it gently, but she caught Marion's frown of annoyance.

They made their way to the lift, Marion walking slowly, focusing on each step.

The lift creaked upwards and Hayley began to wonder if she'd made a mistake. She didn't really know anything about Marion, or what kind of mother she was to the girls. They'd only visited her for fifteen minutes at the hospital and the children had been so delighted to see her that Hayley hadn't really got any sense of who she was.

'How are you feeling?' she asked her now.

'Oh, OK. I mean, it's hard. I can't wait to get back to England.'

'I bet. Where are you staying at the moment?'

'In a hotel. I had an apartment before, but when I was in hospital I let it go. I didn't want to be paying rent on somewhere I wasn't using.'

'How long were you in hospital?'

'It's been two months since my accident.' Hayley squeezed Eva's hand, thinking of how difficult it must have been for her not to see her mother for two months.

'It must have seemed like forever.'

'It's been hell. I still can't walk properly. I need to go for appointments at the hospital all the time. I don't think I'll be able to go back to England for at least another month or two.'

'How terrible for you,' Hayley said, as the lift rose higher.

When they stepped out into the clean, ornate corridor, Marion smiled weakly. 'You know, this reminds me of when David and I moved here. Eva was about Chloe's age and we lived here, in this apartment. Seeing you holding Chloe, it's like déjà vu. I remember walking these corridors holding a baby too. I remember what a struggle it was.'

'Oh,' Hayley said. She hadn't realised that David had lived there with Marion before Julie.

'I came here for him, you know, for his job. It was supposed to be an amazing opportunity for our family. A new life together. And look how that turned out.'

'I'm sorry.'

They arrived at the door and Hayley opened it. 'Here we are,' she said, showing Marion in. 'But of course, you know that.'

Marion walked past the neat rack of shoes, while Hayley pulled off her sandals and took the girls' shoes off. She thought of how she would have to clean the floor later if Marion got even the slightest bit of mud inside.

Marion was wandering slowly round the apartment, dragging her bad leg behind her. She picked up a photo of Julie and David on a beach. 'They look happy,' she said blankly. She looked at Hayley. 'Are they happy?' she asked.

'It's hard to say,' Hayley said, thinking of her heart-to-heart with David last night.

'I hope they're not. They don't deserve to be.'

'Why don't you sit down,' Hayley said, indicating the sofa. 'And do you want a drink?'

'I'll have a tea, please.' She followed Hayley into the kitchen. 'I see she's redecorated in here. I really think this blue is tasteless, don't you?'

Hayley turned the kettle on. 'Why don't you go and play with the girls?' she said. She put Chloe down in her baby seat and fetched a mug and teabag from the cupboard.

'Sure,' she said. 'Girls,' she called. 'Why don't you take me to your rooms?'

Emily ran up and grabbed her hand, pulling her towards the girls' bedroom. 'We share a room now, Mummy. Isn't that exciting?'

Marion's face was ashen. 'What happened to Eva's room?'

'It's Chloe's room now. She needs it more. That's what Julie said.'

'OK, love.' Hayley was grateful that Marion didn't say anything more. She didn't want her to upset the girls. Eva was warming up now and she followed Marion and Emily to their room. Hayley soon heard the sound of the girls' laughter and she felt a flood of relief. This was why she'd invited Marion. To make them happy.

Hayley took Marion her tea and the girls some apple juice and then decided to leave them alone to play together while she fed Chloe in the living room.

After an hour, Hayley started to cook the girls' dinner and then she called them through when it was ready. There was colour in their cheeks and they seemed excited, full of life, the opposite of how they were around Julie.

'It's horrible watching David's life repeat itself here,' Marion said, as the children ate. 'A new baby, a new wife. Julie stole everything I had. And now I'm on my own. Injured and living in a hotel.'

Hayley nodded, digesting what she was saying. It was strange to think of David living the same life in the same apartment with a different partner. Julie was a bit younger than Marion. Hayley wondered what had happened between them all, and whether David's relationship with Julie would last.

Eva knocked into her water and spilt it on the floor and Marion bent awkwardly to pick it up.

'Don't worry, I'll do that,' Hayley said, seeing her wince. She picked up the cup and grabbed a cloth and started mopping, just as Chloe started to scream.

Marion reached into the baby chair and picked her up. 'She reminds me so much of Eva,' she said, 'when she was little. I'd stand in this kitchen rocking her at all times of the day and night.' She stared at the baby, and Hayley could see a mix of emotions in her eyes: affection, interest, envy, and something darker.

'You know Julie was my best friend here when I moved to Bangkok with David. She was my only friend. We met at the British Club. Do you know it? A lot of expats hang out there. It has a swimming pool and a bar, but a lot of people go there to meet people. Julie and I just seemed to click when we met. And her husband got on with David too. The four of us hung around together a lot. Julie showed me the sights and took me to restaurants. I confided in her about my marriage, how it hadn't been the same since we'd had kids and how we were trying to revitalise it in a new city. She took all that and used it against me. To get David.'

'That's awful,' Hayley said.

'Do they treat the girls OK here?' Marion asked.

Hayley didn't know how to answer. She thought of Julie getting cross with Eva, telling her she wasn't her mother. 'It's a nice lifestyle here,' she said. 'And they like the school.'

'You know, I would have always trusted David to be a good father to them. But not her. Not Julie. She'd prefer them not to be in her life. They're an inconvenience to her.'

Hayley couldn't deny it.

Marion continued. 'But perhaps I shouldn't trust David either. After all, he cheated on me with her. I thought I could trust him, but I couldn't.'

She kissed the top of the baby's head. 'I bet he loves you, though, doesn't he?' she said to Hayley. 'Looking after his children for him.' She looked at her intently, until Hayley averted her eyes. 'I wish I could look after them myself, but I'm just not well enough yet.'

'David loves the girls. He was talking to me about them last night. He really cares about them.'

Marion looked down at Chloe, so small and innocent in her arms. 'That's good,' she said. 'Because if either of them ever did anything to hurt my girls, I'd make sure they paid for it.'

TWENTY-SIX

NOW

Hayley wandered round the exhibits in the Science Museum. Alice had run on ahead with Johanna and was showing her one of the interactive displays, which involved shooting imaginary balls. As Hayley approached they both wore the same puzzled frown of concentration as they pressed the buttons and tried to get their aim as accurate as possible.

Hayley smiled at Lars as they watched the competition, and took his hand. His face was lined and he had dark bags under his eyes. She knew that a part of him wanted to be in his office, working flat out on his business, but she had insisted he take time off today.

Lars glanced back at her. 'Are you OK?' she asked, squeezing his hand.

He nodded.

'They're both so competitive,' she said, trying to get a smile out of him.

'Johanna fits in really well,' Lars said.

Hayley had wanted to take Johanna out to thank her for all her help with Alice. The state of their finances meant taking her to a restaurant wasn't possible, so she'd decided to take her to the Science Museum, which was free. Johanna had been delighted, keen to spend the day with the family.

Alice and Johanna eventually moved away from the exhibit, smiling and laughing. Alice ran ahead again to a human body display, and pointed out different organs to them all, trying to name each of them and asking lots of questions about how everything fitted together, and what each part of the body did. Johanna was happy to explain. Although she was studying for a master's in biochemistry, she had a knack of breaking everything down into simple parts, and explained things clearly to Alice in a way that a child would understand.

'I really enjoyed that,' Johanna said, as they headed towards the exit. 'Thank you. It was really thoughtful of you to let me join you on your family trip.'

'No problem at all. Alice loved having you there.' More than she'd loved having Hayley there, she thought, with a twinge of jealousy. She remembered Julie and Chloe, how jealous Julie had become of Hayley's relationship with Chloe. So this was how it felt to be on the other side, to see someone develop a closer bond with your daughter than you had yourself.

'I love spending time with her,' Johanna said simply, and it reminded Hayley so much of herself, how much she used to like playing with Emily and Eva.

'That's great,' Hayley said. 'We're really hoping you'll stick around.' She was worried that after their conversation the other day, Johanna wouldn't want to stay. She thought briefly of Ryan, of the possibility that he might blow everything in her life apart, if he spoke to Johanna.

'Oh, I want to stay on as your lodger. I've said before, it's nice to feel part of a family,' Johanna said with a smile. 'I wanted to ask you about my parents, though. You said you knew them in Thailand. Did you know who I was when I turned up?'

Hayley shook her head. 'No. I wasn't expecting their

daughter to turn up in my home. And—' She cut herself off, trying to stop herself over-explaining.

Johanna sighed. 'There's still so much that doesn't make sense. They left Thailand pretty suddenly. And they don't have many photos of that time in their lives.'

'It would have been normal to leave Thailand and go back to your home country after having a baby. People like to be near family and to have support. And the photos – well, people didn't take so many in those days.'

'Do you have any from that time?'

'What – from Thailand?'

'Yeah. I just want to understand what their lives were like back then. They never talk about it. They're so closed off. It's like they didn't have a life before me.'

'I can dig around,' Hayley said, thinking about what she'd say to Lars. 'I'm sure I have some photos somewhere.' She knew exactly where they were. In the old rucksack at the top of her cupboard, hidden behind some old sheets.

'That would be great,' Johanna said. 'You know, it was good to talk to you about it. I've been so confused about my parents the last few months. I've been questioning who I really am, who they really are. I don't look like either of them. They both have blond hair. I have dark hair. I have completely different features to my father.'

'I don't think that means anything. Features can skip generations.'

'Maybe. But I think it's more than that. I've decided to take a DNA test. Just in case.'

Hayley's heart sank. 'I don't think that's necessary,' she said.

'Well, probably not. But if I'm not their child, perhaps it will connect me to other relatives. And if I am, nothing will come up. I've thought about it and there's really no bad outcome.'

Hayley swallowed, putting a comforting hand on Johanna's

shoulder, trying to keep her voice steady. She mustn't panic. 'Well, I think you should think it through a bit more. I mean, you might find out something you don't want to know. Not necessarily a relative, but perhaps a genetic disposition to an illness.' Hayley was sure she'd read something like that a long time ago in an online article about the risks of DNA testing.

'Don't worry about me,' Johanna said, lightly. 'If I have some awful disease, I'd want to know about it. Besides, I've already sent off the test.'

TWENTY-SEVEN

1999

Hayley rocked Chloe gently in her arms. It was the fifth time she'd been up in the night with her, and now she could see a dim light starting to peek through the sides of the blinds and she knew the sun was coming up. There would be no more sleep for her. She held Chloe close to her, enjoying the warmth of her body, and thought of the day ahead. She needed to get Emily and Eva up, feed them and get them to school.

Things had been more difficult since Julie had got back from her conference. Although David had been true to his word and employed a daytime cleaner, Julie was never completely satisfied with her work and was always in a bad mood. She took it out on Hayley, constantly sniping at her.

At the breakfast table, Chloe was still crying and Hayley held her bottle to her lips as she encouraged Eva to eat her cereal.

She would have to eat later. Glancing up, she saw Julie glaring at her, her eyes on her daughter.

'Do you want to hold her?' Hayley asked hopefully.

'No,' Julie said. 'I can't see how I can compete with you. You're all she ever wants.' Hayley couldn't deny it. It was her the little baby looked for when she was upset; her Chloe's arms reached out towards.

'She loves you,' Hayley said softly. 'Look, she's crying with me. Maybe you could calm her down.' Julie took her tentatively, and Hayley took the opportunity to help Eva with her cereal. Chloe cried harder as Julie rocked her ineffectively.

'I think she wants you,' she said, handing the little bundle back unceremoniously.

'She's tired from being up all night,' Hayley said. Hayley was too. She longed for a hot shower to revitalise her, but she hadn't had time yet.

Just then David came in and Julie kissed him on the cheek. 'Good morning, honey,' she said.

'Morning,' he said, his eyes finding Hayley's. 'How is everyone this morning?'

'I'm great,' Julie said, with false enthusiasm. 'It's so good to be back with my family after my conference. I missed you while I was away.'

David didn't pick up on the hint. He was busy getting his own breakfast.

'Did you have a good time without me?' Julie asked. She'd been back two days already but she insisted on asking the same question. Something about her time away was bothering her, and she kept making little digs at Hayley.

'It was OK,' David said, glancing at Hayley.

Julie went over to David. 'You know, at the conference, there was a plastic surgery specialist speaking. He said you can fix anything now if you have the money. You can look like a completely different person.'

David nodded. 'I don't think I need surgery,' he said.

'Fair enough,' Julie said. 'What about you, Hayley? Have you ever thought about it?'

'Not really,' she said. She looked closer at Julie's face and realised that she had probably had surgery herself.

Julie walked over to her and put her hands on Hayley's cheeks, turning her head from side to side. 'You could get your nosed fixed.'

'What?' Hayley said, her hand flying to her face. She hadn't realised there was anything wrong with her nose.

'Oh, don't look like that,' Julie said. 'It's a compliment. You're good-looking. If you fixed your nose, you'd be truly beautiful. What do you think, David?'

David just grunted, knowing better than to get involved. Hayley blushed.

'Oh well,' Julie said. 'I suppose she's not your type, so you can't really judge. But we could definitely make some improvements.'

'I need to have a shower,' Hayley said, irritated. 'Can someone hold Chloe?'

'Why didn't you have one this morning?' Julie asked. 'We need to leave for work in a minute.'

'I was up from three a.m. with Chloe. There wasn't time.'

'You should get these personal things done when the baby sleeps. That's the expert advice, isn't it?'

'I don't know,' Hayley said. She wanted to tell them they weren't paying for an expert nanny, they were paying for her, a student, who knew very little about babies.

David came over and took Chloe from her arms. 'I'll hold her while you have a shower,' he said.

'I'll be quick,' Hayley said, and jumped up from the table.

When she switched the shower on in her bathroom, it was freezing cold. Hayley turned the dial to the right and then it began to alternate between freezing cold and boiling hot, and she jumped in and out of the stream of water in order to not get scalded. She thought of the week when Julie was away when David had let her use the en suite bathroom in their room with its huge rainforest shower, set to exactly the right temperature and easily adjustable.

When she got back to the kitchen, David handed Chloe back to her and picked up his briefcase. Julie was slipping on her shoes.

'I was planning to see my friends one evening this week. When would be convenient?' Hayley asked. She was usually too busy in the evenings with the children, but this was another thing she and David had discussed when Julie was away – giving her an evening a week off. She was planning to go over to Sunita and Lyndsey's hostel for drinks. She'd have to find time to go to an internet café and email them to arrange her visit. She wasn't allowed to use the internet in David's study any more.

'What do you mean?' Julie said. 'You're working in the week.'

'David said it would be fine.'

'Did he now?' Julie glared at David.

'Yes, I just want to see my friends. They're going away soon and I want to say goodbye.' Hayley realised with a shock that she didn't have any other friends in Bangkok, and that after Lyndsey and Sunita were gone she wouldn't have anything to do on the negotiated evenings off.

'Well, I'm sorry, but that's just not possible. You're needed here.' With that, Julie left.

'Now's not a good time to ask,' David said softly, his voice a warning. He walked out of the apartment and shut the door behind him.

TWENTY-EIGHT

NOW

When they got back from their trip to the museum, Hayley went straight upstairs to check on her mother. She was sitting up in bed, staring blankly at an old TV that they'd recently put in her room. A programme where people were choosing between staying in the UK or moving and starting a new life abroad was playing.

'Hi, Mum,' Hayley said gently, kissing her on the head. 'We're back.' She didn't look up. 'We had a really nice time at the Science Museum today. Alice loved it. And Johanna too.'

'Who's Johanna?' her mother asked.

'Our lodger.' Hayley sighed.

'We don't have a lodger,' Susan said forcefully, and Hayley realised she thought she was still living in her own house. At times like this it was best not to contradict her. It only made her stressed.

Hayley went over to the window and tied the curtains back to let in more daylight. A man was standing across the road typing rapidly into his phone. She recognised Ryan's brown leather jacket. He glanced up, as if sensing her eyes on him, and then started walking quickly away.

Hayley watched him retreating, wondering if he was cutting through to get to the corner shop further down the road. He walked straight past it.

Alice's laughter from downstairs pulled her out of her thoughts, and she turned back to Susan, who was still watching the TV.

'Did you have a nice lunch, Mum?'

'Yes, the previous girl gave it to me.' Hayley winced. Her mother's sense of reality had shifted again and now she seemed to think that Hayley was someone who'd been paid to help her. Michelle had been round today, and she thought Hayley was here to help too.

'Oh, that's good,' she said, trying to keep the tears out of her voice.

Susan stared at the television. 'All these people are silly,' she said. 'Thinking they can have a new life abroad. A happy life just like they have here. Why don't they think things through?'

'I don't know, Mum.'

'My daughter lived in Thailand. Did you know that?' Hayley froze. Her time in Thailand was never mentioned by her mum after she came back. She'd assumed that her mother's dementia would have meant she'd forgotten about it entirely, but clearly she still remembered.

'I knew that,' Hayley said softly.

'She had an awful time of it. Worst decision she ever made.'

The programme moved on and Hayley was grateful.

'What happened in Thailand?' she asked. She needed to know what her mother would say to Johanna if she ever thought to ask her.

'Thailand?' she replied blankly. 'What about Thailand?'

'Nothing,' Hayley said. 'Don't worry about it. Enjoy your programme.'

Hayley wondered how long her mother would be able to continue to live with them. She liked having her in the house and was glad to be able to keep an eye on her. Her brothers had all moved far away, and Hayley was the closest family she had. And yet, her mother's mental capacities were deteriorating rapidly. Six months ago, when she had come to live with them, Hayley hadn't really understood why she'd employed Michelle to help her. Now it was very clear. Hayley was starting to think her mother might need some more permanent care, or something more official. She would have to look at it. They might need to apply for support from the council.

Hayley sighed and went up the stairs to her bedroom, to look for some pictures of Thailand to show Johanna. Opening her cupboard, she dug around in the sheets at the back, looking for the old rucksack where she kept all her photos and memories from her trip. Her hand wrapped around one of the straps and she felt a rush of relief. It was still there. She hadn't checked for years; hadn't had any reason to look at the photos to relive the memories. It was a time she'd rather forget.

But now she held the rucksack and everything came back to her. She remembered the photos she'd taken. The happy photos of her and Emily and Eva. The three photos she had of her and Chloe; one standing outside a shopping mall, which she'd asked the driver to take, one of them sitting on one of the low sofas at the hostel, and a final one of her and Chloe by the swimming pool, that Lyndsey had taken one day when she and Sunita had come over to the apartment. She'd always found them so hard to look at, but she couldn't throw them away either.

She unfastened the rucksack. It seemed emptier than she remembered, with only a shoebox inside. She had been sure there had been a red blanket in here as well. Chloe's blanket. The last thing that Hayley had bought her before everything went wrong. It wasn't here now, and she wracked her brain to think whether she had moved it somewhere else. She was sure she hadn't.

Hayley pulled out the shoebox and opened it carefully.

There were lots of things in there, as well as photos. Old tickets for the boat, a blue shawl she had bought and couldn't bear to part with, a tiny lilac-coloured babygrow, dotted with little red roses. She put it to her face, expecting the fresh baby smell she remembered, but it was musty and mouldy. She swallowed. There was a reason she never looked in this rucksack.

She found the packs of photos, four of them, and started looking through. Most of them were scenery and tourist sites: rows of yellow tuk-tuks outside extravagant shopping malls, sparkling temples, river boats at the floating market. Just looking at them she could almost feel the heat, smell the curries cooking on the street. She remembered how excited she'd been to land in Bangkok, how ready she'd felt for an adventure. She wasn't sure if she could keep looking at the pictures. She didn't want to be reminded of how little Chloe had been, how innocent.

She paused and wiped away tears. What was she going to show Johanna? She didn't mind sharing the photos of scenery, but she wasn't sure she could bear to share Chloe with her. It was too painful.

She kept flicking through the pack of photos, bracing herself for the image of that tiny face. The first pack only contained photos of places. No people at all, not even Lyndsey or Sunita. Which was strange, because when she first arrived in Thailand they were always taking photos of each other.

Hayley went to the second pack and flicked through. Again, only scenery and tourist sites. No people in a single photo. Not Sunita, not Lyndsey, not the children. Not even Hayley herself. Hayley felt sick.

She flicked through the remaining two packs of photos. Nothing in them either.

Someone had been in this room, gone through this bag and taken out all the photos of Chloe and everyone else. They must have taken the red blanket too. Her only links to Chloe were gone. Hayley collapsed into tears. She had nothing left.

TWENTY-NINE

1999

After she'd dropped the kids off at school, Hayley made her way to an internet café further down Sukhumvit Road. The driver waited outside and she paid the attendant and sat at a computer with Chloe on her lap.

Sometimes she wished she could go out alone without the driver, just wander down the street and explore Bangkok. But she couldn't go out alone, and she couldn't walk around with Chloe. Bangkok's uneven pavements didn't allow for a buggy, and Julie and David didn't possess any kind of baby carrier. She had to go everywhere by car.

Julie had been constantly making digs at Hayley since she'd got back from her conference two weeks before. Hayley didn't understand what had changed between them and she wondered if she was struggling with going back to work, leaving Chloe in Hayley's care. Perhaps she felt like she should be at home with her baby, even though she clearly hadn't enjoyed that.

Hayley opened up the internet on the computer. Chloe started to grizzle and Hayley shifted position so she was against her shoulder, and typed her email password with one hand. There were three messages from her mother and one from

Sunita. Hayley put her hand to her temple. She hadn't emailed her mother since she'd first moved into David and Julie's, when they'd let her use David's study.

The first email from her mother was chatty, keeping Hayley updated on family news: her uncle's back operation, her dad's work, her youngest brother getting into trouble at school. The second email was five days later, and was shorter, still chatty but asking her how she was and what her news was. The third email was from two days ago and her mother had sounded worried, asking more about the nannying job and whether she was being treated well. Hayley could read between the lines and knew that her mother must be worried something awful had happened to her. Hayley wished there was a way to communicate other than email. She'd brought a cheap mobile phone with her but she hadn't been able to get it to work once she was in Thailand, and even if she had it would have been far too expensive to call.

She replied to her mother quickly, putting her mind at rest and reassuring her everything was fine. At the end of the email, she put the phone number for the apartment, told her if she needed to, she should call her there.

Then she read Sunita's email, asking when she was next coming over to Khao San for a night out. She explained she was still trying to figure out when she could as Julie wasn't keen on her going out in the evening, but she definitely wanted to see her and Lyndsey soon. She reminded them of the phone number for the apartment at the end of the email.

When she'd finished, she browsed the news. Chloe had fallen asleep on her shoulder, and for the first time in a long time, she felt calm.

Back at the apartment, she was making herself a cup of tea when the phone rang. The noise took her by surprise, the sound reverberating around the flat.

'Hello?' she said, answering the phone, expecting someone speaking in Thai.

'Hi! Hayley? It's Sunita! We got your email.'

'I'm so sorry, it's difficult for me to come out and see you at the moment. Julie's being awkward.'

'Don't worry. We're coming to you. Remember, last time you saw us you said we could come over. And I would totally love a properly hot shower. And a bathroom with a bath mat. I've actually been fantasising about it.'

'Oh yeah,' Hayley said, although she wasn't sure it was a good idea. She knew Julie wouldn't want her friends in her apartment, let alone using her shower. So far she'd managed to avoid telling her that Marion had been round, but she was terrified she'd find out.

'So we thought maybe tomorrow? When the kids are at school?'

'Ummm...' Hayley said, trying to think of a way to say no.

'We need to see you, Hayley. We miss you!'

Hayley thought of Julie, how hard she made her work, how she didn't want her to go out in the evenings. She felt a rising anger. Julie couldn't deny her access to her friends entirely. Hayley had every right to see them.

'Yeah,' she said. 'Sure. Come over tomorrow. I'd love to see you.'

THIRTY

NOW

Hayley looked down at her floor, at the piles of photos before her. She'd been through the four packs. No photos of people in any of them. She went through each pack again. She lifted up the lilac babygrow and her shawl to see if any photos had got stuck underneath them in the shoebox. Nothing. Then she looked back in the rucksack, delving into each pocket. There were ancient receipts in one of the side pockets, and a few coins. That was it. She thought of Chloe's red blanket. That was gone too. But not the babygrow. She shivered. Whoever had taken the red blanket must have known its significance. But how? She'd never mentioned it to anyone.

Opening the packs of photos again, she peered at the negatives, looking at each in turn, holding them up to the light. She could see the pictures she remembered, of her and Sunita and Lyndsey grinning in front of a temple. There was a negative of the photo of her and Chloe. The photos had definitely been here, in this rucksack. But someone had taken them. Now they were gone.

Johanna, Lars and Alice were laughing downstairs, and she remembered that Lars would want to come up to his study soon to work. He'd wonder why she was in their bedroom. She needed to put everything back quickly. She remembered she'd been looking at the photos to find some to show Johanna, and now she selected a few of the temples in Bangkok and some more of her hostel in Chiang Mai. She wondered if Johanna would feel a connection to any of them. She needed to indulge her curiosity without giving any fuel to her idea that she might be Chloe.

She cleared everything away, taking the photos she'd selected and putting them in a black folder, which she shoved in a handbag and carried downstairs with her. She'd discuss the photos with Johanna once Lars was back in his study, working.

In the living room, Lars, Alice and Johanna were immersed in a game of cards. Susan had come downstairs, and had set herself up on the sofa in front of the TV.

'We tried to include her,' Lars said, 'but she wanted to watch her programme.' A repeat of *Emmerdale* was playing on the TV. 'I made her a cup of tea. She's comfortable.'

Hayley nodded. It seemed that 'comfortable' was the best she could hope for for her mother's life these days. Suddenly she remembered finding the photo of Emily and Eva in her mother's room. Could Susan have taken the other photos too? But why?

'Mum!' Alice was shouting, pulling her out of her thoughts. 'Come and play with us. Dad needs you to take over his hand. He's got to work.'

'Sorry, love,' Lars said, as his lips brushed Hayley's cheek. 'Got to get back to it.'

'Good luck,' Hayley said.

'*Förlåt*,' Alice said. 'That's sorry in Swedish. Johanna's been teaching me Swedish words.'

'You never listened to me when I tried to teach you Swedish,' Lars said, ruffling her hair, before he left the room and went upstairs.

. . .

Hayley finished the round of cards with Alice and Johanna, then turned to Alice. 'Why don't you practise your reading with Granny?'

Alice scowled and scrunched in on herself, shaking her head vigorously. 'I want to play another game.'

'I'm sorry, darling, but you need to do your reading before school on Monday. Granny will listen to you.'

They both looked doubtfully over at Hayley's mother. Hayley wondered if she was expecting too much of both of them.

'Can't *you* listen to me read, Mummy?'

'Sorry, Alice. I want to show Johanna some photos.'

'You found photos of Thailand?' Johanna said, her face stretching into a smile.

'I did.' Hayley wondered if she should ask Johanna about the missing photos, if it could have been her that took them. But there was no hint that she was hiding anything. She seemed so excited to see them, it didn't seem possible that she had gone through them before.

'Do you have any of my parents?'

'Afraid not. It's just scenery mainly.'

'Can I see the photos, Mummy?'

'I suppose so,' Hayley said to Alice, patting her head.

They tidied the cards away and then sat on the sofa together, Alice snuggling up with Johanna. Hayley took out the photos and showed them to Johanna in turn. Johanna stared at the picture of the Grand Palace.

'I'd love to go to Thailand,' she said wistfully. 'See all the sights. See where I was born.'

Hayley swallowed, thinking back, remembering when she was born. There was so much she couldn't say.

'I'd love to go too,' Alice said.

'Maybe you will one day,' Johanna replied.

'I'm not sure,' Hayley said. 'It's very expensive.' She'd never wanted to go back. She wanted to put the past behind her.

'Well, if I go, I'll take you,' Johanna said with a smile.

'Really?' Alice said.

'If I can ever afford it.'

Hayley frowned. She didn't like to think about it, but Johanna would be gone when she finished her degree. She'd never take Alice anywhere. She shouldn't make false promises.

'There'll be plenty of time to travel the world when you're older,' she said.

'Like your mum,' Johanna said. 'She went on an adventure to Thailand when she was a teenager.'

'Do you think I'll go on an adventure like you?' Alice asked.

'I expect so,' Hayley said. Although she hoped with all her heart that Alice would never have to go through anything like what she'd been through in Thailand.

Later that evening, she went upstairs to see if her mother wanted help with her bath before bed. She'd only started doing this recently, since the night when she'd walked past the bathroom and heard heavy breathing and groaning and realised her mother couldn't get out of the bath.

She knocked on the door of her mother's room. 'Are you ready for your bath?' she asked.

'I'll just get ready,' her mother replied.

'Do you want some help?'

'No thank you, dear.'

Hayley nodded through the door. Her mother seemed more coherent today. She went downstairs and put some washing on, then came back and started running the bath.

'Are you ready, Mum?' she said, knocking on her bedroom door.

'For what?'

Hayley sighed and entered the room. She guided her mother in undressing, then helped her get into the bath. She and Lars needed to add bars and perhaps a bath chair to make it easier for her. Looking into that was another thing on her to-do list. She felt like she hardly had time to even think lately.

She went back into her mother's room and put her head in her hands. It couldn't go on like this. Not forever. She didn't think she was up to it.

She thought of the photos of Thailand, how they were missing, and remembered finding the photo of Eva and Emily in her mother's room. She opened her mother's bedside table drawers and rooted through creams and tubes of lipstick and jewellery. No photos.

Then she looked in the cupboard, going through her mother's clothes. It saddened her to see how few belongings her mother had. When she'd moved out of her house, she'd had so many things, all the clutter of a life. But they'd thrown away lots of it, and moved more of it into storage, for when her mother got her own place. The idea had been that she would move into warden-assisted accommodation, but now her health had declined Hayley didn't think Susan would qualify for the housing nearest them. She swallowed, not wanting to think about it.

Hayley called out to her mother. 'Are you OK in the bath, Mum?' It was what she also called out to Alice when she was in the bath. Alice had just started to manage the bath alone, washing herself, while Hayley or Lars popped in and out to check on her.

'I'm fine,' her mother called back.

'I'll be in to help you out in a minute.'

Hayley turned to the chest of drawers in the bedroom, and started to look through. In the third drawer she found the photos. They were hidden away in an old Tesco bag. Why had her mother taken them? Why did she have a sudden interest in this after all these years? And where was the blanket? She thought warily of Ryan, remembered him in her house, going upstairs to use the toilet before he left. How long had he been upstairs? She hadn't been paying attention as she'd been trying to clean up. Her mother had been upstairs in her room. Could he have spoken to her about Thailand? He'd promised he wouldn't speak to anyone in her family. Perhaps Johanna had spoken to her, or found the photos. The pictures had been so well hidden in the rucksack at the top of her cupboard, and her mother would have only just been able to reach. Hayley pulled the pictures out and flicked through them, seeing her teenaged self smiling with Lyndsey and Sunita, then Emily, Eva and Chloe. Tears formed in her eyes as she looked at the pictures of baby Chloe. She ran her finger over the face on the photo, wishing she could still feel the baby's soft skin.

THIRTY-ONE

1999

Hayley was giving Chloe her bottle when the apartment reception rang her to tell her that Sunita and Lyndsey were here to see her. A ball of worry formed in the pit of her stomach. She had forgotten that they would have to speak to reception to be allowed up. She hoped the woman at the desk wouldn't think to tell Julie.

When they got to the apartment she greeted them with huge hugs. It was so long since she'd seen anyone outside of the family, and she wasn't prepared for the well of love she felt springing up in her chest.

'Oh my god, this apartment block is amazing,' Sunita said, gazing all around her. 'I can't believe you live here.'

'I bet it has a pool,' Lyndsey said, putting her huge dusty rucksack down on the floor. 'Does it have a pool?'

'It does,' Hayley said, with a smile. She'd almost forgotten about the pool and the gym on the rooftop. David sometimes used the gym, but she'd never had time to use it herself. And she hadn't used the pool since before Chloe was born.

Lyndsey turned to Sunita. 'I told you it would have a pool.' She looked at Hayley. 'We've brought our swimming stuff.'

'Oh, great,' Hayley said. Lyndsey was already walking into the flat, leaving a trail of dirt from her sandals.

'Could you take off your shoes, please?' Hayley called after her. 'Julie likes to keep the place clean.'

'Oh, sure.' They both took off their shoes.

'Do you mind if we do some washing while we're here?' Sunita asked, indicating her big rucksack. 'We put it all in one bag before we came. It's easier than going to the launderette.'

'It won't be dry in time,' Hayley said weakly.

'Don't you have a tumble drier?' There was one in the back room. But there wouldn't be time for them to dry their clothes as well. They had come later than she had expected and it was only two hours before she was due to collect the girls.

'I don't think there'll be time to do washing. I have to collect the girls at three.'

'What time's Julie back?' Lyndsey asked. 'Should we stay and meet her?'

'No!' Hayley said quickly. Why did they think that would be a good idea? She'd told them about all Julie's rules. 'I haven't told Julie you're here.'

'Well, we could come and pick up the girls with you, at least?'

'That's not a good idea.'

'OK, then. Maybe we can meet them when you're back. Then we can sort out the washing while you're out.'

'I guess so,' Hayley said. She wanted to have enough time to spend with her friends, but already everything felt rushed. She'd have to tell the girls not to mention anything to Julie. She sighed.

'This flat is amazing,' Lyndsey said. 'You're so lucky.'

Half an hour later, Lyndsey and Sunita's clothes were in the washing machine in the apartment and the three of them were up at the pool with Chloe. Hayley had even managed to have a swim, while Lyndsey held Chloe.

'This is the life,' Sunita said. 'You know, this is more what I had in mind when I imagined backpacking round Thailand. I'm fed up with that grotty hostel.'

'When are you off to Australia?' Hayley asked.

'We're going in a month's time. Sure you don't want to come?'

'I can't afford it.'

'And you have a pretty nice life here,' Lyndsey said.

'I'm not sure,' Hayley said. 'I don't usually have time to use the pool.'

'What? Not even after work?'

'I work all the time.' She looked at Chloe down in her arms. 'She keeps me busy. Plus they expect me to do some cleaning too.'

'Don't the parents do anything?'

'Not much. David does a bit. But Julie does nothing at all. She's completely disinterested in the children. It's crazy, really. I don't know why she had a child.'

'Why don't you quit?'

Hayley sighed. 'I should really.' She looked down at Chloe. 'But I love the children. It's not just Chloe. It's the girls – Emily and Eva. They're not Julie's biological children and she doesn't care about them. I couldn't leave them alone with her.'

'But you'll have to, won't you?' Lyndsey said. 'Eventually.'

'Well, no. Their mother is taking them back to England soon. She's been in hospital but she's out now, getting better. Once they go back to England, then I might leave. It will be good, because I'll have saved up a bit more money by then. I can do a bit more travelling.'

'Oh, great. We're going to be a couple of months in Oz then we're heading back to Asia,' Sunita said. 'Maybe you can join us. Where were you thinking of going?'

'I don't know,' Hayley said. 'I want to see a bit more of Thailand.' Her money would last longer if she stayed in the country and besides, there was so much more to see.

'Maybe we could all meet up. We haven't seen any of the south of Thailand yet. We could go to Khao Lak together. That's supposed to be a really chilled-out place. We could go trekking through the jungle.'

'That would be good,' Hayley said, closing her eyes for a second, with Chloe in her arms, imagining a life without any responsibility except for herself. It felt good to picture an end to her time with Julie and David, a future travelling around Thailand, having carefree adventures and trying new things. She looked down at Chloe. Even after Emily and Eva had left with their mother, the baby would still be left behind with her parents. It would be so hard to leave her.

THIRTY-TWO

NOW

Hayley walked past the shops, weaving round people with overloaded shopping bags, and made her way to the old pub at the end of the high street. She'd been there with Lars once when she was younger. It was the kind of pub that had live bands on a Friday night and 2-for-1 burgers. The kind of pub she would have met friends at before she had children, and nights out had become such a rarity that cheap food and drinks in a loud bar didn't cut it any more. They wanted to go somewhere nice, somewhere *where they could hear themselves think*.

Hayley smiled as she pushed the door open, her eyes adjusting to the dim lighting, accentuated by the dark wood panelling, low ceiling and tiny windows covered in posters. She saw Michelle was already there, seated at the back, with a glass of wine.

'Did you want one?' she asked. 'I didn't know what you drank.'

'I should be getting the wine,' Hayley said. 'You've done so much for Mum.'

'Oh, it's no bother,' Michelle said. 'I actually wanted to talk to you about something too, pick your brains about living abroad. I was thinking I might try and find work, maybe in Asia. Your mum said you'd worked in Thailand.'

Thailand again. Why did it keep coming up?

'That will be a real shame for your clients,' Hayley said kindly. 'I don't know what Mum would do without you.'

'Don't worry, I won't be going yet. It's just a pipe dream.' She laughed nervously. 'I'll probably never go anywhere. But you said you needed to talk to me?' After Hayley had found the photos in her mother's room, she'd phoned Michelle, suggesting a meeting. She'd thought she might be able to come back home from work at lunchtime to meet her, but it was Michelle who preferred to meet her here, at the pub. She'd said she was in town anyway and it was more convenient.

'Yeah, I'm worried about Mum. Have you noticed she's been getting even more confused?'

Michelle sighed. 'I think she's got worse, even since we last spoke. Keeps asking who I am, who Johanna is, even sometimes who you are.'

Hayley nodded, thinking of the other day, in her mother's room, when she hadn't recognised her. 'I'm going to take her to the doctor again. Get her checked out. Do you think she needs more intensive help?'

'I can come round more often,' Michelle said. 'I think that would be a good idea. I can help her in the mornings and stay through until after lunch every day, if that would be useful?'

Hayley swallowed. They simply couldn't afford that. 'I don't know,' she said. 'I was thinking more of moving her some-where else, somewhere that would have staff to help her.'

'A home?' Michelle said, visibly shocked. 'I don't think she's ill enough for that.'

'Maybe not. I'll speak to the GP, see what she says.'

'Good idea.' Michelle was quiet and Hayley got the impression she was holding something back. Hayley paused, wondering if Michelle would say more. But she just sipped her wine in silence.

'There's something else...' Hayley said. 'I think she's been taking things from my room. Some photos were missing and I found them in her room.'

'Maybe she's just reminiscing about the old days. They could be triggers to help her remember the past.'

'They weren't photos of anything to do with her. They were my photos. From a long time ago.'

'Oh,' Michelle said. 'What were they of?'

'My gap year in Thailand.'

'Thailand?' Michelle's eyebrows shot up. 'Susan's suddenly been talking about Thailand. That's how I got the idea of maybe working abroad.'

'Has she? What's she said?'

'Something about someone called Chloe. How you didn't do it. To be honest, it doesn't make any sense. Do you know what she's talking about?'

Hayley tucked her hair behind her ears, and tried to meet Michelle's eyes. 'Chloe was someone I used to know.'

Michelle looked down into her wine. 'She seemed to say that she was a baby. And that someone thought you'd killed her... I mean, I know Susan gets confused, but what's that about? It's so odd.'

'Maybe it was just something she saw on the TV,' Hayley said quickly. 'She keeps watching those programmes where people move abroad. And too many crime dramas. Maybe she's somehow combined the two in her head.'

'That could be it. Plus the fact you actually were in Thailand. Maybe that's what's making her confused.'

'Maybe.' Hayley flushed. This conversation suddenly seemed risky, like she might let something slip.

'She gets so agitated when she talks about it. But maybe

there's some way I can correct what she's saying by reminding her of what really happened. What did you do in Thailand?'

'I was a nanny,' Hayley said, without thinking.

'To Chloe?'

'Yes. You know, I'm not sure it would be helpful for Mum to remember all the details about my life. It would be better for her to think about her own life. She's never even been to Thailand.'

Michelle nodded. 'I'm sorry, I didn't mean to intrude. I just want to help Susan. I don't like to see her so confused.'

'When did she start talking about Thailand?' Hayley asked.

'Just in the last couple of weeks.'

Hayley frowned. This couldn't be a coincidence. She thought of Ryan researching his book, of him talking to Michelle. 'Do you remember that man I told you not to talk to?' she asked.

'The one hanging around outside? Tall with dark hair?'

'Yes, him.'

'He has a niece the same age as Alice.'

'Oh yeah, I think he does.' Hayley frowned. Ryan had mentioned his niece, but she hadn't realised that she and Alice were the same age.

'Yes. He was telling me about her. Being friendly, I thought at the time. But obviously, since your text I haven't spoken to him,' she said hurriedly.

'Has Mum spoken to him?' Hayley said urgently.

Michelle flushed. 'Well, I think so, yes. Before you told me to avoid him. We were chatting to him a few weeks ago, and I had to go back into Sainsbury's because I'd forgotten something. I left her talking to him when I went back in.'

'Oh,' Hayley said. Maybe Ryan had asked her mother about Thailand. Johanna might have spoken to her too, which would mean it was on her mind.

Michelle went even redder. 'I'm sorry. Have I done something wrong?'

'No, no. You weren't to know. Just don't talk to him again.'

'I won't. He just asked so many questions. He seemed so friendly.'

'What kind of questions?'

'It was all more about Alice. How old she was. What school she went to.'

'Did you tell him?' Hayley said, panic rising in her chest. *What did any of this have to do with Alice?*

Michelle looked confused. 'Yeah, I did. He said he had a niece the same age, wanted to see if they went to the same school. He looks after his niece a lot and he said she had a schoolfriend called Alice, that it might be the same Alice.'

Hayley felt a growing dread. What was Ryan playing at? 'And were they friends?' she asked.

'No, it turned out they weren't. They go to different schools.'

'OK, Michelle. Please don't speak to him again. He's been creeping around and it makes me uncomfortable.'

'OK, sure. I'm sorry.' Michelle looked flustered. 'I haven't spoken to him since your message.'

'Don't worry about it now. Just stay away from him.'

THIRTY-THREE

1999

Hayley's driver pulled up into the underground parking for the apartments and Hayley got Emily, Eva and Chloe out of the car. Emily was chatting happily about a certificate she'd received at school for good handwriting. She told Hayley that she couldn't wait to show it to her once they got up to the apartment. Hayley nodded distractedly. She felt nervous about going up. She'd left Sunita and Lyndsey there on their own and she hoped they'd treated the apartment carefully.

Hayley said goodbye to the driver, took the children up in the lift and opened the door to their home. There was a strong smell of washing liquid, and the empty rucksack was in the middle of the hallway. Emily looked quizzically up at Hayley, as Lyndsey and Sunita came towards them.

'You must be Emily and Eva,' Sunita said, reaching down to pat Eva's head.

Emily reached for Hayley's hand and Eva hid behind her leg. They weren't used to strangers in the apartment in the daytime. It was usually a quiet time for her and the children to relax after school.

'It's OK,' Hayley said gently. 'These are my friends.'

'I'm Sunita,' Sunita said. 'And this is Lyndsey.' Lyndsey beamed at them and Emily gripped Hayley's hand so hard it hurt.

'Are you allowed to have friends round?' Emily asked.

'Well, we don't have to tell Julie and your dad, do we?' She handed Chloe to Lyndsey and crouched down to Emily's height. 'Like when your mum comes round. We don't let Julie know.'

'Because it would make her cross.'

'Yes, because we don't want to worry her.'

'Why would she be worried?' Emily frowned.

'It's more like a game,' Lyndsey said. 'A secret game.'

'Yes,' Hayley continued. 'We all have to keep the secret. Not tell Julie and your dad that Lyndsey and Sunita were here. Can you do that?'

Emily nodded slowly.

Hayley took the children through to the living room and turned the TV on, then turned back to Sunita and Lyndsey.

'Did your washing come out OK?'

'Yeah. It was fine. Most of the stuff is in the tumble dryer, but we've hung a few bits in the bedroom.'

'Which bedroom?'

'That one.' Lyndsey pointed to the door to Julie and David's room. Hayley swallowed and walked into the room. There were bras hanging from the doorknobs of all the wardrobes and a couple of smart tops hanging from the curtain rails. Hayley couldn't imagine what Julie would say if she saw this. She started laughing.

'This stuff can't be tumble-dried,' Lyndsey said.

'OK, I get it. Let's just make sure there's no sign you've been in this room afterwards.'

'Is this their room? The parents?'

'Yep.'

'It's lovely, isn't it?' Sunita said, stroking the dark knotted wood of a chest of drawers.

'Yeah, it is.'

'And where's your room?' Lyndsey asked.

'We looked round but we couldn't find it,' Sunita said.

Hayley took them through to the back of the flat and to the inconspicuous door that marked the maid's quarters. 'Here it is,' she said. When she'd moved in she was comparing it to the hostel, but now, for the first time, she realised how shabby it was compared to the rest of the apartment. She hadn't even put new pictures up after Mae had taken hers back.

Her friends looked at each other. 'It's nice,' Lyndsey said finally.

'It's en suite,' Hayley said weakly, pointing to the small toilet and shower room.

'Much nicer than the hostel anyway,' Sunita said. 'By the way, I hope you don't mind. We used the shower in the bathroom by the girls' room. We borrowed some towels.' Hayley felt her heart sink. She'd been given old towels for her bathroom. She wasn't allowed to use the pristine white ones in the rest of the house. She'd need to wash and dry them before Julie got back. Or else somehow blame it on Eva and Emily. But she didn't want them punished.

'No problem,' Hayley said. 'I'll put them in the wash now.'

'Julie's really strict, isn't she?' Lyndsey said, after Hayley had put another wash on and was making up a bottle for Chloe in the kitchen.

'Yeah, she's difficult.'

They took the bottle into the living room and sat on the sofas while Eva and Emily watched TV and Chloe drank from her bottle.

'She doesn't like me to go out in the evening,' Hayley continued. 'And she told me I could do with plastic surgery.'

'What? Really?' Her friends' eyes were wide. 'That's ridiculous.'

'Yeah, I know. She seems to really hate me.' Somehow it all sounded worse when she said it out loud. She felt tears of frustration starting to form in her eyes. She loved the children. If she only had to deal with them, then she'd love her job too. David was OK, but she wished Julie would treat her like more of a person, and less of a servant.

'Was she always like this?'

'She was nice to me at the beginning, before she had Chloe. But she's changed.'

'Do you know why?'

'The baby, I guess. It's stressful. And she doesn't like me talking to David.'

'What – is she jealous?' Lyndsey said incredulously.

'Yeah, she must be.'

'You're younger than her, prettier than her,' Sunita said. 'Maybe that's why.'

'Maybe,' Hayley said. Although she wondered if that wasn't the only reason. David could be a bit flirty sometimes. Maybe Julie suspected something was going on between them.

'As if you'd be interested in David!' Lyndsey said. 'He's over forty, isn't he?'

Forty-three, Hayley thought, but she didn't say it out loud.

'Look,' she said. 'I'm going to need to clean up before they get home from work. It's important it looks like no one has been round.'

'Oh, we'll help,' Sunita said.

'Yeah, of course,' Lyndsey agreed, and they set to work, straightening the cushions, mopping the floor and removing all traces that they'd been there.

'You have to get out of here,' Sunita said, when they left. 'You can't live like this.'

THIRTY-FOUR

NOW

Hayley sorted through her work on her desk. While she'd been on the training course her colleagues had added a stack of new student files which she needed to put on the system. The work had built up, and now she was faced with a full diary of students, as well as a pile of admin.

She went out to the kitchen to get a coffee and saw Ryan there, by the coffee machine. She froze, remembering what Michelle had told her about him speaking to her mother.

'I didn't realise you were volunteering today,' she said, trying to keep her voice calm.

He smiled. 'I changed my shifts around. I was supposed to be on last week, but I swapped to this week.' She wondered if he'd switched things around because she was away on her course.

He pulled his cup out of the coffee machine and stepped closer to her. 'I wanted to speak to you again. About Chloe. I have more questions.'

'I'm so busy...'

'It's important,' he said. 'I heard from Hans.'

Hayley panicked, thinking of Johanna. She was going to

have to delay her first student and find out what Ryan knew. 'OK,' she said quickly. 'I have ten minutes, if you can make it quick. Come to my office.'

In her office, he slid into the student seat like it was the most natural thing in the world and she perched on the edge of her chair opposite him.

'So,' she asked, 'what did Hans say?'

'Not much. Just that he was in Bangkok around that time, that he remembered Chloe's disappearance. And he mentioned you. Said you were a good nanny to them. And that you wouldn't have done anything to hurt her.'

'Oh,' Hayley said, relieved. 'Anything else?'

'No, he doesn't want to talk to me. It's a familiar theme. Everybody clamming up. Including you. It's like people have got something to hide.'

'They don't want to think about it. It was a horrible time.'

'But I need to find out what happened.'

Hayley thought of the photos she'd found in her mother's room. 'Michelle said you spoke to my mother.'

'Michelle?'

'My mother's carer.'

'Oh right, yeah, I did have a brief conversation with them, just small talk, really.'

'OK, because I said that I didn't want you to speak to anyone I knew without asking me first.'

'Of course. But I spoke to them ages ago. I won't do it again.'

'My mother's become more interested in Thailand lately. She took some pictures from my room.' She didn't mention the missing red blanket.

'What? Pictures of Thailand?' He looked confused.

'Yes. Did you have anything to do with that?' Even as she spoke the words they sounded far-fetched and ridiculous. She was being paranoid.

'No, but I'd love to see the pictures.'

Hayley stared at him. She didn't want him looking through the photos, thumbing through her memories. 'You can't,' she said. 'I can't help you any more with your book. What happened isn't any of your business. Lars doesn't know about Chloe. Alice doesn't know. I haven't been able to talk about it. And I don't want to start now.'

He reached out for her hand and squeezed it for a second, before she pulled it out of his grasp. 'I understand that,' he said. 'But this book isn't going to cast you in a bad light. If anything it will show that you're innocent, that you were just a naive young woman, out of your depth.'

'Thanks, Ryan,' she said. 'But I'm done. I've helped you enough already.' She stood up, went to the door, and held it open for him to leave.

For the rest of the day, Hayley couldn't get Ryan out of her head. She knew it was only a matter of time before he found out more about what happened in Thailand. And with Johanna here too... everything had got too risky. On the bus home, she resolved to tell Lars about Chloe, about Thailand. She'd explain how she'd been a nanny, how she'd been locked up for a night in a Thai jail, accused of hurting a baby. She'd tell him every bit of information that was publicly available. She knew he'd be hurt that she'd kept it a secret, but it might be her only opportunity to tell her side of the story.

When she got home that evening, Johanna was playing happily with Alice in the living room. She had collected her from school, cooked her dinner and they were now enjoying their time together. Lars had finally persuaded Hayley that Johanna should look after Alice after school, in exchange for Hayley and Lars providing her meals, and Johanna had started the previous week when Hayley was on her training course. It was going well and had saved them a lot of money. Now

Johanna ate with them every night, and although Hayley enjoyed her company, she felt she never had any time with alone with Lars any more. She loved the fact that Johanna was integrating so well into their family, but she felt worried about how dependent they had all become on her. It felt risky. She felt like she knew Johanna, but how well did she really know her?

'Hello,' she said to Johanna and Alice. 'Good day?'

'Yes,' Alice said. 'Johanna's helping me build a castle out of Lego.'

'Great,' Hayley said.

'She's brilliant at Lego,' Johanna said enthusiastically. 'Must be her Scandinavian genes. She's very creative, too.'

Hayley nodded. 'Well done, Alice.'

She saw some flowers laid out on the kitchen table. Blue delphiniums and white roses. Her favourites. Lars must be home. Her heart lifted. She wondered what she'd done to deserve this. Then her heart sank again when she remembered that she was going to have to tell him about Thailand.

She went upstairs, knocked on the door.

'Lars?'

'Come in.'

'How are you?' she said, as she went through the door.

'Yeah, OK. Busy.' He grunted at the spreadsheet he was looking at.

'Right. Thanks for the flowers.'

'Have you had a proper look at them?'

'No, I only just saw them... I...' She had been planning to talk to him tonight about Thailand, but now seemed like the worst time. He was engrossed in his work, and she didn't want to burst the bubble of positive energy from the flowers.

'Why don't you go and put them in water?' he said, not making eye contact.

She frowned, wondering if something was wrong or if he was just busy.

'Sure,' she said. She walked over to him and kissed him lightly on his sandy-blond hair.

He didn't look up.

She went downstairs to the kitchen and got out a vase and filled it with water.

Picking up the flowers, she saw the card that had come with them and stared at it in surprise. She'd assumed Lars had bought the flowers from a shop, but there was a logo for an online flower delivery company.

She opened the card and gasped.

The message was short, but to the point.

I'm going to tell your husband everything. Ryan x

THIRTY-FIVE

1999

Hayley wandered through the market with Chloe strapped to her in a makeshift sling she'd made from an old bedsheet. She had started to get out of the house more in the daytime since she'd seen Sunita and Lyndsey and heard all their stories of everything they'd seen in Bangkok. She'd wanted to go to the big market for ages, which was listed as a shopping mecca in the *Lonely Planet* guide. Now Chloe was a bit older, it was easier to take her with her. She'd got into more of a routine and could go for a few hours without crying for milk.

Hayley strolled past rows and rows of fake branded T-shirts, and displays of ceramic plates. She moved on to the wooden toy section and bought two tiny carved dragons for Emily and Eva. In the outside area, she turned away from the animals in cages in the wildlife section, not wanting to look.

It was sweltering in the market, and busy, and she worried about how Chloe was coping. She was wearing a thin cloth hat to shield her face from the sun, and was sleeping peacefully. But her little body was hot against Hayley's. Hayley kept walking, looking for somewhere to sit down so she could give her some milk. She reached into her bag and took the milk out of the cooler so it would start to warm up. It would take no time at all in the intense heat. After a few minutes she saw a little café, shaded under expansive blue and white umbrellas. She ordered a can of Coke and carefully took Chloe out of the sling. She was still asleep, but Hayley reluctantly woke her, and put the bottle to her mouth. She sucked it hungrily, finishing it quickly. Hayley put a cloth over her shoulder and burped her, then sat with her on her knee while she sipped her Coke and watched the world go by.

As she sat there she noticed the sky darken. It felt like the rain came out of nowhere. Torrential. Falling from the sky in sheets of water. Pounding the people and the stalls. Under the umbrella, Hayley and Chloe were safe, and dozens of people crowded in with them, huddling in the tiny space. Hayley held Chloe tight as everyone watched the rain. Around them the stallholders were hurriedly unwinding plastic sheets to protect their wares.

As time passed and the rain continued, people sighed, dug out umbrellas and left the shelter of the parasols, jumping over puddles as they dashed inside the covered part of the market. Hayley looked down at her bare arms, her backpack, then looked at Chloe. She had no umbrella and nothing to cover either of them. She swallowed. She'd have to wait it out. She'd read about the rainy season in her guidebook, but she hadn't understood how apocalyptic it would feel, how dark the world would go. There was something beautifully angry about it. She'd just have to sit here and wait for it to pass.

An hour later, she was still there and the rain was still falling, while Chloe grizzled. She regretted taking the bus here, her desire for independence leading her to bypass Julie and David's driver, who she knew would disapprove of her trip. She needed to leave soon, so she'd be back in time to pick up Emily and Eva.

She put Chloe back in the sling, then dug around in her bag, found the cloth that she'd used to burp her and placed it over Chloe's head. Then she made a run for it, her sandals splashing through the puddles and filling with water. She'd only run less than twenty metres to the indoor market, but she was soaked through, water running off her arms, her hair clinging to her face. Chloe was crying now, the cloth on her head sodden.

Hayley sighed. At least it was warm. She needed to go straight out of the market to the bus stop. She still had an hour and a half to get back, but she had no idea how long the bus would take in the traffic. If she could find a taxi, she'd get one instead, but it was still likely to be a long journey. When it rained, the Bangkok traffic was heavier than ever.

'Hayley?' Hayley turned at the sound of her name, but didn't see anyone. She hardly knew anyone in Thailand.

'Hayley?' She turned and saw a woman striding towards her. It took a moment to recognise her. Karolina.

'Hi,' she said uncertainly. She hadn't seen her since Karolina had come round with presents for Chloe when she was a newborn. 'How are you?'

'I'm good,' she said. 'Thanks. You got caught in the rain, did you?'

'Yeah. I didn't predict the weather. It's always so hot, it's hardly rained since I've been here.'

'It's the start of the rainy season. You can look forward to lots more days like this in Bangkok. Have you got an umbrella with you?'

'No,' Hayley said. Her vest top clung to her and she was starting to feel shivery.

'How are you getting back?'

'I was going to take the bus back. Or a taxi.'

'All the taxis will be taken in this weather. And the bus will be overflowing. You wouldn't want to take a baby on it.'

'But I need to get back and pick up the girls.'

'Oh, of course. Does your driver take you to the school? What time do you pick them up?'

'Yeah, he takes me to the school for three o'clock.'

'That's still a while away. I live near here. Why don't you come back to my apartment with me, and then I can phone your driver and he can pick you up from there? It's on his way to the school.'

'That sounds great. Thank you.'

Outside, Karolina managed to hail a tuk-tuk and they clambered in, Hayley holding Chloe tightly in her arms as the driver wove in and out of the traffic. Five minutes later they arrived, and Karolina took them up the stairs and into her apartment.

It was beautifully decorated, and full of natural light. Hayley went to the window and looked down at the metropolis of the city, the buildings rolling on and on.

'How are you getting on?' Karolina asked, when they had both sat down on the sofas with cups of tea in their hands. 'Is Julie treating you OK?'

Hayley felt the tears well up in her eyes. 'Not really,' she said.

'Oh no, how awful,' Karolina said. 'She's so lucky to have Chloe, and you to help her. I'd kill for that.' Clearly Karolina still hadn't fallen pregnant and Hayley felt a wave of pity.

'Can I hold her?' Karolina asked.

'Sure.' Hayley handed Chloe over. Hayley's clothes were nearly dry now and she felt less shivery. She watched as Karolina cooed at the baby, smiling at her and holding her close. She thought how she'd never seen Julie do that.

'So what's happening with Julie?' Karolina asked.

Hayley explained how hard she had to work, the nasty way in which Julie spoke to her, and how horrible she was to Emily and Eva. 'She's even strange with Chloe,' she said. 'I'm not sure she really loves her.' It felt like such an awful thing to say, but she knew it was true.

'Gosh, that's appalling,' Karolina said, gazing into Chloe's eyes. 'She's perfect.'

'Emily and Eva are going back to England with their mum in a few weeks. After that I'm going to leave too. If it wasn't for them, I'd go sooner.'

'But what about Chloe?' Karolina said, her eyes full of concern. 'Will she be OK without you?'

THIRTY-SIX

NOW

Hayley read the message on the flowers again. Ryan was going to tell Lars everything. But what did he actually know? She thought of Lars upstairs, how she'd thanked him for the flowers and he hadn't said anything. He'd just suggested she put them in water. *He'd seen the card. He knew they were from Ryan.*

'Lovely flowers,' Johanna said, coming into the kitchen.

'Thanks.' Hayley shoved the card into her pocket. 'Excuse me a minute.'

'Do you want me to put them in a vase?'

'No, no, I'll do it later,' Hayley said. She left the room and hurried back up the stairs to see Lars.

'Lars?' she called out, knocking on the door of his study.

He grunted, and she pushed the door open.

'I've seen the flowers,' she said. 'And the note.'

He swung round in his chair. 'Who's Ryan?'

'He's no one... he—'

'You've been having an affair, haven't you?' He spat out the words. 'Are you unhappy with me? Because we don't have the money we used to, is that what it is?'

'No,' she said. 'This isn't about you. It's—'

'So it's about you, is it? You just fancied a bit of fun? Didn't care about me at all.'

'I'm not having an affair, Lars. Ryan is, well, he's a writer. A crime writer.'

'What's that got to do with anything? Or are you trying to say he's more exciting than me?'

'No.' Hayley sighed. 'He's someone who... well, he's been watching me. He's investigating something that happened a long time ago. I was planning to tell you what was going on, but...'

Lars got up from his seat and started pacing up and down his office. 'What were you planning to tell me? What does he mean when he says he's going to tell me everything? And why would he send you flowers? Your favourites, too. He must know you well enough to know that.' He stopped and looked at Hayley, narrowing his eyes.

'He asked my work colleagues what flowers I like. He volunteers in student support with me.'

'So you got to know him at work? Does he have a crush on you? Is that what this is? Did you do something to lead him on?'

'No, nothing like that. He... he's interested in me for other reasons.'

'What other reasons?'

Hayley swallowed, unable to form the words. 'You might have seen him around here. He's been hanging around outside the house, watching me. He's spoken to Michelle and Mum. He's digging for information.'

Lars shook his head, his anger shifting to concern. 'I haven't noticed anyone hanging around. But that behaviour sounds threatening. Why didn't you tell me? Something about this whole thing doesn't add up.'

At least Ryan hadn't spoken to Lars already. But that meant

Lars was completely in the dark. He had no idea what was going on.

'Look,' Hayley said. 'Ryan has become obsessed with something that happened a long time ago. Over twenty years ago. When I was in Thailand.'

'When you were on your gap year?'

Hayley nodded. 'Yeah.'

'But what happened? I thought you had a great time.' She'd never told Lars about working as a nanny on her gap year.

'I did. But while I was in Bangkok, a baby went missing.'

'OK... But what did that have to do with you?'

Hayley took a deep breath. She had never wanted to discuss this part of her past with him, had wanted to put it all behind her. 'I was the baby's nanny,' she said. 'And for a short time I was held in custody. Because I was arrested on suspicion of kidnapping. The police thought... well, they seemed to think I might have killed her and then disposed of the body.'

'What?' Lars said incredulously. He started to laugh. 'They thought you were a murderer? But you've never hurt anyone in your life.'

'It's not funny,' Hayley said tersely, remembering Chloe's tiny little face. 'It was a difficult time for me, and I'd rather forget it. But for Ryan it's an interesting cold case he wants to solve, that he wants to write a book about. The baby was never found. And Ryan wants to use me to help me work out what happened.'

Lars was staring at Hayley, trying to process what she'd said.

'Look,' she continued quickly. 'We really need to all be keeping an eye out for Ryan. His behaviour's become... intimidating. He's sent the flowers, he's hung around outside our house, he's even spoken to my mother. In fact, I think he may have asked her to find out more about what happened in Thailand from me. She's suddenly developed an interest in Thailand and I found some old photos of mine in her room.'

Lars stared. 'What does he look like? If I see him, I'll give him a piece of my mind.'

Hayley swallowed. She didn't want Lars talking to Ryan. 'I don't think it's a good idea to say anything at all to him. You don't know how he might use it in his book.'

'But you've got nothing to hide.' Hayley felt a surge of love for him. He was so sure she'd done nothing wrong.

'Still, you don't know how he might spin things, how he might make things look. And I don't want Alice to ever know anything about this. She's too young to understand.'

Lars nodded. 'But why didn't you tell me any of this was going on? Why didn't you trust me?'

'I don't know,' Hayley said. 'I suppose... it wasn't that I didn't trust you, it was just that I didn't want to talk about it. It was a horrible time for me. I didn't really want to think about it all. I knew you were caught up in your business, and I hoped Ryan would just go away.'

Lars frowned. 'Well, it doesn't look like he's going away. But if you ever see him outside the house again, then call me. And the police. We can't have him harassing you like this.'

He sat back in his chair and returned to his spreadsheet. The conversation was over. Hayley felt dismissed.

She walked slowly down the stairs. Johanna was on the first-floor landing. 'Is everything all right?' she asked. Hayley nodded, wondering how much she'd overheard. She should have shut the door when she'd been talking to Lars.

'It's fine,' she said.

'Are you sure?' Johanna reached out and touched her arm.

'Yeah,' said Hayley. 'I'll go down and start on the dinner.'

Johanna squeezed her arm. 'Wait. I want to tell you something. I've had good news and I wanted to share it with you first.'

Hayley felt a tingling sense of dread in her chest.

'What is it?' she asked, trying to sound cheerful.

'You won't believe this. I was right. My parents have been hiding something from me.' Hayley's heart sank. 'I got my DNA results today. I had a match. I think I've found a half-sibling.'

THIRTY-SEVEN

1999

Hayley played with Chloe, shaking a rattle at her and watching her smile and giggle. As she was developing her coordination and starting to engage with the world, Hayley was becoming more and more entranced by her. She always smiled when Hayley entered a room, always seemed to be looking for her. It wasn't the same with Julie. When Chloe saw her mother, her eyes would follow her round the room, but she never tried to reach out to be picked up, the way she did with Hayley.

Julie often ignored Chloe. She seemed unsure what to do with her, how to engage. She didn't seem interested in holding her and she had said herself that she was just waiting for her to grow up so that she could talk to her properly. Hayley thought wistfully of Karolina, how much she'd loved playing with Chloe, but how she couldn't have her own child. Sometimes life seemed so cruel, the hands people were dealt felt unfair.

Hayley put Chloe down in her rocker and strapped her in, then carried her to the children's bathroom so she could watch Hayley clean it. Emily and Eva were out with their mother for a few hours. Marion had taken them for dinner and ice cream, picking them up straight from school. They'd be back soon. Hayley had missed them. She was used to the girls being there late afternoon, the apartment full of noise and laughter without Julie and David.

As Hayley was scrubbing the children's toothpaste off the bathroom sink, there was a knock on the door. She opened it and the children rushed in and hugged her. Hayley fought back tears. Soon the fragile daytime equilibrium of her, Chloe, Emily and Eva would be gone. The girls would go back to England and she'd miss them intensely. She would leave, and this whole life would be over.

'How was the ice cream?' Hayley asked.

'De-li-cious!' Emily shouted. 'I had chocolate and strawberry and coconut.'

'I can still see some of it round your mouth,' Hayley said with a smile, pulling a baby wipe out of a packet in her pocket to wipe Emily's mouth.

'And how did you cope?' she asked Marion, gently. It was the first time she had taken the girls out on her own.

'OK,' Marion said. 'But I'm absolutely exhausted now. I'm dying for a cup of tea.'

'I'll make you one.' Hayley went to the kitchen to switch on the kettle as Marion took her shoes off.

They sat down at the table together, while Emily and Eva watched TV in the living room. Julie and David wouldn't be back from work for another couple of hours.

'So, how are you feeling?' Hayley asked.

'I'm definitely getting better. But I'm not a hundred per cent yet. I still get a lot of pain in my leg and I get tired so easily.'

'It's hard looking after a four- and a five-year-old.'

'When I get back to the UK, I'll have my parents to help. They can't wait to see their grandchildren. We're going to move in with them.'

'That will be good. It will help make the move easier,' Hayley said.

'Do you think Emily and Eva will be OK moving across the world?'

'They're young. They'll adjust.' Hayley didn't want to tell her that their life with Julie and David wouldn't be something to miss. Although she supposed they'd miss the school. And her. 'I'll miss them a lot,' she said. 'They're lovely children. But I imagine they'll soon forget me. They're so young. In a few years' time, they might not even remember they lived in Thailand, if you don't talk about it.'

'My parents never wanted me to move to Thailand with David,' Marion said with a sigh. 'Told me it was a huge mistake. They turned out to be right.'

'When are you flying back?' Hayley asked. She needed to know, because as soon as Emily and Eva were gone, then she'd go too, away from Julie and David.

'I'm going to book soon,' Marion said. 'Hopefully we'll leave in the next month. I just need to get my strength up a bit first.'

Just then, they heard a key in the lock. Hayley froze, her eyes widening as she looked at Marion. She prayed it was David and not Julie.

'This apartment is a mess.' Julie's voice. She was already in the living room.

'You're going to need to leave,' Hayley whispered urgently to Marion, as she got up to see Julie. She went into the living room, leaving Marion in the kitchen.

'You're home early,' she said to Julie.

'Yeah,' Julie snapped. 'And I need a glass of wine. Can you pour me one? I've had an awful day with a patient. And I don't expect to come home to find my apartment in this kind of a state.' She gestured at the toys scattered over the living room floor, that Emily and Eva must have brought from their room when Hayley had been talking to Marion. The girls weren't allowed toys in the living room, but Hayley let them when Julie and David weren't there.

'I'll get you that wine, and then clear up,' Hayley said meekly. She hurried into the kitchen, trying to think of a way of getting Marion out of the apartment without Julie seeing her. She pulled out a bottle of Chilean Merlot, Julie's favourite, and started to open it.

'And can I have some crackers too?' Julie was saying.

'Sure!' Hayley called out, glancing at Marion.

Julie pushed open the door to the kitchen. 'The wholegrain ones—'

She stopped mid-sentence when she saw Marion. Her face flushed.

She turned to Hayley. 'What is *she* doing in my home?'

'She came to see Emily and Eva. She hasn't been here long—'

'Get her out of my home! Now!'

Marion was making no attempt to move, smiling as she sat at the table, enjoying Julie's anger.

'It used to be my home,' Marion said softly. 'David and I chose it together. I've cooked in this kitchen, I've washed in your bath, I've slept in your bed with David. Doesn't that bother you? That everything you do, I've done before?'

'Get out!' Julie screamed. 'Get out now!'

Marion laughed. 'Don't worry, I'm leaving.' She got up slowly, taking her time. 'I'll just say goodbye to the girls.'

'No, you won't. Get out.'

Marion ignored her, entering the living room and shouting cheerfully, 'Bye, girls!'

They ran up and hugged her, and then returned to watching the TV.

Marion bent over Chloe's chair and gave her a kiss on the cheek. 'Bye, little one, see you soon.'

'Don't touch her!' Julie screamed.

'I'm going now,' Marion said.

'Get out, right now,' Julie shouted, 'if you want to see your girls again.'

'You can't keep them, Julie. I'm taking them back to England.'

'As if I'd want to keep them!' Julie laughed viciously. 'You're welcome to them.'

She pushed Marion out of the door and threw her shoes into the corridor behind her. 'Get out of *my* apartment.'

She slammed the door behind her and then turned to Hayley. 'How could you be so stupid, letting that woman in?'

THIRTY-EIGHT

NOW

'Sorry?' Hayley said, not sure if she'd heard Johanna correctly about the results of the DNA test. She gripped the banister on the landing and stared at her, the blood rushing to her head.

'I have a half-sibling,' Johanna repeated, excitedly.

'Oh, that's brilliant.' Hayley tried to reflect Johanna's enthusiasm. 'What's their name?' Hayley knew she would recognise it.

'I don't know yet. I've just got the email about the match. I wanted you to be the first to know.' Johanna smiled nervously. 'I haven't dared open it yet. I know Chloe had two sisters, Emily and Eva. Do you think it's one of them? Do you think this match means I'm her? That I'm Chloe?'

'Umm...' Hayley said, trying to unjumble her thoughts. 'No – I mean, probably not. I think half-siblings are quite common. It could be from a previous relationship that one of your parents had before they met. Or an affair. There are so many possible explanations.'

'It would mean my parents lied to me.'

'Not necessarily. If it was on your dad's side he might not even know. I wouldn't jump to conclusions.' Hayley felt sick.

As soon as Johanna saw the result, Hayley knew what conclusion she would draw. She just hoped it didn't say what she thought it would say. There could be other half-siblings too, that Hayley didn't know about. This person could be one of them.

'That's the thing. I don't think it can be on my dad's side. From what I've seen, I don't think Hans is my father.'

'Why not? Have your parents done DNA tests too?' Hayley's stomach clenched with anxiety.

'No, I didn't feel I could ask them. I didn't want to tell them that I thought they'd been lying to me. I just wanted to find out for myself.'

'So why don't you think Hans is your father?'

'My cousin on my father's side did the test a while ago. And he hasn't come up as related to me. I haven't had any notifications about cousins.'

'Oh,' Hayley said. 'That's strange.'

'It is – isn't it? I think if I just speak to the half-sibling I'll be able to find out what's going on. Maybe he or she is related to my real father.'

Hayley felt sick.

'Are you sure you're ready for this?' she asked.

'Oh, god, no, I'm not sure.' Johanna started pacing up and down the landing. 'Is this going to blow my whole life apart?'

'I don't know,' Hayley said. 'Maybe you should think about it some more before you do it.'

Johanna shook her head decisively. 'No,' she said. 'I know it's what I want to do. I mean, I've come this far. I'm just scared. Will you stay with me while I open the match on the website? Then I'll be able to see the name and email address and I'll be able to contact her or him.' She suddenly grinned. 'I'm going to find out if I have a sister or a brother. It's actually quite exciting, isn't it? I always wanted a sibling when I was younger. I hated being an only child.'

Hayley took a deep breath. 'I guess you've finally got your wish.'

'Yeah. Right. I'm going to open it now. Just stay beside me.' Johanna pulled out her phone and Hayley peered over her shoulder. She watched as Johanna logged onto her account and then clicked 'family connections'. She frowned. There was nothing listed under 'siblings', just a long list of distant relatives.

'Oh,' Johanna said, disappointment filling her voice. 'I don't understand. Where's it gone? Maybe it's in a different part of the site.'

She clicked the menu at the top of the page, but there was only one link to genetic connections – the page she was already on. 'I don't understand,' she said. 'I had an email notification saying I had a connection, a suspected half-sibling.' She went into her emails and found the message. Hayley could see she was right. There had been a connection. But now it was gone.

Johanna clicked the link, but now it just said, 'Page no longer available'.

'Why would this happen?' she asked. 'I don't get it.'

'Maybe they changed their privacy settings.' Hayley tried to think what this meant. Had they seen Johanna's match and decided they didn't want to be found? 'What are you going to do now?' she asked gently, trying to hide her relief. She saw tears running down Johanna's cheeks.

'I don't know,' Johanna said. 'I was so excited about the new sibling. It kind of detracted from the bad stuff, my dad not being my dad.'

'You don't know that for sure.'

'No, I suppose not. I'll have to look into it more.'

'It could be your cousin that isn't the biological child of his parents. Not you.'

'I hadn't thought of that. I guess I'm no further than I was before.'

'I'm sorry, Johanna.'

'I feel so lost. I just want to find out who I really am,' Johanna said.

'I know.' For a moment, Hayley had a desire to tell her. She had always thought it was for the best that she didn't know her history, that she had an opportunity for a fresh start. But now she wasn't sure.

'I'm going to go to my room,' Johanna said. 'Don't bother saving any dinner for me. I'm not hungry.'

That night, Hayley lay in bed, trying to sleep, thinking of Johanna. She'd dodged a bullet when her half-sibling hadn't wanted to connect after all. But how much longer could Hayley keep everything hidden? She rolled over again in the bed, trying to get comfortable.

'Can't sleep?' Lars said from the bed beside her.

'No, my mind's spinning.'

'Mine too,' he replied. 'I can't understand why you never told me about Thailand. We've been together so long. We got married. And yet you've kept such a major thing from me.'

'I didn't do it,' Hayley said, picturing Chloe's tiny face. 'I didn't take her.'

'I know you didn't. Of course I wouldn't ever think that. But it must have been traumatic for you. You were arrested. What's bothering me is that you never trusted me enough to tell me. All our heart-to-hearts, all the things we confided in each other, I thought we had no secrets.'

'It was before we got together... so far in the past it didn't feel worth bringing up.'

Lars sighed heavily and rolled towards her, wrapping his arms round her.

'You've kept this from me all these years. It makes me wonder what else you might have kept from me. We can't hide anything from each other. We have to be open and honest if this marriage is going to work.'

'You're right,' she said, 'of course.'

'No more secrets?' Lars murmured, his arms hugging her tighter. She remembered how comforted she used to feel by his warm body next to hers.

'No more secrets,' she replied, to draw the conversation to a close. She listened to Lars' breathing calm and then heard his gentle snores. Despite what she had just said, the truth was there was a lot Lars didn't know. A lot she never wanted him to find out.

THIRTY-NINE

1999

Hayley wandered around the temple, enjoying the sense of calm and peace that radiated from it. Since Marion had started collecting Eva and Emily from school, she had more time with just Chloe in the day. She was trying to visit all the minor temples in her area that were shown on the *Lonely Planet* map. Now she had the sling she had made for Chloe there was no stopping her, and Chloe loved being out and about, absorbing the sights and sounds of the city. Hayley was sure it was good for her development.

It was amazing that this tiny, inconspicuous temple sat in the middle of the city, on the corner of two major roads. It was ornately decorated in gold, and intricately designed. For hundreds of years monks and ordinary people had come here and left offerings to the gods. Inside, she stopped beside the large gold Buddha that dominated the back wall and dropped a few coins into the collection box to pay her respects.

What do you wish for, Chloe? she asked in her head, feeling the comfort of the baby's body against her in the sling. *I pray you have a good life. I pray Julie and David are kind to you.*

She looked down at Chloe. She'd fallen asleep. Hayley

stroked her head and then walked out of the temple and into an air-conditioned café, where she took her out of the sling and let her rest in her arms for a while. When she woke she gave her a bottle and then wandered back to the apartment.

She was meeting Marion shortly, in the McDonald's a few roads away. She would hand over the children there, as Marion wasn't allowed in the apartment. Julie hadn't forgiven Hayley for inviting her in.

It wasn't long until Marion would be taking Emily and Eva back to England. Each day it got closer, Hayley felt a sense of longing in the pit of her stomach. She was going to miss them so much.

When Hayley returned from meeting Marion, with Emily and Eva in the car, she felt happier. The children were so much more at ease in their mother's company, and for the first time she had genuine faith that the three of them would build a good relationship, and that Emily and Eva would have a good life with their mother. Marion herself was looking better and better each time Hayley saw her, with more colour in her face.

Hayley bathed the children and put them to bed, and then curled up with Chloe on the sofa. It was the first time in ages that she'd finished all the cleaning and childcare before Julie and David came home. Emily and Eva had had an exhausting day, with school and then meeting their mother, and they had fallen asleep easily during story time.

Hayley put the TV on and sat back to watch the news. She was starting to relax, when she heard the door open.

Julie.

Hayley stood up to go and take Chloe to her bedroom. She had no desire to speak to Julie.

'Hello, Hayley,' Julie said, appearing behind her, before she managed to escape. 'How are you?'

Hayley regarded her suspiciously. Julie never asked her how she was. 'I'm fine,' she said.

'I hear you've had an interesting day,' Julie said sarcastically.

'What do you mean?'

'Panit just picked me up in the car. He said he'd been driving you all over the city. McDonald's today, wasn't it?'

'I was meeting Marion there, now she can't come to the apartment.'

'Why there?'

'She was looking after the girls. McDonald's was the easiest place to meet her.'

'You know how bad that food is for them?'

'I think she gave it to them as a one-off treat.' Hayley knew that Marion was trying to save money. 'I'm just putting Chloe down to bed,' she said, trying to close down Julie's questioning.

'Don't go yet,' Julie said, grabbing her arm so hard it hurt. 'Come and sit down with me. There are more things I need to talk to you about. A lot of things have come to light recently. I'm not happy with the way you've been performing your role.'

Hayley swallowed. 'How can you be unhappy? I do everything.'

'Come and sit down.'

Hayley followed her reluctantly back into the living room and perched on the edge of the sofa.

'I've learnt some things about you and what you've been doing,' Julie said, 'which are truly shocking.' Hayley's heart jumped in her chest. She thought of David, how kind he'd been to her at first. Everything had turned on its head. She waited for Julie to speak.

'You had your friends here, in my home, using my things.'

Hayley stared. They'd cleaned up so thoroughly. How had Julie found out?

'A friend of ours from another apartment saw the three of

you at the swimming pool. Having the time of your lives, she said. When you were supposed to be looking after Chloe.'

'I had them round because you wouldn't let me go out and see them.'

'That's no excuse. You have to understand – this place isn't your home to show off. You're part of the staff.'

Hayley stared miserably at the floor. She couldn't wait to get out of here.

'And Panit says he drove you all the way over to Khao San once to meet your friends, and he collected you from a friend's place near the market. I pay you to look after the children, not to socialise.'

'You won't let me go out at night,' Hayley said weakly. 'So I have to go out in the day.' She thought of the joy she got from exploring with Chloe. It had become the highlight of her days. 'I want to see the city. I've been taking Chloe round the temples.'

'I don't pay you to be a tourist. I pay you to work.' Hayley wondered what her hourly rate actually was. It must be less than a pound an hour.

Julie leant in closer to her. 'And that's not the worst of it. Panit told me you lost Chloe.'

Hayley gasped, remembering the supermarket, how Panit had been there. Why had he told Julie?

'You handed Chloe over to a stranger. How could you do that? You nearly lost her!'

'That was a misunderstanding. The woman was nearby the whole time. It was fine. I found her really quickly.'

'You think that's fine?' Julie's voice rose to a crescendo now. 'Losing the baby you're supposed to be looking after? I could report you to the police for neglect.'

Hayley swallowed. That couldn't be right, could it? It was only a moment of inattention. She was sure Julie was bluffing.

'I'm sorry,' she said. 'There's really no need to involve the police.'

Julie sneered. 'I'll let you off this time. But I'm watching you. You're on your final warning. You're only still here because I haven't found a professional nanny for Chloe yet.'

'Can I go now?' Hayley said.

Julie frowned. 'Yeah, get out of my sight,' she said. 'But if you mess up again, I'll throw you out onto the street.'

FORTY

NOW

Hayley walked round the park by the university at lunchtime, trying to slow her racing mind and get some exercise. It was a sunny day and the park was full of dog-walkers, new mothers pushing prams and clutching coffees, and screaming toddlers heading for the playground. Hayley thought of Lars. Things hadn't been the same between them since her confession. He was polite, but distant, always lost in thought. And when he looked at her, it was almost like he did a double take, as if he didn't quite recognise her.

Hayley headed back inside. She'd brought a sandwich from home, but forgotten a drink, so she went to the cafeteria and bought a water. She was in the queue when she spotted him. Ryan. Staring over at her. She shivered. It was inevitable that she'd bump into him. She'd prepared for this, running through in her head the different ways of telling him to leave her alone.

He ambled over as she waited to pay. 'Fancy seeing you here,' he said jovially, as if they were friends.

'Hi,' she replied weakly.

'Thanks for talking to me the other day.'

The man in the queue in front of her moved away with his

food, and the cashier smiled at her. Hayley turned away from
Ryan. 'Just this, please,' she said. She paid for the water and
walked rapidly away, longing to get back to her desk.

Ryan was following behind her. 'I wanted to speak to you
again,' he said, catching up and falling into step beside her. 'I've
been trying to get hold of you. There are a few things I want to
follow up.'

'No,' she said. 'I don't want to talk to you. You need to stop
harassing my family.' Hayley could hear her voice become
increasingly panicked.

Ryan acted like he hadn't heard. 'Did you like the flowers?'
he asked.

She glared at him. 'Of course not. But if you think they've
come between me and Lars, you're wrong. I've told him everything that happened in Thailand. He was sympathetic. He felt
sorry for me.'

Ryan laughed. 'That's an odd response. Considering what
you did.' Hayley jumped. What did he mean, 'what you did'?
He'd always said he was on her side. Had he always been trying
to catch her out? Did he think she'd hurt Chloe?

'I didn't do anything.'

Ryan smirked. 'Everything will come out in the end,
Hayley. It's just a question of how. Don't you think it's better
you speak to me, get your side of the story across?'

Hayley shook her head. 'Just stay away from me and my
family.'

When Hayley got home that evening, she still felt unsettled by
what Ryan had said. She was sure he was bluffing, but everything about Hayley's life seemed so precarious lately. It felt like
the past was careering towards her like a speeding train.

She heard voices when she went through the door of her
home and saw Johanna sitting with her mother in the kitchen.

She wondered what they were talking about and thought again of the photos of Thailand. Could Johanna be the one who'd found them, the one who'd been grilling her mother about them?

'How's Mum been?' she asked Johanna.

'I'm right here!' her mother said, irritably. 'You don't need to ask Johanna, you can just ask me.'

'Sorry, Mum,' Hayley said. 'How are you?'

'Fine. I had a good day, thanks.' Hayley waited to see if she had any more to say, but she didn't.

'How was Michelle?' Hayley prompted. 'Did you do anything today?'

'Just a quick walk. I could have done it on my own without her, really. She talks incessantly, asks so many questions. Sometimes I just want some time for myself.'

Hayley smiled. Her mother seemed entirely lucid today. She knew where she was, who Hayley was, who Michelle was. Maybe Hayley could take her out, spend some time with her. It had been so long since they'd had a proper chat. She was always too busy trying to work out the best way to take care of her.

'Where's Alice?' she asked Johanna.

'She's colouring in the living room. She's had her dinner.'

Hayley smiled. 'The weather's nice. I think I'd like to get out of the house. I'll take Alice to the playground. Give you a bit of a break. I'll go and get changed first. Is Lars upstairs?'

'Yeah, he's in his office.'

Hayley went upstairs to say hello to Lars, who completely immersed in his work. He was always too busy to talk to her these days, and he'd become worse since she'd told him about Thailand. She told him she was going out with Alice, but he barely acknowledged her.

While she was changing in her room, she heard footsteps on the stairs, and then a conversation in Swedish. A peal of laughter came, deep and loud. Hayley frowned. What had Johanna said to him?

When she'd finished changing into her jeans and T-shirt, she went across the hallway to Lars' study. Johanna was standing over his desk, looking at something on his screen, leaning forward slightly.

'Hi.' Lars caught sight of her. 'Johanna and I were just talking about something in the Swedish news. Another political scandal. There's a really funny cartoon about it.'

Johanna stepped away from the desk. 'I just came up to see what Lars wanted for dinner. I thought I'd cook tonight.'

'Oh, that's very kind of you,' Hayley said. 'You don't need to.'

'I want to,' Johanna said. 'To say thank you. You've really made me feel like part of the family.'

In the playground, Alice went on the swing and then climbed to the top of the climbing frame.

'Look at me!' she shouted. 'Mum, look at me!'

The walk over had been slow and when they'd got to the park, Hayley had let Alice run ahead and into the playground. It was busy and it was hard to keep track of her as she ran from one thing to another. At least now she was older there was little risk of her leaving the park of her own accord. It wasn't like when she was a toddler and she'd been determined to explore everything, always trying to open the gates to get out. Now, Alice knew to stay inside the park.

Hayley turned to her mother. 'So, how's it going?' she asked her.

'Fine,' her mother said. 'Although I hate getting old. I used to see older people on the wards all the time when I was a nurse. And I never really understood what it was like to slowly lose your physical and mental abilities and to know that you weren't going to improve again, that things were only going to get worse.'

'You're not old, Mum. You're only seventy.' Hayley didn't know what else to say, because although her mother was not that old, her health was in a much worse state than others she knew who were the same age.

'Past my sell-by date,' her mother said with a bitter laugh. 'Don't work too hard, you'll regret it when you're older. I thought I'd enjoy my retirement. But then your stepfather died. And since then it's all been downhill.'

'At least you can live with us. You get to see your grand-daughter growing up.' Hayley was searching for a silver lining.

'Yes, it's lovely to spend time with Alice.'

They watched as Alice raced over to the slide. She seemed to have made a friend and they ran together, holding hands.

'She's at a lovely age. They're more difficult when they get older. At least, you were.'

Hayley laughed. 'Teenagers are always difficult.'

'Maybe.'

'Mum – have you met someone called Ryan?' Hayley asked, taking advantage of the fact that her mother's thinking seemed clearer today.

Her mother frowned. 'I don't think so. Or at least, I don't remember. But then I can be forgetful these days.'

'You'd have seen him outside the house. On your way to the supermarket, maybe?'

Her mother shook her head.

Hayley bit the bullet. 'I found some photos in your room. Of my time in Thailand. I wondered – did Ryan ask you to get them for him?'

Her mother looked at her, confusion clouding her eyes. 'I don't know about any photos,' she said. She seemed distressed by the thought, shaking her head a little too hard. 'But every-one's been asking about Thailand.'

'Who, Mum? Who's been asking?'

Her mother shook her head, her mind lost in a fog. 'I don't know,' she said. 'Everyone.'

Hayley sighed. The sky was starting to darken. They should head back.

She looked around the playground for Alice, but couldn't see her. She left her mother where she was and walked round quickly, looking at each piece of equipment. There were kids on the swings, the slides, the climbing frame. None of them was Alice. She couldn't spot her pink coat.

'Alice?' she called out. She suddenly remembered Michelle saying that Ryan sometimes looked after his niece who was Alice's age and lived locally. Hayley's mind spun. What if she was the girl Alice had been playing with? Alice would never leave the playground of her own accord, but she might if a 'friend' suggested it.

'Alice!' she called out, more urgently.

No answer. She went round the playground once more, looking on every level of the climbing structure and under the slide, then searching behind the bushes in the middle of the playground. Her heart was pounding now, and she couldn't help imagining the worst-case scenario – police in her house, a search party, pictures of Alice pinned to trees.

And then she spotted it. Her pink coat. Behind the little hut that the children sometimes had picnics in. Hayley ran up to her.

'Alice!' she said, trying to calm her voice. 'What are you doing?'

Alice had mud splashed all over her trousers and coat. 'We're making a mud pie,' she said.

Her friend nodded. 'Do you want some?' she asked.

Hayley smiled at her friend. 'It looks amazing, but no thanks,' she said, already thinking about whether she had time to put a wash on when she got home.

'Alice has to go now,' she said. 'Alice, say goodbye to your friend.'

Alice stood up and waved to the girl. The girl got up and ran over to her own mother. A woman with short blonde hair. Not Ryan. This child was nothing to do with Ryan. It had all been her imagination.

FORTY-ONE

1999

Hayley was reading in her room when the argument started. Chloe, Emily and Eva were asleep and she was having a rare moment to herself. She was trying to distract herself from the fact that Lyndsey and Sunita were flying to Australia tomorrow and she'd no longer have friends in the city.

But then she heard the voices. They murmured at first and then rose to a crescendo.

'Whose is it, then?' Julie screamed.

'I've no idea how it got there.' David sounded frustrated.

Hayley held her breath, hoping the children wouldn't wake up.

'Don't treat me like a fool. Of course you know how it got there! You've been having an affair.'

Hayley swallowed. Then Chloe started screaming. They'd woken her up.

Hayley shut her book and crept out of her room, stepping carefully past Julie and David's bedroom, not wanting to get embroiled in their fight.

David was muttering something, denying an affair. She

peered into the room as she went by. Julie was holding up a red bra. Hayley stared at it. She'd seen it before. Suddenly she had a flash of memory.

When Lyndsey and Sunita had come round and done their washing, weeks before, Lyndsey had hung her underwear up in David and Julie's bedroom. She must have left it behind and it had only resurfaced now.

Hayley hurried to Chloe's room, picked her up and held her close.

She kept the door open so she could hear the conversation.

'Who was it?' Julie was shouting. 'Was it Marion? She's been in this apartment. Was she getting some twisted little revenge on me? Paying me back for stealing you from her?'

'No, of course not!'

'Or was it the nanny? That would fit your way of operating, wouldn't it? Trading me in for someone younger.'

'You know I wouldn't look twice at her.'

Hayley winced.

'But it could be her bra. I mean, maybe it got mixed up in the washing.' Hayley felt her face reddening.

Chloe cried harder and Hayley rocked her.

'Do you think I'm stupid? What a ridiculous excuse. She does her own washing.'

'I don't know then...'

Emily and Eva crept into Chloe's room now, and Hayley welcomed them into her arms, wrapping them in a hug. She held their warm bodies close as she listened to the argument. David was still denying any affair.

'I'm going to find her,' Julie said suddenly. 'Ask her myself.' Hayley tensed as she heard footsteps in the hallway walking determinedly her way.

Julie appeared at the door, her face thunder.

'You've been sleeping with my husband, haven't you?'

Hayley hugged the children tighter, suddenly fearful. 'No!' she said.

'I mean, he's had affairs before. But I never thought he'd cheat with you. Part of the reason I chose you was because you were so unattractive.' Hayley flinched.

'There's nothing between me and David,' she said firmly, glancing at him standing behind her.

Julie glared at her. 'Of course there isn't,' she said. 'He'd never be interested in scum like you.'

'She's not scum,' Emily piped up.

'It's OK,' Hayley said, stroking her hair.

'You children need to get back to bed,' David said. 'Come with me.' He took them by the hands and led them to their room.

'Night night,' Hayley whispered as they left. 'Sleep well.'

Chloe was asleep again now, and Hayley placed her carefully in her cot.

'You've made a big mistake.' Julie pushed her face close to Hayley's as she rose from the cot. 'But don't worry. We're interviewing for a new nanny in the next few days. And as soon as I find someone, you'll be straight out the door.'

Hayley stayed silent. She wanted desperately to tell Julie to stick her job, that she was leaving now. But she couldn't. She needed to stay until Emily and Eva left. It wouldn't be much longer.

'I'm not interested in David,' she said. 'And I'll try harder at work.' *And as soon as the girls are gone*, she thought, *I'll pack my things and leave without a word. Leave you to sort everything out.*

Julie glared at her. 'Go to your room,' she said, pointing in that direction, as if she was a child. 'Go to your room and I'll see you in the morning. Ready to work.'

Hayley stared at Julie, unable to believe how she was being treated.

She went to her tiny bedroom, grabbed her bag and went back into the living room.

'I'm going out,' she said. 'You can deal with your own children when they wake up in the night.'

And with that, she went to the door and left the apartment.

FORTY-TWO

NOW

Hayley changed the sheets on her mother's bed, dropping the dirty ones into the washing basket to take downstairs. Michelle was due to arrive any minute to take Susan to the shops. She went to draw the curtains, which her mother seemed to always keep closed. Outside the window, the street was quiet, except for two people talking at the corner.

She recognised Ryan first and felt her body tense, his tall, hunched posture one she'd become familiar with. And then she saw who he was with. Michelle. They seemed to be having some kind of argument, Michelle gesticulating wildly as she spoke. Suddenly, as if sensing someone watching, Michelle turned her head towards the window. Her eyes locked with Hayley's for a second, and then she said something to Ryan and walked rapidly away.

When she came through the door of the house, Michelle came straight up to see Hayley.

'I've given him a piece of my mind,' she said breathlessly.

'Yeah, I saw you talking,' Hayley said. 'What did you say?' She hoped she hadn't angered him. He was so unpredictable.

'It was the first time I'd seen him since you told me what he was like,' Michelle said. 'I told him what I thought of him, how he shouldn't have started a conversation with me under false pretences. I told him to stay away from you and your family. And never to talk to me again.'

Hayley was surprised by the passion in Michelle's voice. She clearly felt bad about speaking to Ryan in the first place.

'How did he react?'

'He didn't say much. I think he got the message.' Michelle smiled.

'OK, thanks, Michelle,' she said. 'I think we should just try and avoid him from now on. Why don't you see how Mum's getting on? She's in the living room.'

'Sure,' Michelle said.

Hayley went upstairs to tell Lars what had happened.

'Ryan was here again,' she said, as she walked into his study. He glanced up from his work and put his fingers to his lips and then muted the call. 'What did you say?' he asked.

'Ryan was here.'

'At the house? Is he still here?'

'No, he's gone. He was talking to Michelle. She told him to get lost.'

'That's good,' Lars said. 'Let's talk about it tonight.'

He turned back round to the screen and Hayley took it as her cue to leave.

That evening, Hayley was making the dinner, thinking about what she could do to make Ryan leave her alone.

'Hi.' Lars' voice made her jump. 'I just checked on Alice. She's had a nightmare. Didn't you hear her call out?'

Hayley shook her head. 'No, sorry. I didn't. What was it about?'

'Something about someone hurting her. Standard childhood stuff. I sat with her until she went back to sleep.'

Hayley nodded and poured herself a glass of red wine. 'Want one?' she asked Lars.

'Sure,' he said.

'Just us and my mother for dinner, tonight. Johanna's out.' She had told Hayley she was driving out of London for the evening, to meet some friends in a country pub.

'Have you spoken to her recently?' Lars asked.

Hayley shook her head, remembering her and Lars giggling together. 'No, why?'

'I've been having some odd conversations with her lately. I didn't realise she knew about the missing baby in Thailand. She must have found out about it. And somehow she's come to the conclusion that *she* is this missing baby, this Chloe.' Lars cocked his head to the side, looking at her questioningly.

Hayley sighed. 'I know, she told me. She's confused.' She wondered why Johanna was talking to Lars about this now, and not her. She'd noticed Johanna had been more distant with her recently, but she wasn't sure why.

'Yeah, very. I think she might be mentally unwell. She's become fixated on this idea. I think that's why she's been friendlier to me lately. So she could gain my trust and ask me questions.'

'Oh,' Hayley said. If Johanna was trying to get information from Lars, that meant that she hadn't been satisfied with her denials. She tried to think of something to say to Lars, to explain Johanna's behaviour. 'I think she had an unhappy childhood,' she said. 'She's become convinced her parents aren't her biological parents. And she was born in Thailand. I think she's put two and two together and made five.'

Lars stood up and turned to her. 'She's really taken it and run with it. She's thought up a whole theory about what happened to her as a child. She thinks that you took her away and gave her to her parents.'

'She's wrong.'

Lars frowned. 'Of course she's wrong! I think her behaviour is very concerning.'

'Concerning? What do you mean?'

'Well, she's completely integrated herself into this family. She eats every meal with us, looks after Alice for free. Surely you have to ask why she wants to do all that? Doesn't she have her own friends?'

'She's with her own friends now,' Hayley said weakly.

'She seems obsessed with us.'

'We're like a surrogate family for her. That's all.' She wished he'd go easier on her.

Lars shook his head. 'It's all so odd...' he said. 'Does she know Ryan?'

'I don't think so. But he might have spoken to her. He's tried to speak to everyone connected to me.' She thought of Michelle. She really hoped he hadn't spoken to Johanna as well.

'The timing just seems too much of a coincidence, doesn't it? Until now, you've never mentioned what happened in Thailand. It's never come up. And then suddenly two people appear out of nowhere who are interested in what happened back then. A student crime writer and someone who's convinced they're the baby. Someone who actually moves in with us. Johanna and Ryan must be connected. I think she's come into our lives for a reason. And I think we need to get her out of our house.'

Hayley shook her head. 'No, we can't do that. She needs our support. She's vulnerable at the moment. She just found out she has a half-sibling on a DNA test, but they don't want to meet her.'

'A half-sibling? Then why does she think she's Chloe?'

'Chloe had half-sisters, so I can see how she could think it might be possible.'

'It's so bizarre, though. She moves in here and then becomes convinced she's a missing baby you used to nanny? I'm telling you, she's not quite right.'

She came to live here because she thought she was the missing baby, Hayley thought. But explaining that to Lars would only make him more suspicious of Johanna. And the last thing she wanted was for her to move out. She liked finally having her close by.

'Just give her a chance,' she said. 'Honestly, she's not a threat.'

At that moment, they heard the letter box open and then shut.

'It's late for post,' Lars said, frowning.

Hayley got up and went quickly to the window. She saw a man walking away from the house, his hood up, his body hunched over. Ryan. She was sure of it.

She ran to the doormat and intercepted Lars as he reached for the folded note, grabbing it before he did.

He looked at her in confusion. 'I saw Ryan walking away from the house,' she said.

'He left this?'

'Yes,' Hayley said, her heart pounding. 'Let me see what this says.'

She stood with her back to the wall, so Lars couldn't see the contents of the note. She was worried it would reveal what he knew about her, or accuse her of hurting Chloe. But it did neither of those.

Instead, it was a typed threat.

It's time you told the truth. Otherwise Alice will disappear. Just like Chloe.

FORTY-THREE

1999

Hayley ran down the stairs of the apartment block, through the lobby area and out the front door to freedom. She felt the warmth of the night air on her face as she left the building, and shivered with anticipation. It was the first time in ages she'd been out after dark, and the city buzzed with life. She hailed a taxi to Khao San Road and they drove past the bright lights advertising massage parlours and go-go girls, fast food and convenience stores.

In Khao San, she got out by the hostel. Lyndsey and Sunita were flying to Australia tomorrow. Time had flown, and she hadn't seen them since they'd come to the apartment a month ago. She wanted to say goodbye properly. And then she'd go back to the apartment, back to Julie and David. Back to the children.

At the hostel, she spoke to the man on the desk and asked if he'd seen them. He let her look in their dorm but they were out. Usually their clothes and belongings were spread out everywhere, but now their rucksacks were neatly packed, leaning against the wall, ready for the morning. Hayley felt a sliver of envy. She wished she could join them.

Hayley looked in the hostel bar, but they weren't there. Disappointment filled her. What if she couldn't find them? Perhaps this was a bad idea, to just turn up without letting them know she was coming. What was she doing here?

She couldn't go back to the apartment, not yet. She wanted Julie to get up in the night with Chloe, to see how intense her job actually was, perhaps to even feel some gratitude for everything Hayley did.

For a moment Hayley wondered if she ever had to go back at all. But she knew she did. The girls were there. And all her things.

Khao San was alive with noise and smells and people. Food was cooking at the stalls in the middle of the street, and backpackers wandered aimlessly, zigzagging through the crowds. Many of the stools at the outdoor bars were already full. She walked the whole way up the road, but didn't see Sunita or Lyndsey. Eventually she sat down on an empty bar stool and ordered a rum and Coke. It slipped down easily and she had a second. She sipped this one slowly, wanting to delay the inevitable moment when she had to go back to the apartment.

Watching the crowd, she suddenly caught sight of Sunita, wobbling on her heels as she walked, swaying slightly. Lyndsey caught her by the arm. They were in a big group of revellers, enjoying their last night in Bangkok.

'Sunita!' she shouted. 'Lyndsey!'

Lyndsey turned towards her and then beamed as she caught sight of her. She came over, dragging Sunita behind her.

'Hayley! What are you doing here?'

'I came to see you. To say goodbye.'

'You're allowed out then?'

'No, I left.'

'You left? As in, you quit?'

'No, I'm going back. But only for a couple of weeks. They're looking for a new nanny.' She didn't want to go into the details. She just wanted to relax and forget about it.

'Come on,' Lyndsey called out to their group of friends, 'let's go to this bar.' She sat down on the stool next to Hayley, and Sunita sat down next to her. A group of about ten people wandered over and all pulled up stools to their table.

'Let's get buckets,' one of them said.

Before Hayley knew it, five buckets of bright blue alcohol were on the table. Everyone leant in and drank through the straws, their heads bowed together. Hayley grabbed a straw and joined them.

Soon the alcohol was coursing through their veins and Hayley felt relaxed.

'You should come with us,' Sunita said. 'To Australia. You could work there, you know. They have fruit picking.'

'I'm sorry. You know I can't. I have to go back to the apartment tonight.'

'You'll join us later, won't you? When we're back in Asia?' Lyndsey asked.

Hayley nodded slowly. The alcohol had gone to her head and everything looked blurry and sounded fuzzy. She leant back on her chair to steady herself, but there was only air. She had been on a stool. Her head hit the tarmac with a crunch and her world went dark.

FORTY-FOUR

NOW

Lars grabbed the note from Hayley's hand.

'So now Ryan's threatening Alice?' He opened the front door. 'I can't see him. Which way did he go?'

'Left,' Hayley said.

Lars ran down the street, looking for him. 'Where are you, you coward? Come out and face us rather than threatening my daughter!'

But Ryan was gone.

Lars came back inside. 'Do you think Johanna had something to do with this?'

Hayley shook her head. 'No, of course not. We saw Ryan.'

Lars nodded. 'I'm going to call the police.'

Hayley's mind raced. She felt the terror fill her. She'd tried to avoid having any dealings with the police since Thailand. But Lars was right, they needed to report this.

'Good idea,' she said.

The next day, Hayley tapped the steering wheel impatiently as she sat in traffic, on the way back from Alice's swimming lesson.

'Are we nearly home yet?' Alice whined. 'I'm hungry.'

Hayley reached into her handbag on the passenger seat and found some biscuits. 'Have these to keep you going.'

'Thanks, Mum.'

Hayley thought about the note she'd received through the door. The police hadn't been too concerned, just thanked her for reporting it, and told her to let them know if anything else happened. They'd told her to be watchful, just in case.

'Alice,' she said, 'has the school taught you about strangers?'

'What do you mean?'

'I mean, if a stranger approaches you, you shouldn't ever go off with them.'

'I know that. You told me that.'

Hayley remembered how she'd thought she'd lost Alice in the park. 'Even if it's a child you've made friends with at the park, they're still a stranger. You shouldn't go anywhere with them.'

'Why would I, if I was already in the park?'

'I suppose you wouldn't. But make sure you do what I say. It's important, Alice.'

'Who's a stranger?' Alice asked. 'Is Johanna a stranger?'

Hayley thought for a minute. 'No, not really. I mean, we know her, don't we?' She heard the hesitation in her own voice, thought of what Lars had said about her. But Hayley was sure she could trust her.

'So is a stranger someone I've never met at all?'

'Well, yes.'

'What about someone I'd met once?'

'Well, I suppose they'd be a stranger.'

'Like Uncle Ray?'

'No, he's family. And you've met him more than once.' Hayley was losing patience now, with both Alice and the traffic, which still wasn't moving. 'Look,' she said. 'Just be careful, OK? Only ever listen to people that you trust. So that would be me and your dad, anyone living in our house, and your teachers. No one else. Especially not any strange men. Understand?'

Alice didn't say anything, and Hayley thought again of the note that had come through the door. She hoped it was an empty threat. 'Look, Alice, this is really important. Do you understand?'

'Yes, Mum,' Alice said sullenly. 'Do you have any more biscuits? I'm still hungry.'

When they got home, Johanna was eating lunch with Michelle and Susan. Michelle had heated up a supermarket shepherd's pie and some frozen peas and they were all digging in. Alice immediately sat down at the table. 'Is there any for me?' she asked.

'Don't worry,' Johanna said, laughing. 'I asked Michelle to save you a bit.' She went to the oven and took out the last bit of the shepherd's pie and dished it up for Alice. 'I'm so sorry,' she said, turning to Hayley. 'There wasn't enough for you and Lars.'

'Don't worry, I'm just going to have a sandwich,' she said.

'Sure.'

Hayley had noticed that Johanna had been acting strangely around her lately. It felt like she'd been avoiding her.

'Are you OK?' she asked Johanna.

'Yeah, sure. Why?'

'No reason.' Johanna turned back to her conversation with Michelle. They were talking about a film playing at the cinema, making plans to see it together. Hayley felt a twinge of jealousy. It was a thriller she would have liked to have seen herself. But they wouldn't have thought to ask her, probably thought she was too old.

'I wanted to speak to you both,' Hayley said quickly, thinking of her conversation with Alice in the car.

'What about?' Michelle asked.

'You know there's been a man lurking around outside?' As she said it, Hayley realised she'd never mentioned it to Johanna.

But Johanna nodded. 'Michelle told me about him,' she said.

'I want you both to make sure you keep a close eye on Alice. And tell me or Lars if either of you sees him near the house.'

'I always watch her carefully,' Johanna said.

'I know. But just make sure you always hold her hand, and never let her out of your sight.'

'I wouldn't,' Johanna said. 'But why the sudden concern?'

Hayley paused, wondering if she should tell them about the note. She decided not to. It would lead to more questions than it answered.

'No real reason,' she said. 'I've read some dreadful things in the papers lately. I just want to keep Alice safe.'

FORTY-FIVE

1999

Hayley's head was hammering as she woke up to banging on the door of her room. She groaned and rolled over, putting the pillow over her head. She thought back to last night in Khao San. She'd had a great time, but she'd had far too much to drink.

The banging continued. 'Hayley!' Julie shouted. Luckily there was a small bolt on the door, that Hayley had remembered to pull across last night. Julie couldn't come in. 'You're needed at breakfast,' Julie shouted again.

'I'll come soon,' Hayley shouted back, the sound of her own voice making her head pound harder.

'Not soon. Now.' Julie sounded furious. In the background Hayley could hear Chloe crying and it tugged at her heart. But why should she get up to care for her? They'd have to cope without her soon.

Eventually she heard Julie's footsteps retreat and the door to the kitchen bang shut. Chloe was still crying.

Hayley reached her hand round to the back of her head. There was a small sticky patch of dried blood and the memory of falling off her stool came back to her. She'd hit her head and been knocked unconscious for a few seconds. When she'd come to, everyone had been gathered around her. She'd tried to get up, but fallen down again immediately, this time saving herself with her hands. They'd all thought it was hilarious, including her.

She remembered Lyndsey and Sunita's hands on her, pulling her up, Lyndsey stumbling as she did so. They'd checked her over, and she'd insisted she was fine. They'd considered and dismissed going to get her checked out at the hospital and then carried on drinking. No wonder she felt awful now.

Chloe was still crying and no one seemed to be going to her. Hayley would have to. She ran her fingers through her hair, unlocked the door and crept out of her room. When she picked up Chloe she felt shaky, as if she might drop her. She put her down on a mat on the floor and changed her nappy, then tickled her tummy. She seemed to calm down. Hayley thought she was probably hungry, but for now she seemed happy, so she decided to have a shower before she got the bottle. Someone else must have given her her night-time milk. She couldn't imagine Julie doing it. It must have been David.

Julie walked past her as she was going back to her room. She glared at her and moved away from her. 'What were you doing with Chloe?' she asked.

'She was crying. I was looking after her.'

'You stink,' she said. 'You must still be drunk. Go to your room and sort yourself out. David will take the day off to look after the girls. He can say it's a family emergency. Because it is. It would be dangerous to leave them in your care.'

Hayley slunk back to her room, fuming, as Julie left the apartment. She crawled back into bed and listened to the noise in the house rise as David struggled to get the girls ready for school, and then fall as they left the apartment and their footsteps retreated down the corridor. It was the first time she'd ever had the house to herself, without any children. She got up slowly and eased her way into the shower. Julie was right. She was still drunk.

Later, she helped David with Chloe, showing him once again the best way to feed her from the bottle, how to change her nappy. She was amazed that he still struggled with it, that he didn't know the basics about looking after his own daughter. But at least he was nice to her, and together they worked as a team to make the day go quicker. He didn't mention the bra in the bedroom, or the argument last night. That was best forgotten.

In the evening, Hayley got out of their way after she'd put Chloe to bed. The doorbell rang at 8.30 p.m. and she jumped in surprise, putting her book down. She pretended that she needed to check on Chloe and crept into her room. She sat in the nursing chair and listened to the conversation in the living room.

'So what are your qualifications as a nanny?'

The woman listed her qualifications, and the previous jobs she'd had. She'd worked with many families before, brought up their children. She must be in her forties. So different to Hayley. Perhaps she'd be kind to Chloe, care for her properly. Hayley prayed that would be the case. She didn't want to leave her with someone unkind.

Hayley heard her ask who was looking after Chloe now, whether they currently had a nanny.

'We did have one, but she wasn't qualified. Just a pissed teenager on a gap year,' Julie said. David and the nanny laughed along with her.

When the interview was over, the woman asked about

salary and there was a notable silence after she was told. Then they took her to see Hayley's room. They didn't knock, just barged in. Luckily she wasn't there.

Then Julie and David walked the nanny to the door.

'When can you start?' Julie asked her.

FORTY-SIX

NOW

When Hayley got in from work, exhausted from her day, she found red roses on the kitchen table, already carefully arranged in a vase. She swallowed. It couldn't be Ryan again, could it? If they'd been delivered then Johanna might have put them in a vase for her, without checking who they were from.

She searched around the kitchen, looking for a note. Nothing.

Lars appeared in the kitchen. 'They're from me,' he said. He smiled and then the smile dropped from his face. 'You didn't think they were from someone else?'

'No, of course not. Just after last time, with Ryan, I was worried... that's all.'

'Right,' Lars said. 'So this time they're from your one and only husband.'

'What have I done to deserve this?' Hayley asked. She couldn't help sounding wary. He'd been acting so distant lately, and he hardly ever bought her flowers.

'I have some good news,' Lars said, grinning. 'That I want to celebrate with you.'

'What is it?'

'I won the new client. The contract's worth over two million. It will keep the business ticking over for a while. I don't need to make anyone redundant. And our house is safe. Our whole lifestyle is safe.'

'That's amazing news,' Hayley said, her stomach unknotting. She hadn't realised how anxious she'd been about their financial future, but now relief flooded through her.

'So tonight, I'm taking you out to celebrate. I've booked a babysitter and I'm taking you for an expensive meal, at the new steak restaurant in town.'

'Great,' Hayley said, swallowing her exhaustion. It was a long time since she and Lars had been out for a nice meal. 'Who have you found to babysit? Do I know them?'

'I found someone on one of the babysitting apps. Overqualified. Worked as a nanny previously. Expensive. They'll be perfect.'

'Great,' Hayley said. Really, she'd prefer Johanna to babysit, but she knew Lars would never agree to that. Not any more.

'Things have been tense between us lately, haven't they?' Lars said, when they were halfway through their main course.

'A little, maybe... it's been hard not knowing whether we're going to be able to afford things.'

'I know. And I've been completely distracted by the business. I haven't had much time to think about anything else.'

'I'm so glad you got the new client.' Hayley lifted her glass to toast him. 'Here's to you. To us.'

He smiled at her as their glasses clinked. 'I've been thinking about what you said about Thailand,' Lars said. 'I still don't understand why Ryan is so interested in it or in you.'

Hayley sighed. 'He wants to write a bestselling true-crime book. He thinks I can give him more details about what happened.'

'What exactly did happen?'

'I was the baby's nanny. And the baby disappeared one night. I was arrested because one of the half-sisters said she'd seen me taking the baby. But she didn't. She was only four and she got confused.' Hayley tried to sound matter-of-fact, to control her emotions. 'I was released the next day without charge.'

'You had nothing to do with it?'

'No, but I did feel guilty.' Hayley pushed down the feelings rising up inside her, holding back tears. 'Because I was there that night. And I felt so sad about Chloe. I really loved her.'

'But you didn't know where she went?'

Hayley frowned. Had Lars started to doubt her? 'No,' she said.

He nodded and then looked at her intently, his eyes boring into her. 'I've been speaking to Johanna,' he said.

'Oh?'

'She seems to trust me, wants to confide in me.'

'About what?'

'She told me that she'd found her half-sister.'

'What?' Hayley felt the blood drain from her face.

'They met up, got on well. They'd had a match on the DNA test. At first the sister didn't want to connect, but then she changed her mind and got in touch.'

Emily. Hayley thought. *Eva*. She felt a twinge of longing. She'd always wished she'd known what had happened to them after they'd gone back to England. Their mother had rushed them back to their grandparents' home in Milton Keynes shortly after Chloe's disappearance. Marion had said she hoped they'd forget what they'd been through. Hayley wasn't so sure.

'The half-sister's father is David McFarlane. She shares a dad with Johanna. David McFarlane is Johanna's father.'

Hayley stared at Lars, her mind racing. How far was

Johanna from working out the truth? Was it time to tell her?
'Oh,' she said slowly.

'Yep. It's indisputable. Johanna is part of that family. The family you nannied for.'

'Are you sure?' Hayley couldn't think of anything else to say.

'It was in the DNA results. DNA doesn't lie.'

'Wow, this is big news.'

'Her sister thinks she's Chloe, too. It was very emotional for them. The sister was so pleased to discover Johanna was alive.'

Hayley's heart sank, imagining all the hope that had gone into that meeting. They thought they finally knew what had happened to Chloe, that she was safe. How long was it before they found out the truth?

'She's not Chloe,' she said.

'How do you know?'

'Sorry?' Hayley said, confused.

'If Chloe disappeared, how can you be so sure what happened to her?'

'I suppose I don't know for sure,' Hayley had to say. 'But David... he was a philanderer. He had several affairs. Johanna could easily be his child, without it meaning she's Chloe.'

'Johanna said you used to know her parents. In Thailand.'

'I did.' This was starting to feel like an interrogation.

'And they moved to Stockholm when she was a baby. Shortly after Chloe's disappearance.'

'No,' Hayley said, shaking her head. 'It was a long time later. Nearly a year.'

'So you knew them well enough to know that?'

'A mutual friend told me.' Hayley remembered the sinking feeling in her stomach when she'd found out, the sense of an ending.

Lars looked at her, his eyes quizzical. 'There's a whole side of you I don't think I know at all.'

'That's not true. You know me better than anyone.'

'But you never told me about all this.' She swallowed. There was so much more she hadn't told him.

'I've explained why.'

'OK, so it was a time you wanted to forget. But after you left Thailand, you spent lots of time in Stockholm. You always said you liked travelling in the Nordics. But you didn't really travel round, did you? You kept coming back to Stockholm. Even before we started seeing each other you were often there. Why was that?'

'I just liked the city,' Hayley said weakly.

'But you didn't have any connections with it. Except for the fact that Johanna's parents were living there. Johanna herself was living there.'

Hayley stared down into her wine, her thoughts swirling.

'Johanna thinks,' Lars said, 'that you took Chloe from David and Julie and gave her to your friends, her parents, Hans and Karolina.' He gazed intently at Hayley. 'You've got a lot of explaining to do.'

FORTY-SEVEN

1999

Hayley swam up and down in the swimming pool, trying to clear her head. She was counting down the days until she would leave the apartment, leave Julie and David far behind. Marion had booked flights for herself and the girls to leave in a week's time.

If Julie had her way, Hayley would have left as soon as she'd found the bra and Hayley had disobeyed her and gone out. It was David who had insisted that she stay until they found a replacement. Of the two of them, he was the one who understood how much work she did, how difficult it would be to manage without her. Julie had no idea, and she had reluctantly agreed to let Hayley stay on for a bit longer.

Hayley had gone on a kind of half-strike. For the last week and a half she hadn't done any cleaning or washing or ironing. She simply did the childcare. David had asked the cleaner to do more hours in the week, but still the apartment was messy, and he was forever putting things back in the right place.

Hayley felt the sun on her back as she swam in the pool. David had Chloe downstairs. The first nanny they'd interviewed hadn't been interested in the job, so he'd taken the morning off work to conduct more interviews. He was introducing each candidate to Chloe to see how they were with her. Emily and Eva were at school. Marion was picking them up later to take them out to dinner, before bringing them back well before Julie got home. Then tomorrow, at the weekend, Marion and the girls were going shopping for warm clothes for England and had invited Hayley. She was going to join them, and leave Chloe with David and Julie.

As the swimming pool water washed over her, she thought how good this job could have been if Julie and David had only asked her to look after the children, had allowed her to take breaks, to use the apartment block's facilities. It could have been a dream life. But it hadn't been.

Eventually, Hayley got out of the pool. She lay on a sunlounger reading a book until she was sure the interviews would be finished. Then she wrapped a towel around her, slipped on her flip-flops and went down in the lift to the apartment.

'Hello!' David greeted her, as she wandered in.

She put her towel down while she took off her flip-flops and then picked it up again to go to her room to shower.

David whistled. 'God, that bikini looks good on you,' he said, eyeing her up appraisingly.

'I'm just going to have a shower,' she said.

'You can use the one in our bedroom if you like.' She hesitated, remembering when she had last used their bathroom. It had been when Julie was away at the conference. The rainforest shower had pummelled her shoulders and it had felt luxurious.

'OK,' she said. 'Thanks.'

She showered, enjoying the sensation of the warm water running down her body. She stayed in there for ages, unwilling to get out, to go back to her room. When she finally got out, she had to walk back through David and Julie's bedroom to get to her room.

David was sitting on his bed, waiting.

'Looking good,' he said, as she emerged in her towel, making her jump. 'Come here.' He reached out, touched her bare shoulder.

She was tempted for a moment, thinking of when Julie had been away, how they'd drunk too much wine, he'd let her use their shower and then they'd sunk onto the bed together; how exciting and wrong that had felt, but she'd got caught up in the moment. She'd felt awful in the morning, and had sworn to herself it wouldn't happen again. She couldn't deny that David was attractive, but she didn't want to keep sleeping with her boss. It was just a drunken mistake. One that Julie must never find out about.

'No,' she said to David, scurrying past him and back to the safety of her room.

When they got back from the restaurant, Hayley went up to Alice's room and looked at her sleeping form. She looked so peaceful, and so fragile. It was hard to believe that she was the age Emily had been when she'd looked after her. She'd loved Emily and Eva, but it hadn't been like the all-consuming, overwhelming love she had for Alice. She wondered what they were like now. One of them must have spoken to Johanna. What could they have told her about Thailand? About her?

She'd managed to convince Lars that Johanna must have been a product of David having an affair, and had hinted that it was probably with Karolina. But what was she going to say to Johanna? Did she finally need to tell the truth? She felt a sliver of fear shooting through her. She could wreck everything.

The door to Johanna's room had been closed when she passed by. She must have already gone to bed. She would text her in the morning from work, suggest they spoke. She needed to understand what Johanna thought had happened in the past, needed to battle this head-on.

On Alice's dressing table, there were three groups of Sylvanian families. Hayley frowned as she noticed that one of the families only had three members, not the usual four. There was a mother squirrel, a father squirrel and a boy squirrel, but no girl squirrel. That was Alice's favourite set and she played with it a lot, the girl always representing her.

Now Hayley looked round the room for the missing toy, on the floor, under the bed, by Alice's pillow. It wasn't there. She moved the bedside table slightly. And there it was. It must have fallen down into the dust, its little feet sticking into the air.

She pulled it up. And then she saw. Its body was there, but its head was missing. Broken off. On the floor below it.

She stared at it for a moment, wondering if it meant anything. Toys often broke more easily than you'd think. Alice had played with this one a lot; it would have had a lot of wear and tear. And if it had been wedged behind the bedside table for a while, the head could have broken off.

She tried to push the two parts together, but they didn't slot into each other. Could it have been deliberately broken? She thought of the note through the door, the threat to Alice. Hayley frowned and then kissed Alice on the cheek, taking the broken doll out of the room with her.

The next day, Hayley rushed to finish her paperwork in the office, completing the referrals to financial support for two students. She'd explained to Kim that she needed to get back early this afternoon to look after Alice. She'd messaged Johanna to say she'd pick Alice up from school, and that she wanted to speak to her that evening after Alice had gone to bed. Johanna had replied to say that she had wanted to speak to Hayley too, and Hayley's stomach had knotted with fear, unsure what she wanted to say.

'Why isn't Johanna picking me up any more?' Alice asked, as soon as she saw it was Hayley collecting her.

'She's busy today.' Hayley couldn't think of a better answer.

She thought about the decapitated toy in Alice's room, Lars' concerns about Johanna's mental health, the note through her door from Ryan. It had made her want to keep Alice close to her, made her anxious about trusting Johanna to look after her.

'Do you like Johanna? Is she nice to you?' she asked Alice.

'Yeah, she always plays with me. Whatever I want to play. She lets me choose.'

Hayley had seen that Johanna was always patient with Alice. She liked to watch them together, having fun and laughing. In those moments it felt like things were exactly right, like this was how her household should be. But she had always known it couldn't last forever.

When they got to the house, there were voices in the kitchen.

'Johanna!' Alice said, running into the kitchen. 'Guess what happened at school today?'

Johanna swept her into her arms. 'What?' she asked. She was sitting at the table with Michelle and Susan, drinking coffee.

'I was selected as team captain for bench ball.'

'Wow, that's amazing.' Hayley felt a twinge of jealousy as she wondered why Alice hadn't told her this on the walk home.

'Come on, Alice,' she said. 'Let's go up and get changed.'

'I want to play with Johanna.'

'Johanna's busy,' Hayley said.

'Listen to your mum,' Johanna said.

After Alice was changed from school, Hayley let her play for a bit while she cooked her a quick dinner. Lars was still upstairs working on the project for his new client. She called up to him to see if he wanted to put Alice to bed, but he didn't hear her. When she knocked on his office door, he had his headphones on and was engrossed in a meeting. She shut the door quietly behind her.

She put Alice to bed and kissed her good night and then

went downstairs to find Johanna. She was playing cards in the kitchen, with Michelle and Susan. Michelle had said it would help boost her mother's memory.

'Did you want to talk?' Johanna said anxiously, standing up from the table.

'Yes, I did, actually. Do you have time now?'

'Of course.' Johanna smiled.

'I'd better be off,' Michelle said, and Hayley suddenly realised that she'd stayed well beyond her usual hours. Hayley would have to make sure she paid her properly. It was such a relief that Lars' business had picked up.

'Thanks, Michelle. Have a lovely evening.'

'Do you want me to put something on the TV for Susan?' she said as she stood up.

'Yes, that would be good.'

'Sure. Come on, Susan.'

'See you tomorrow,' Johanna called after Michelle.

Johanna and Hayley sat down at the kitchen table. They waited until they heard the sound of the TV. Michelle turned it up loud, just how her mother liked it.

Then they heard the thud of the front door closing as Michelle left.

Hayley looked at Johanna and hesitated. There was so much to say. She ran her hands over the decapitated toy in her pocket. She'd start there. Hayley pulled it out to show Johanna.

'This was Alice's favourite toy. And someone's taken the head off. I found it down the back of the bedside table last night.' She studied Johanna carefully for her reaction.

Johanna stared. 'It could have just broken on its own,' she said. 'I think that's the most likely explanation.'

'OK,' Hayley said. 'I've just been worried about Alice. I had a threatening note through the door...'

'Oh – is that why you picked Alice up from school yourself?'

'Partly… look, Johanna… Lars mentioned you'd met your half-sister.'

Johanna's face darkened. 'That's what I wanted to talk to you about. You've been lying to me.'

'What do you mean?' Hayley's stomach clenched. How much did she know?

'David's my father. My sister showed me photos. I look just like him. You must have known as soon as you saw me.'

Hayley sighed. 'I suppose I suspected.'

'You didn't just suspect. You knew.'

Hayley couldn't meet her eyes. She needed to know about Emily and Eva. How they were now. She changed the subject. 'Was it Emily you met? Or Eva?' Not that it mattered. She hadn't seen either of them since. She wondered how much they remembered.

'Eva.'

'What was it like? Meeting her? How is she?'

'Why do you want to know?'

'I used to nanny for them. I… I really missed them after I left. I loved them.'

'She was really nice and kind. And pleased to meet me at last. We both cried. We couldn't believe we had finally found each other again.'

'Again?'

Johanna sighed. 'Don't hide it any more. It's obvious what happened now. I'm Chloe. And for whatever reason, you took me from my biological parents, David and Julie, and gave me to Karolina and Hans. Then they escaped Thailand with me, before they could be found out. Why did you do that?'

For a moment Hayley wondered if it would be easier to let Johanna believe that she was Chloe. Everyone would be happy then. Emily and Eva reunited with their sister. Chloe still alive. Hayley couldn't be accused of murder.

But maybe it was finally time to tell the truth.

'You're right about one thing,' Hayley said. 'When you were a baby, I gave you to Karolina and Hans. And it was for all the right reasons. They desperately wanted a child. And I knew they'd make good parents for you. I knew they'd love and protect you.'

'So you took me away from my birth parents? From David and Julie? You thought that was the right thing to do? To let them believe that I had been stolen or murdered?' Johanna's face was pale.

Hayley sighed. 'I didn't take you away from them. David is your father. And Emily and Eva are your half-sisters. But Julie isn't your mother. I am.'

FORTY-NINE

1999

Hayley walked beside Marion through the shopping centre, carrying a sleeping Chloe in her handmade sling. In the air-conditioned centre she didn't need to worry about Chloe getting too hot and dehydrated.

The shopping mall made her feel comfortable, and she loved seeing all the branded shops and the well-dressed shoppers, arms overflowing with bags. It was nothing like Ealing, but somehow the cool air and piped music made her long for home. It didn't help that Emily and Eva were shopping for clothes to wear in England's cold climate. Their bags were full of jumpers and tights. Now Emily was running her hand over a new coat, hundreds of little dogs forming a pattern over it. 'I love this one,' she said, while Marion looked at the price tag and then made her try it on. Hayley tried to think of the last time she'd needed a coat. She'd recently bought a poncho for the rainy season in Bangkok, but she hadn't needed a proper coat since she'd been in England. She longed to feel the cold air, the wind on her face, see the terraced houses and the green trees. Maybe after she left Bangkok, she'd head up north, to Chiang Mai. She could stop off on the way, see some of the Thai countryside before Sunita and Lyndsey came back. She was done with the city. It was time to have an adventure.

In the shop, she saw a red blanket with grey stars on it. She ran her fingers over its soft material and thought how nice it would look in Chloe's crib. She looked at the price tag and saw it was on offer, and decided to buy it as a parting gift for Chloe. She was going to miss her so much.

'Are you looking forward to going back to England?' she said to Emily and Eva.

They looked at each other.

'I don't think they can even remember what England's like. Eva was a baby when we left,' Marion said.

She turned to the girls. 'I bet you can't wait to see your grandparents?'

They looked up uncertainly. For them the move only represented change, moving away from everything that was familiar.

Emily glanced at Hayley and suddenly threw her arms around her. 'What about you? Can you come with us?'

Hayley shook her head. 'No, I'm sorry.' She crouched down to Emily's level. 'But I'll miss you so much.'

'I'll miss you too,' Emily said, tears flowing down her face.

That evening, it sank in that Hayley's time in the apartment was coming to an end. She'd miss the children. It would be hard to be apart from them.

She looked sadly at her rucksack in the corner. She'd imagined carrying it everywhere as she backpacked round Asia, but instead it had spent most of the time sat in the corner of this room. But that was going to change. She and the backpack were going to have a proper gap year, see new things, meet new people, go on a proper adventure.

She started to pack the things she wouldn't need over the next two days. She put her spare trainers in a plastic bag at the bottom of the rucksack, and then took her clothes out of the wardrobe, neatly folding and packing them. She was surprised by how little she'd accumulated while she was here. Aside from the poncho she'd bought at a market, and a tiny silver bracelet, she'd hardly bought anything for herself. When she'd gone out to the shops it had always been to buy tins of formula for Chloe or school supplies for Emily and Eva.

She went into her tiny bathroom, opened the little cupboard and saw the packs of tampons and sanitary towels she'd brought with her for her trip. She'd hardly used any since she was here. It must be something about the heat, but her periods had been far lighter than usual, hardly there at all. She stared at the sanitary products. It was obvious to her now that she really had used very few. She thought of her periods, how light they had been. When had she had her last one?

She reached her hand to her stomach. It felt slightly more bloated than normal, but nothing more. And yet everything was slotting into place. Her slight nausea in the mornings, the strange craving she'd had for a meat feast pizza the other day, which she'd put down to missing home. She did the calculation in her head. She was nearly two months pregnant.

FIFTY

NOW

Johanna stared at Hayley in shock. 'What?' she asked.

Hayley repeated herself. 'I'm your mother,' she said. 'David's your father and I'm your mother.'

'I don't understand,' Johanna said slowly, putting her head in her hands. 'Julie's not my mother? You are?'

Hayley wanted to reach out and comfort her, to hold her hand. But instead she reached into her handbag and pulled out her wallet. She reached into the small zip pocket and pulled out four tiny photos. Three of them were of Alice, showing her as she grew older: a newborn baby, then a toddler pushing a toy buggy, then aged four, holding a balloon at her birthday party. But there was a photo she'd carried for longer than the others, one she'd told Lars was a photo of her god-daughter, who she rarely saw since the parents had moved abroad.

'This is you,' Hayley said, pulling out the photo. 'When you were a baby, in Thailand. I've always carried it with me.'

Johanna took the photo and studied it, tears in her eyes. The baby in the photo was tiny, scrunched up and red, clearly a newborn.

'Wow,' she said, studying the photo. 'I've seen photos of

when I was a baby, but none from when I was this tiny. I can't quite believe this.'

'I've always kept you close to me. I used to look at this photo every day.'

'Do you have any more photos?'

'I have a few, but they're all from the first couple of days. I gave you away after that. I can dig them out later.' They were in the cupboard with the other family photos. Lars thought they were her god-daughter too. 'And I still have a babygrow from when you were first born. I can show that to you as well.' Hayley blinked back tears.

'Oh wow. This is crazy, I can't take this in.' She looked up at Hayley. 'You're my mother. I don't know how to feel about that.'

'Take your time,' Hayley said. 'It must be a huge shock.' She wanted to hug Johanna, to hold her like a mother would hold a daughter, to comfort her. She'd longed to feel her embrace for years. But she knew that now was not the right moment, that Johanna needed to process what she'd said.

'Why didn't you tell me before?'

'I was too scared. I was worried I'd lose you.'

'You must have been young when you had me,' Johanna said gently.

'I was nineteen. When you were born I was so overwhelmed by love for you.' Hayley swallowed down her emotions, trying to stop the tears falling. 'You always had such beautiful eyes. I just wanted to cuddle you forever. But I knew I couldn't support you. I had no income. No money at all. And I was living in a foreign country.'

'What about my father? David?'

'He didn't want to know. And he'd just lost Chloe.'

'But didn't you have any family who could support you? Or friends who could help?'

'I didn't tell anyone I was pregnant. I was ashamed, embarrassed. Maybe I was in denial. I was so young. I couldn't face it.'

'So you decided to give me to Karolina and Hans? Why them?'

Hayley felt tears running down her face, and wiped them with the back of her hand, remembering.

'I didn't plan to give you to them, not initially. After Chloe disappeared, I moved to Chiang Mai. I stayed in a cheap hostel, and helped the owners serve the breakfasts to get a discount on the room rate. I taught English there. I was saving up enough money to fly home and have you there. I was planning to give you away in England. So that I knew you'd go to a good home. I wasn't sure about the orphanages in Thailand, where you might end up. I'd booked my flight back home. I was going to spend a few days in Bangkok, then get on the flight. I hadn't told anyone I was coming back to the UK. I couldn't risk them seeing that I was pregnant, and I wasn't sure if I'd still look different after I'd had the baby. I thought I'd let people know I was back once I'd lost the baby weight. I had it all planned.'

'So what happened? Why didn't you go back?'

'You came early,' Hayley said in a whisper, remembering how terrified she'd been when her contractions had started. 'In the hotel bathroom in Bangkok, in the middle of the night, two days before I was due to fly. I was so scared, I thought I was going to have to call an ambulance and then I would be exposed. Everyone would find out and the baby would be taken to a Thai orphanage. So I endured the pain and had you in the bathroom of the hotel. I cut the cord myself, with scissors I'd run under boiling water to sterilise.'

'You gave birth alone,' Johanna said incredulously. 'At nineteen? That's younger than me.'

'At the time I felt it was my only option. I didn't want anyone to know about the baby. And I didn't want it to be taken somewhere it wouldn't be cared for properly. You know, when I first looked into your eyes, when you first fed from my breast, I didn't think I could give you up. But I knew I had to. If I wanted a good life for you, I had to. And I thought of Karolina and Hans. They'd been trying for a baby for a long time with no luck. I knew they'd be good parents. So after a couple of days, I made myself take you to them.'

'You just gave me away? And then you left? You didn't you want to be part of my life?'

Hayley winced. It hadn't been like that. She hadn't been thinking about the future, about how the baby would turn into a child, then a teenager, then an adult. She had only been thinking about what was best for the baby right then.

'I was messed up. All I could think of was finding the best home for you. I didn't want anyone to know you were mine. I took you in a taxi and got out a few blocks from their apartment. I was wearing long, loose clothes, and you were a very calm baby. I put you under my shirt, held you to my breast to keep you from screaming. When I walked into the apartment block, my heart was racing. But no one noticed me. The block wasn't very secure and I went up the back staircase to Karolina and Hans' apartment. It was early on a Sunday morning, and everyone was asleep. I started to worry that they might not be in, might be away for a weekend. I wrapped you in a blanket and laid you gently on the floor outside the door to their apartment. You immediately started crying when you were separated from me and my heart broke. I left a bag with nappies and formula and a couple of spare sleepsuits and then I rang the bell. I darted back to the staircase to hide. I heard the door open, the astonishment in both their voices. They didn't speak for long. Then the door shut. I peered out from the staircase. You were gone. I was completely alone again. I couldn't stop crying, but I knew I'd done the right thing.'

Tears rolled down Hayley's cheeks and Johanna reached out to touch her arm. 'I'm sorry,' she said.

'It was so hard to leave you,' Hayley said. 'But I was

convinced you were going to have a better life without me. You did, didn't you? You had a good childhood?'

'My parents did everything for me,' Johanna said.

'I'm so glad,' Hayley said, her voice cracking. 'I tried to come and check on you as much as I could, but I could never visit you, never hold you. I found out your parents' address but I could only try and catch a glimpse of you from a distance. I never even knew your name. Karolina and Hans had no idea I was your biological mother and I wanted it to stay that way. To tell them would have been too complicated and I just wanted to get on with my life. I stayed in Thailand until your parents left for Sweden with you a few months later. They must have registered you as their biological child. I understood why. Since I'd given you away, I'd done my research. If the Thai authorities had realised you'd been abandoned, you wouldn't have been able to stay with them. You'd have been in the care of the state while they looked for your birth parents, and then tried to place you with a new family. It might have taken years, and all the while you'd have been in a state orphanage. They did the right thing, taking you away.'

'But they took me illegally?'

'It was the best outcome you could have had.'

Johanna shook her head. 'I can't get my head round this. You left me.'

'I checked on you in Sweden. Any money I could save up from my job, I spent on cheap flights to Stockholm. I used to watch your parents' house. Not all the time, just long enough to see you come and play out in the garden. Long enough to see that you were happy, that I'd made the right decision.'

Johanna looked at her, tears in her eyes. Then she reached out and put her arms round Hayley. For the first time in years, Hayley felt complete.

FIFTY-ONE

1999

Hayley sat in the internet café on Sukhumvit Road, hugging Chloe close. She'd been researching the law in Thailand for the last half an hour. She felt so torn. A part of her already felt attached to the life that was growing inside her. But the pragmatic part of her knew she wouldn't be able to support a baby without any money. And her horizons would narrow, at least temporarily. If she had the baby, she wouldn't be going to university this year. But she wanted to understand what her options were. Her research had shown that if she stayed in Thailand, she would have to have the baby. Abortion was illegal and she could face up to three years in a Thai prison.

Chloe grizzled and Hayley shifted her position to make her more comfortable. Soon she was asleep. Hayley put a hand to her own stomach. She wouldn't be able to look after her baby on her own. She thought of David, in his big apartment. She'd have to tell him. See if he would support her and his baby. Perhaps he would even leave Julie, move in with Hayley in Bangkok. They could be a family. But the thought made Hayley uncomfortable. David was so much older than her. The night she'd slept with him had been a drunken mistake. She didn't want to live with him, although she liked the idea of him breaking up with Julie.

She just needed to ask him to support her and the child. Perhaps she could stay in Thailand in a flat he paid for. But she'd have to go back to England eventually, tell her parents what had happened. She thought of their disappointed faces. She wouldn't be going to university, or fulfilling their dreams for her. She'd be looking after a child for the next eighteen years.

That evening, Hayley sat in her room contemplating her future and waiting for Julie to go to bed. Julie always turned in before David. David liked to listen to the radio for a bit on his own before he retreated to the bedroom. Eventually she heard Julie's footsteps leaving the living room. She waited for the bedroom door to shut, then came out of her room and checked on Emily, Eva and Chloe.

Then she went into the living room.

'David?'

'Yes?' he said, clearly irritated at being interrupted.

'I need to talk to you.'

He hadn't turned round.

'I'm pregnant,' she said quietly. It was easier to blurt it out while he wasn't looking at her.

He turned suddenly, and got up to face her. 'What?'

'What should I do? Will you help me?'

'Help you?' David said, his eyes wide.

'The baby's yours.'

'Are you sure?'

'Yeah,' she said. 'It can't be anyone else's.'

'Well, then.' He started pacing up and down the room. 'I know someone, I think. Someone who can get you sorted.'

'An abortion, you mean?'

'Yeah, what else?'

'Aren't they illegal?'

'Only if you're caught. The call girls here have them all the time.' He glanced up and saw the expression on her face. 'Don't worry, it's perfectly safe. I can arrange it at a lovely clinic I know. You'll be looked after.'

'I don't want an abortion. I want you to support me.'

'You'd have the baby, you mean?' He shook his head and then came over and put his hands on her shoulders. 'You need to think this through. Give yourself time to work out what's best for you. Having this baby at your age – well, it could really mess up your life.'

'But not yours,' Hayley said bitterly. He seemed so unconcerned about the baby, dismissing the problem so easily with an upmarket abortion clinic.

'It doesn't have to mess up either of our lives,' he said. 'If you don't let it.'

'But it's your responsibility too. It's your baby.'

'Is it?' The high voice came from behind her, and she turned to see Julie. And then Julie ran at her. 'You little bitch!' she screamed, her hand stretching out to hit her.

FIFTY-TWO

NOW

Johanna hugged Hayley tightly. 'I can't believe you're my real mother,' she said.

Relief flooded through Hayley and she sank into Johanna's embrace. It felt like a huge weight had been lifted. 'I've been fantasising about this moment for so many years.'

Johanna pulled away. 'I'm still trying to process this. It's so confusing... You loved me, but you gave me away.'

'I know, and I'm sorry. All I want now is for us to have a proper relationship. I know it will take time, but I'd love it if we could be close, if we could build a real mother–daughter bond.' Hayley's voice cracked.

'I have a mother – Karolina.'

'Of course,' Hayley said quickly. 'She's brought you up. I could never replace her.'

'This is such a lot to take in,' Johanna said. 'My head's spinning. I think I'm going to go out, have a walk, reflect on what you've said.'

'Do you want me to come with you?'

'No, I need to be on my own.'

'It's dark out,' Hayley said, looking at her watch. 'Are you sure?'

'I'll be fine,' Johanna said softly. 'I'll be back soon.'

After Johanna left, Hayley went to the fridge and poured herself a glass of wine. She'd been both hoping for and dreading the moment Johanna found out. And now it had finally happened. Johanna just needed a bit of time to process it.

She sat at the kitchen table and sipped her wine, feeling the cool liquid slide down her throat. She had her daughter back after all these years. And nothing had blown up in her face, not yet.

When she finished her drink, Johanna wasn't back. Hayley could still hear the roar of the police television show her mother was watching in the other room; all shooting and shouting. She had no idea when and why her mother had acquired a taste for these violent television programmes.

Hayley went out into the corridor and then opened the door to the living room. Susan wasn't on the sofa. She must have already gone to bed, forgetting to turn the TV off. Hayley flicked it off and felt the silence of the house. Lars would still be in his office on the top floor. She wondered if her mother had managed to get changed for bed on her own. She'd look in on her after she'd checked on Alice.

Hayley climbed the stairs and pushed open the door to Alice's room. It was pitch-black and she couldn't make out the shadow of her daughter in the bed. She walked closer as her eyes adjusted to the dark. She could see the smooth top of the duvet.

Alice wasn't there.

Hayley flicked on the light with a building sense of dread. The bed was empty. She remembered Ryan's note. *Alice will disappear. Just like Chloe.*

Hayley swallowed and looked over the other side of the bed to see if Alice had fallen out, as she sometimes did in the night.

Then she rushed to the bathroom, pushed the door open and checked in there. Alice wasn't in there. Where was she? Maybe she hadn't been able to sleep and Lars had taken her into their bedroom. They used to do that sometimes when she was little; let her sleep in their bed until they moved her when it was time to go to bed themselves.

She rushed up the stairs into their bedroom. No one in the bed. No one in their en suite bathroom. She ran into Lars' study.

'Alice is gone!' she screamed at him.

'What?' he said, removing his headphones and glancing away from his screen.

'I can't find Alice.'

He got up quickly. 'Have you looked everywhere? In every room?'

'No.'

'Right, I'll check upstairs, you check downstairs.' She heard him opening the door to the cupboard under the eaves, peering inside. She ran down the stairs, checked the kitchen, the living room, the dining room. She checked behind the curtains, under every table. Alice wasn't there.

She ran back upstairs. 'Have you found her?' she screamed at Lars.

He shook his head, and she could see her own fear reflected on his face. 'No,' he said, 'and your mother's missing too. Do you think she's got confused and taken her somewhere?'

'She could have,' Hayley said, her voice faltering.

'I'll check the back garden,' Lars said. 'You check the front and the street. Then I'm calling the police.'

Hayley nodded, and she ran out into the front garden. Alice wasn't there. Or her mother. She ran up and down the quiet street, looking left and right, peering into people's gardens.

Alice was gone.

FIFTY-THREE

1999

Hayley ducked as Julie came towards her, her arms flailing. David pulled her away and she wriggled in his arms, trying to break free.

'What do you mean, the baby's his?'

'I mean he slept with me. And I'm having his baby.' Hayley spat out the words. She didn't care how Julie felt any more. At first she hadn't wanted Julie to find out about her stupid mistake, sleeping with David. But now things were different. Now there was a baby involved, Julie needed to know the truth. David would need to support his child.

Julie nearly escaped David's clutches, her arms clawing at Hayley. But David pulled her back.

'It wasn't like that,' he said weakly. 'It was a huge mistake. You were away and she came on to me.'

Hayley glared at David. 'No, I didn't!' she said, angrily. She remembered the feel of his breath on her ear as he whispered, his hand creeping up her thigh. It was him who'd come on to her. He had instigated the whole thing.

'But you *slept* with her? With our nanny?'

Hayley wanted to run to her room, to finish packing her bag

and leave immediately. But she couldn't step away from the conversation. She needed to hear what David had to say. And she needed him to agree to support his baby.

'I can explain,' David said to Julie. 'But we need to talk properly, just the two of us.' He took Julie by the shoulders and led her towards the door. 'Let's get out of here. Let's talk.'

Julie relaxed slightly and let David pull her towards the door.

She glared back at Hayley. 'I welcomed you into my home,' she said. 'But you betrayed me. How could you?'

David didn't look back, leaving the apartment and shutting the door behind them.

Hayley sank down to the floor, drained by the confrontation.

In her room, Chloe started screaming.

Hayley rose and went to her and rocked her in her arms. She must finish packing her bag, get ready to go. It took her a moment to realise that she couldn't leave even if she wanted to. She'd been left alone in the apartment with the children. Tears of frustration and regret filled her eyes. If only the job had been different. If only she'd been treated respectfully. If only she hadn't got drunk and slept with David.

She held Chloe's face to hers, breathing in her smell, trying to calm down. She touched her stomach and thought of her own baby, how David wanted her to get rid of it. She cried harder, tears streaming down her face. If she had the baby, it would never have the life Chloe had, or the advantages. Hayley couldn't afford to look after it. Everything seemed stacked against her.

Chloe's screams started to calm and eventually she settled, her breathing steadied and she went back to sleep. Hayley would miss her so much. She placed her carefully in her cot and then went into Emily and Eva's room and gave them each a kiss on the cheek and stroked their hair. Emily stirred in her sleep.

She wished they were both awake to say goodbye to. They'd be upset when she was gone in the morning. But, she reminded herself, they'd be off to their new life in England in a couple of days. Everything would be exciting and new for them. Marion and her parents would look after them. They'd be OK. They were so young. They'd probably soon forget about Hayley and their time in Bangkok. She touched their cheeks one last time, whispered goodbye and then left the room. In Chloe's room, she stared at the sleeping baby. Eva and Emily would leave, but Chloe would have to stay with her parents. Hayley prayed they'd treat her properly, look after her. She leant into the cot and stroked the baby's head.

Then she went to her room and started packing her remaining things into her rucksack. She would leave tonight, as soon as David and Julie got back. It was time to go.

FIFTY-FOUR

NOW

Hayley ran back inside the house. Lars had his mobile up to his ear.

'I'm phoning the police,' he said.

When he got off the phone, he turned to Hayley, his face pale. 'I've told them we have two missing people, Alice and your mother.'

'When will they be here?' Hayley asked desperately, her heart pounding as she paced up and down the room.

'I don't know. As soon as they can. In the meantime, we should keep searching. And ring round everyone who might have seen them. Or any places Alice might have gone or your mother might have taken her.'

'OK.' Hayley unlocked her phone, adrenalin pumping through her.

'Where's Johanna? Maybe she saw or heard something.'

'She went out for a walk,' Hayley said. If only she was here now to help. She got on so well with Alice. She might know where she would go.

When had Alice and her mother gone missing? Why hadn't she or Johanna heard them leave? They'd been so engrossed in their conversation, and the television in the other room had been so loud. Why hadn't she thought to check on them?

'Ring her. Tell her to come back,' Lars said.

Hayley was already dialling her number. The phone rang and rang and then went to voicemail. She left a brief message asking her to call her back as soon as she could. 'She's not answering,' she said to Lars.

'Do you think that means something?' Lars asked.

'I don't know.' Hayley reached for the wall to steady herself.

The doorbell rang, and when they opened it they were confronted by two police officers, a man and a woman.

'I'm Constable Harris and this is Constable Devine,' the woman said, as they stepped into the house. She explained that the police had split into two teams. One team was searching the local area for Alice and Susan. Harris and Devine were here to interview Hayley and Lars to get as much information out of them as possible to help with the search.

'Do you want a drink?' Hayley said automatically, and then instantly regretted it. Any time making drinks could delay finding her daughter.

'No thank you,' they said in turn.

'So, first things first,' PC Harris said. 'We need a picture of Alice. And one of Susan.'

'Sure,' Hayley said. While she searched through her pictures in her phone, her stomach knotted as she thought of all the pictures of missing children she'd seen in newspapers. There were two types: smiling, happy children on family holidays or more demure school uniform photos. The pictures were first used for the search, then as time went on they were shown underneath less hopeful newspaper headlines, or, in the worst case, became the public memory of a dead child.

But she couldn't think like that. She'd seen Alice only a couple of hours ago as she tucked her into bed. Of course she was still alive. She found a picture of Alice standing proudly by the big slide in the playground and showed it to the officer.

'Is that a recent photo?'

'From about six months ago.'

'Hmm... the light's slightly off. Her face is a bit in shadow. Do you have another one? School photos are usually good.'

Hayley flicked through her photos until she found a school photo from a couple of months ago. She reluctantly showed it to the police officer. 'It's from two months ago,' she said.

'Perfect,' the police officer said. She handed her a business card. 'Send it to the email address on here with your daughter's name as the subject and we'll get it sent out to all our police forces on the ground asap.'

Hayley did what she was told. She sent them a photo of Susan too. Then the questioning turned to when they had last seen Alice, what kind of mood she'd been in, who her friends were, her favourite places to go.

'And do you have any reason to believe anyone would want to hurt Alice?'

'Yes,' Lars said. 'There's a man who's been hanging around outside our house. Ryan Davies. He put a note through our door last week, threatening Alice.'

The police officer's eyebrows shot through the roof. 'Someone was threatening your daughter? Did you go to the police?'

'Yes, we did,' Hayley said. 'There should be a report. Don't you have that already?'

'I'm sure we do,' the female officer said. 'I'll get someone to look that up immediately and link the file.'

Hayley swallowed the bile rising in her throat. This was really happening. Her daughter was missing. She thought of Chloe, of the Thai police trying to find her, how futile it had been. She thought of the note with the threat to Alice. *Alice will disappear. Just like Chloe.* The past was finally catching up with her.

PC Devine asked for Ryan's number and to see any text messages between them. She handed over her phone, numbly.

'OK,' the policeman said. 'We'll try and trace this number urgently and find Ryan. But in the meantime, we need to ask you some more questions.'

The interview went on and on, the police combing over every element of their lives. They were planning to speak to all their friends and family, and check if they knew anything. They asked about Susan, how advanced her dementia was, whether she could persuade Alice to leave the house with her.

'And your lodger...' The policeman looked down at his notes. 'Johanna – where's she?'

'She went out for a walk. She'll be back soon.'

'Very late to have gone out.'

'I've tried to call her. She's not answering.' Hayley felt dread rising up from the pit of her stomach. It was after midnight. Why wasn't Johanna back?

'And any reason why she'd want to take Alice?'

She'd just found out they were sisters, Hayley thought.

'We'd just had a heart-to-heart, actually. A long chat.' She looked at Lars. She was going to have to drop a bombshell on him in front of the police. There was no alternative.

'What were you talking about?'

Lars jumped in. 'Johanna's been confused lately. She thought she was a missing baby, and she was confused about who her parents were. She spoke to me about it too.'

'Lars—' Hayley said, just as the policewoman said, 'A missing baby?'

'Years ago,' Lars continued. 'Hayley was a nanny in Thailand and a baby went missing. Johanna thought she was that baby.'

'This sounds very odd. Why did she think that?'

Hayley couldn't stand it any more. Going over this was a waste of everyone's time. She had to set the record straight. 'Lars,' she said again, speaking over everyone. 'I spoke to Johanna tonight. I... I was keeping a secret. I finally told her. Johanna is my daughter.' She swallowed.

'What?' Lars said, his eyebrows raised in surprise.

'Johanna is my daughter. I got pregnant in Thailand. And I gave her up.' She rushed the words out. She didn't want to talk about this now. They needed to focus on finding Alice.

'Why didn't you tell me?' Lars' forehead scrunched into a frown.

'And this conversation,' PC Harris said urgently, 'the one where you told Johanna she was your daughter. That's a lot for her to take in. How did she seem afterwards?'

'I don't know.' Hayley struggled to think back. She'd thought Johanna had been fine. But had she? 'She went for a walk,' she said again, unsure what else she could say.

'I think we need to find out where she's gone. Do you have a picture of her? I'll get our officers onto it.'

PC Harris went out of the room into their kitchen and Hayley could hear her on the phone informing the person on the other end that they had a person of interest to look out for.

PC Devine continued to question them.

'Do we really need all these questions?' Lars said. 'Shouldn't we be out looking for Alice? And Ryan? And Johanna?'

'As I said when we arrived, we have a team of officers doing just that,' he said reasonably. 'But we need to get as much information as we can to maximise the efficiency of our search. Now, back to Johanna – she lived in your house?'

'Yes, she's lodged with us for a couple of months.' Hayley swallowed. Had it been a mistake to let her stay?

'Does she have a car?' the police officer asked.

'Yes,' Hayley said. She went over to the window, looked out

onto the street. 'Her car's not parked outside,' she said, her heart sinking. Johanna always parked in the same place. Could she have taken Alice?

'OK, so she's taken her car. If you give me the registration number, then we might be able to track her down.'

'Sure,' Hayley said. She'd had to register Johanna for the on-street parking, and had taken her registration then, recording it on the notes app on her phone. She looked up the number, wrote it down and handed it over, her mind spinning.

'And have you checked the house? Checked whether anything is missing? Other than your mother and daughter, of course.' He coughed and reddened, realising he'd made an attempt at a joke in the most inappropriate circumstances.

'I haven't checked,' Hayley said. 'I didn't notice anything. But then I was so caught up in looking for Alice. And my mother.'

'Right, let's check now then.'

'Things have gone missing before, though,' Hayley said. 'Some old photos of when I was in Thailand. But they turned up again. In my mother's room.'

'Oh? You think someone moved them?' PC Devine asked.

'They must have done. They were in a rucksack at the top of my cupboard. It could have been my mother who moved them, but I doubt it.' She looked at Lars, who was staring at her intently. It was obvious she had hidden the photos from him. Everything was starting to unravel.

'What were the photos of?'

'Just photos of people in Thailand. Chloe. Emily. Eva. Those were the children I looked after.'

'And Chloe was the one that Ryan was interested in?'

'Yeah.'

'OK, well, we should look at the photos. But first take me up to Alice's room.'

They went up together. Lars stayed downstairs, phoning

round everyone he could think of that Alice knew, asking if they'd seen or heard from her.

In Alice's room PC Devine went through every drawer, her wardrobe and her toybox. Nothing seemed to be missing. Hayley showed the police officer the beheaded toy and he seemed to take it seriously. If only she hadn't dismissed it so easily as an accident, then Alice might be with her now.

Hayley felt exhaustion wash over her. She looked at the Mickey Mouse clock on Alice's wall. It was nearly 2 a.m. So much time had already passed.

PC Devine moved on to her mother's room, searching her disorganised belongings. He was meticulous in his search, and Hayley felt impotent standing there as the minutes ticked by. She wondered if she should be out on the streets looking for Alice. But the officer wanted her here so she could tell him if there were any items missing. As far as Hayley could tell, everything was there.

'Where do you keep the passports?' he asked, when he'd finished his painstaking search.

'The passports?' Hayley's stomach clenched with worry. 'They're upstairs. In the study.'

Hayley walked him up to Lars' home office. All the passports were there in the drawer where she'd left them. She sighed with relief. It hadn't occurred to her before, that whoever had taken Alice might want to take her out of the country. She watched as he searched the rest of the room, rifling through every drawer. 'We're going to have to search the whole house, I'm afraid.'

'Why?' Hayley asked. 'How's that going to help?'

'Just standard procedure. In case there are any clues as to where she went. Don't worry. We're doing everything we can. As well as the officers on the street, another team is trawling CCTV for her.'

PC Harris appeared at the door of the study. 'Good news,'

she said. 'We've tracked down Johanna. She's staying in a friend's room at the university halls, while her friend is away. Our officers are going over there now to ask her if she saw anything.'

Hayley swallowed, thinking of how Johanna had disappeared without telling her where she was going. She'd said she was going for a walk, just before they'd realised Alice was missing. But she'd taken the car. And now she was staying out overnight. If there was anyone Alice would have willingly gone off with, it was Johanna.

'I think Johanna's taken Alice,' she said quickly, unable to believe quite what she was saying.

'You do?' PC Devine asked.

Hayley felt filled with guilt. This was her fault. For telling Johanna who she was. For thinking Johanna was happy about it, like she was. She had never really known what she was thinking. She wondered if Johanna was connected to Ryan, if she was somehow involved in the note that had been dropped through the door.

'Alice trusts her,' Hayley said. 'I have to come with you. I have to find Alice.'

The police officers exchanged glances. Hayley could see them trying to work out whether she'd be an asset or a liability.

'Look,' she said. 'I think this is about me. About the fact I'm Johanna's mother. And if it is about that, then the person who should talk to her is me.'

PC Harris nodded. 'OK then,' she said. 'I'll tell the other officers to hold fire until we get there. Let's get in the car.'

FIFTY-FIVE

It was dark as they drove through central London, and the roads were close to empty, but the journey still felt like it was too long. Hayley reached for her phone and tried to call Johanna again. No answer. She couldn't expect her to pick up in the middle of the night. She probably had no idea what was going on. Hayley thought how happy she'd been last night when Johanna had accepted her as a mother. What had she really been thinking?

When they finally got to the university halls, PC Harris turned to her. 'We're going to go gently with this,' she said. 'If Johanna has got Alice, then we need to tread carefully. You and I will go in together and talk to her, see what she says. The other officers will be on standby outside the building.'

'OK,' Hayley said, her stomach tightening. 'Sure.'

'And, Hayley?'

'Yeah?'

'Don't pin all your hopes on this. This is just one lead we're following up. We're still trying to track down Ryan. And following up other avenues.'

'OK, thanks,' Hayley said. But she was sure Johanna had Alice.

PC Harris flashed her pass at the sleepy security guard at the front desk of the university halls, then told Hayley the room number. They went up in the lift together, and Hayley knocked on the door of room 327. There was no sound at all from any of the rooms in the corridor. Everyone must be asleep.

'Johanna?' Hayley called out, her voice shaking, despite herself. 'Are you in there?'

There was a stirring and then the door opened a crack.

'Hayley – what are you doing here?' Her eyebrows rose in surprise when she saw PC Harris. *She's pretending*, Hayley thought. *Like she always was, from the moment she came to my door.*

Hayley craned her neck to peer through the gap, but Johanna's body was in the way and she couldn't see anything. She had a desperate urge to push the door open, to force her way in and find Alice. But she needed to take things slowly, go gently with Johanna, like PC Harris had said.

'Can we come in?' PC Harris asked, flashing his badge. 'I'd like to ask you some questions.' She had briefed Hayley that they needed to be non-confrontational. She wanted to see how Johanna reacted to seeing the police, before they asked her about Alice.

Johanna looked confused. She ran her hands through her hair. 'Is everything all right? Has someone died? Is it my parents?' Her face flushed. She was a convincing actress.

'No,' the police officer said. 'We're just making some enquiries. Your parents are fine.'

'Oh, right... I was asleep. You woke me up.' Hayley noticed, for the first time, the faded T-shirt that Johanna must have been sleeping in. 'Can you give me a minute to get changed?'

'Of course, we'll wait,' PC Harris said, letting her shut the door. He turned to Hayley. 'Don't worry, we're on the sixth floor. She can't go anywhere.'

Hayley nodded. PC Harris updated her on the search of the

woodland that the local community were planning a few streets away from their house. Alice played there sometimes, collecting conkers in the autumn. Hayley couldn't face the thought of them finding her there.

Then the door opened again and Johanna stepped out. 'Could we speak somewhere else? It's tiny in there. And messy. And there's nowhere to sit.'

No, Hayley thought. Suddenly she was convinced that Alice was in there.

'I'm sure we've seen worse,' PC Harris said.

'OK,' Johanna said reluctantly, holding the door open so they could step over the threshold. Hayley had to stop herself from racing inside, tearing the room apart to find Alice.

The room was crowded with personal belongings: a clothes rail with dresses packed tightly together, a bedside table covered with jewellery and make-up, a tiny open-plan kitchenette which looked overflowing, despite there only being two pans and a container of utensils on the work surface. The flat was tiny, like Johanna had said – too tiny to be hiding Alice. There were no cupboards. Hayley knelt down and peered under the bed. No one there.

'What are you doing?' Johanna asked, confused. 'What's wrong?'

'Alice is missing,' the police officer said calmly. 'We're conducting a missing persons enquiry.'

Hayley was still looking round the flat. She couldn't help herself. She opened a cupboard door and a pile of shoes slid out from inside. Then she opened the only remaining door. The bathroom door. She saw the grey toilet mat, the shower with mould round the bottom. Nothing there.

Johanna didn't have Alice.

FIFTY-SIX

1999

Hayley lay on her bed, bag packed, waiting for Julie and David to return. The children were all fast asleep. As soon as David and Julie walked back through the door, she was going to leave and find a hostel for the night. She wasn't coming back here. She looked at her watch. It was already after 11 p.m. She wished they'd hurry up. And she prayed they weren't drunk. It was bad enough being on the receiving end of Julie's anger when she was sober.

Chloe started screaming, and Hayley eased herself off the bed and went to her. She could smell the nappy from the hallway; it was a particularly nasty one. Holding her breath, she went into the room. When she lifted Chloe up, the mess was everywhere, leaking through her sleepsuit, down her legs and up her back. Hayley got out the changing mat to change her on the floor and then thought better of it. Why should she always be kneeling on the floor to change their baby's nappy? She was going to change it on a bed, David and Julie's bed. That would be more comfortable for everyone.

She picked up Chloe under her arms, trying to hold her away from her body, so nothing got on her clothes. She grabbed the changing mat from the floor and a nappy, some wipes and a nappy bag. When she got to David and Julie's room she laid the mat out on the bed. She put Chloe on top of it, hoping that the smell would infiltrate the air and the sheets. She eased off her babygrow, and put it into the nappy bag to throw away. It wasn't salvageable.

Just then she heard the door open. David and Julie were back. Julie would be furious. Hayley rushed out of the room to intercept them, but it was only Julie there.

'David's coming later,' she said. 'He's just picking up wine.' Hayley could smell the alcohol fumes on Julie's breath and yet she seemed calmer than before.

'OK,' Hayley said. 'I'm leaving tonight. I'm just changing a nappy, and then I'm going.'

'Good riddance,' Julie snarled. 'I want you out of my apartment, away from my things, away from my baby, away from David.'

'I can't wait!' Hayley said. She went back into David and Julie's bedroom, no longer caring if Julie saw her changing the baby on their bed. As she went through the door, it was like she saw everything in slow motion.

Chloe was trying to push herself over, to roll.

And suddenly she did it, and she was falling from the safety of the bed.

Hayley raced towards her, but it was too late. Her head hit the corner of the bedside cabinet hard, and she bounced off it onto the floor.

FIFTY-SEVEN

NOW

'Alice is missing?' Johanna asked Hayley. Shock filled her face. 'What do you mean? Where's she gone?'

Hayley saw the distress on Johanna's face. She hadn't been pretending. She really didn't know where Alice was.

'I don't know. You didn't see anything, did you?'

'Last night? No. When did she go missing?'

'I don't know. But when I went into her room after our conversation, she was gone.'

'Oh my god!' Johanna said.

'Did you hear or see anything?' PC Harris asked. 'Anything at all?'

'I didn't hear anything,' Johanna said. She turned to Hayley. 'Did she leave while we were speaking?'

'Yeah, while we were in the kitchen. My mother's gone too. They think they left together.'

'Then they can't have gone far, surely?'

Hayley frowned. 'They've disappeared. Do you have any idea where Alice might have gone? Has she mentioned anything or anyone to you?'

'Just her schoolfriends. And there's a teacher at school she talks about a lot. Miss Patel.'

'Lars has already spoken to her schoolfriends' parents. None of them know anything. The police have spoken to the school. I'll mention Miss Patel specifically to them. She's the music teacher, I think.'

Johanna stared at Hayley. 'I can't believe this has happened. I can grab some things and come straight over. Help in whatever way I can.'

'Yeah,' Hayley said. 'That would be great. They're doing a search of the woods later today. The local community are involved. I'm sure they could use more help.'

'Let me interview you first,' PC Harris said. She turned to Hayley. 'If you want to go back, I can get a police car to take you?'

Hayley nodded. 'I want to go home, just in case Alice comes back.'

'Of course,' Johanna said. 'I'll see you soon.' She reached out and held Hayley in a tight hug, before letting her go.

In the car back home, Hayley felt deflated. Lars rang her and asked how it had gone. He told her the police were still trying to track down Ryan and were conducting door-to-door enquiries. His voice was brimming with frustration. They both just wanted to do something, anything, to get her back. Already they felt like the police were being too slow. It was hours since Alice had gone missing. Weren't missing children usually found quickly or not at all? She tried to remember what she'd read about child abduction.

When she got back, Lars put his arms round her and she sank into him. 'It will be all right,' he said. 'We'll find her.' But they were both aware that there was no way that he could know that.

When PC Harris returned from interviewing Johanna, Hayley and Lars were sitting at the kitchen table, going through their phone contacts. They'd already rung everyone who might know where Alice was. 'Why don't you get some sleep?' PC Harris said kindly. 'You've been up all night. You could do with some rest.'

'How can I sleep when Alice is missing?' Hayley said incredulously.

'It's the best thing you can do for her. We'll wake you if there are any developments. But for now you've done all you can. You've told us everything you know. We can get on with our jobs. And when you wake up, you'll be refreshed and ready to deal with whatever the day brings.'

'But what if the kidnapper phones?' Hayley asked.

The police officers looked at each other. 'We don't know she's been kidnapped,' PC Devine said. 'The thing that makes us think she probably hasn't been is the disappearance of your mother. Someone who kidnaps a child doesn't normally kidnap the frail grandmother too. Why would they? It would make them easier to find. And your mother would be a liability for them. It would be much more difficult for them to escape quickly. At the moment, our working theory is that they both wandered off together. We just have to find them.'

PC Harris nodded. 'But this... Ryan... is still a concern. We haven't been able to track him down. The phone is a pay-as-you-go, a so-called burner phone. He used cash to buy it, so we don't have any details. And he's no longer at the address he gave when he was signing up for the class at the university, so we haven't been able to locate him yet. He's definitely got something to hide, but we're not sure how he's connected to Alice, aside from the fact that he works with you – but we can't work out his motivation to send that note or why he might kidnap a child.'

'So it could be him?' Hayley said. 'I could text him, ask him what he's done with her.'

'That's not a good idea. But we're still trying to track him down. So leave your phone with us while you sleep. That way if he gets in contact we can follow up.'

'And you'll wake us if anything happens?' Hayley felt bone-tired, but she was certain she wouldn't be able to sleep. Her mind was whirring with thoughts of Alice.

'Yes.'

'Thank you, officers,' Lars said, tears in his eyes. 'We know you're doing the best you can. But you really need to find Alice as soon as possible. She's only five, and the idea that she's been out in the dark overnight…'

'Understood, sir,' PC Devine said, touching his shoulder. 'Now get some rest.'

Hayley handed her phone to the constables and then Lars took Hayley's arm and guided her towards the stairs.

She lay on her bed, fully dressed, listening to the sounds of the world waking up. Doors slammed, car engines started, and children protested loudly at getting up in the house next door. *I might never get Alice up in the morning again*, she thought. She couldn't just lie there doing nothing, while Alice was missing. She glanced at Lars, who was already tossing and turning in a fitful sleep.

She had to do something. She'd walk the streets, looking for Alice. Check the playgrounds and parks herself.

She pulled herself up out of bed, went down the stairs and found PC Harris in the kitchen.

'I can't sleep,' she said. 'I need to do something. I want to check the playgrounds. I know they've been searched, but I want to look myself.'

PC Harris nodded and handed over her phone. 'Take your phone with you. We'll let you know if there are any developments.'

Hayley left the house, felt the air on her face. Alice was out there somewhere. She wracked her brains to think where her mother might have taken her. She was a slow walker. Surely they wouldn't have gone too far from here? Unless someone had picked them up in a car or a van.

Hayley was only a few steps from her house when a car pulled up beside her and Johanna got out. 'I need to talk to you,' she said breathlessly. 'I've thought of something. I don't know if it's relevant, but I think it might be important.'

'What is it?' Hayley asked urgently.

'Have you spoken to Michelle?'

'No,' Hayley said. 'The police tried to ring her but I don't think they've got through yet. They want to ask her if she has any ideas where Mum might go.'

Johanna frowned. 'The thing is... I'm worried... well, I think she might have had something to do with it. Your mother would follow her anywhere.'

'But Michelle went home long before they went missing. I'd just put Alice to bed when she left.'

Johanna shook her head. 'She didn't go then. She wanted to hear what you said to me, about my background. She was planning to pretend to leave, then stay in the house and listen.'

'What? Why? Why would Michelle care what I had to say to you?' Hayley asked. She knew that Michelle and Johanna had become closer lately, but she felt like there was something huge she was missing here, something important.

Tears formed in Johanna's eyes. 'Michelle's not who you think she is.'

'What do you mean?' Hayley said.

'Michelle's my half-sister. Her real name is Eva.'

'Sorry?' Hayley said, shock rocketing through her. 'Michelle is Eva?' Why hadn't she said anything? Why had she been in her house for so long and never mentioned who she was?

'Yeah. Eva wanted me to ask you again about Chloe, so

when you wanted to talk to me, she thought she'd learn the truth. We both thought that I was Chloe and that eventually you'd admit to it.'

'But you're not Chloe.'

'No. Until she realised that we were half-sisters, Eva was convinced you had something to do with Chloe's disappearance. She thought you might have murdered her.' Hayley thought back to when she was arrested by the police, how Eva had said she'd seen Hayley taking Chloe. What did she remember from that time?

'So you think she took Alice?'

'I don't know. But she would have heard everything we said in our conversation.'

'And she realised that you weren't Chloe.'

'Yeah... if she heard that... it means that Chloe's still missing... and I think she would have gone back to thinking you were responsible for her disappearance.'

FIFTY-EIGHT

Hayley thought of the sweet little girl Eva had been, how much she'd loved her. But now she was someone else entirely, someone who might want to hurt her and Alice. 'We need to tell the police,' she said.

Johanna shook her head. 'I don't know. Let me call her, speak to her myself. Maybe I'm wrong and she has nothing to do with it.'

She pulled her mobile from her pocket. 'Eva, it's me – Alice has gone missing.'

A stream of fast, angry words came from the phone, and Hayley strained to try and hear as Johanna listened to the response in silence, her face paling.

'What's going on?' Hayley asked urgently.

Johanna put her hand over the phone's microphone. 'I was right. She's taken Alice.'

'I'll go inside, get the police.'

'She says no police,' Johanna said quickly. 'Or she'll hurt Alice.'

'What? Is Alice OK? Can I speak to her?' Hayley's heart raced.

Johanna shook her head. 'No. She wants to talk to us face to face. She said to come to her house. It's the other side of Ealing.'

Hayley thought of Lars, upstairs in their home, asleep. She needed to tell him. But then she remembered the police had his phone. She couldn't contact him without telling the police too.

'Let's go,' she said. 'Now!'

Johanna got into her car and Hayley climbed into the passenger seat beside her, her stomach in knots as Johanna sped across Ealing, honking her horn and overtaking. Hayley gripped her seat, her whole body tense. She had felt afraid from the moment Johanna had found her half-sister, had had that creeping sensation that something awful would happen. But she hadn't known the extent of Eva's hatred for her, that she had still blamed her for Chloe's disappearance.

Eva had fooled her so effectively. It had been her mother who had started employing 'Michelle' to help her with little jobs around the house, before she'd come to live with them and before they'd suspected she had dementia. Hayley had never thought much about it. She'd always assumed she was a qualified carer, and she'd trusted her. She'd seemed like such a godsend for her mother. But they hadn't known who she really was.

Johanna reached her hand across the gearstick and held Hayley's for a second. 'It will be all right,' she said.

'Thanks for coming with me,' Hayley said.

'I had to,' Johanna said. 'Alice is my sister too. We'll find her. We'll get her back. I'm sure of it.'

'How long have you known Eva's your sister?' Hayley asked.

'Not long. It was after the DNA test. She'd had her data on the site ever since she'd started trying to find out what happened to Chloe. My test result showed we were half-sisters. She was so shocked when she saw that I was her match that she blocked me at first. But then she got to know me a bit better and told me that we were sisters. We both thought I was Chloe. She'd befriended your mother months ago to try and get close to you and find out what really happened to her sister.'

Hayley swallowed, realising how little she had known 'Michelle'. 'How much further is it to the house?' she said urgently.

'Not far.'

Hayley's phone started ringing. 'It's Lars,' she said.

'Don't tell him where we're going. He'll tell the police.'

'Hi, Lars,' Hayley said.

'Where are you? I woke up and you were gone. The police said you'd gone for a walk.'

'Yeah, I was looking for Alice.'

'Any luck?'

'No.'

'You sound like you're in a car.'

'Yeah. I'm with Johanna.' Hayley glanced over at Johanna. 'We're looking together.'

Lars hesitated for a moment. 'Johanna?' he asked.

'Yeah, she's helping.'

'Are you sure you can trust her?' he said. 'A few hours ago you thought she might have taken Alice.'

'Of course I can,' she said, hoping Johanna couldn't hear his side of the conversation. 'Listen, I've got to go. I'll call you later.' By then maybe she'd have Alice with her and this nightmare would be over.

Hayley looked back at Johanna. She was her daughter. Of course she could trust her, couldn't she? But even though Hayley was Johanna's mother, Eva was her sister. Where did her loyalties really lie?

'We're here,' Johanna said, as she pulled up beside a row of terraced houses, parking haphazardly, the rear of her car sticking out into the road. She jumped out and ran to the door of one of the houses. Hayley followed her through the overgrown front garden, catching sight of an old mattress lurking below the weeds.

Johanna pounded on the door. 'Eva,' she shouted. 'Eva – are you in there?' Hayley stood beside her, shaking with anger. If Eva had done anything to hurt Alice, she didn't know what she'd do to her. Alice was her world.

There was no answer. Hayley couldn't hold it in any more. 'Eva!' she shouted. 'Have you got Alice? We need to come in!'

And then they heard footsteps on the other side of the door, a bolt being pulled across. The door opened slowly, and she saw a flash of dark hair.

Hayley stepped back from the door, her mind racing.

It was Ryan.

'What are you doing here?' Hayley asked.

He smiled at them. 'I'm Eva's boyfriend,' he said.

FIFTY-NINE

1999

Hayley reached for Chloe, lying still on the floor.

'Oh my god!' she screamed. She could barely comprehend what was happening.

Chloe was quiet. Hayley picked her up gently and cradled her, kissing her head over and over again. 'Chloe,' she said. 'Chloe, Chloe, Chloe.' Then suddenly the baby started to cry, her face reddening as she bawled.

Hayley felt sick with relief. She was alive. Her tears fell on the baby's tiny cheeks and she was so distracted that she didn't hear Julie come in. 'What have you done?' Julie shouted at her. 'She's hurt. What have you done?'

'She fell off the bed,' Hayley said, coming to her senses. 'I left her for just a moment and—'

'Why were you changing her on the bed?'

'I'm sorry...' Hayley said. Chloe's unearthly screams were getting louder. 'We need to call an ambulance. Get her to the hospital.'

'I'll do it,' Julie said, snatching Chloe out of her arms. The baby kept screaming. 'Get out!' she shouted at Hayley. 'Get out of my home! And don't come back.'

Hayley ran to her bedroom, grabbed her rucksack and rushed out the door. She walked and walked, tears streaming down her face as she thought about what had happened. How could she have left Chloe alone on the bed? What had she been thinking? She replayed the moment of her falling off the bed over and over again in her mind's eye. How could she make such a huge mistake?

She wiped her tears with the back of her hand as she carried the heavy rucksack down the busy street. Surely Chloe would be all right? Julie would take her to the hospital and they'd find that she hadn't been seriously hurt. It was just an accident.

It was late at night but the street with still alive with traders and small roadside bars serving spirits. She sat down at one and ordered a whisky. She watched the world go by, and thought about how she needed to find a place to stay tonight. A taxi to Khao San would be expensive and it was already late. She should find a hotel here. But she couldn't shake the niggling doubt about Chloe, couldn't get the sound of her head hitting the bedside table out of her mind. She was so tiny, so fragile.

Hayley finished her drink and started walking again, this time towards the apartment. She had to check Chloe was OK.

SIXTY

NOW

Hayley's mouth dropped open. All the time she'd thought Ryan was just a student who was writing a book on the case, he'd been Eva's boyfriend.

Johanna glanced at Hayley. 'She never told me she had a boyfriend,' she said, her eyes darting from Ryan to Hayley as if trying to process the information.

'Why don't you come in?' he said.

Should they go inside? Now Ryan was here, it meant there were at least two adults inside the house; Ryan and Eva. There could be more. They could be outnumbered. What if they turned on them?

But what about Alice? And her mother? Finding them was the only thing that mattered. And Eva had said to come to the house to get her.

Johanna was already following Ryan through the door. Hayley went after them.

'Where's Alice?' Hayley asked desperately, as he took them down the hallway.

'Not here,' he said, dismissively. 'Sorry.'

'What?' Hayley's heart sank. Where was she?

Ryan led them into the messy kitchen, boxes of cereal and dirty plates covering the work surfaces. Susan was sitting at a small table next to a pile of junk mail. She rocked back and forth, muttering to herself.

'Mum,' Hayley said, wrapping her arms around her. 'Are you OK?'

Her mother didn't say anything. At least she was safe. Hayley turned angrily to Ryan. 'You live here then? With Eva? And that's why you were looking into Chloe's death?'

He nodded. 'I met Eva at the university months ago. She'd been hanging around, looking for you, I think. We met at the student bar. She got drunk and told me what had happened to her sister Chloe, told me you were responsible. She was caring for your mother then to get closer to you, but hadn't managed to find out anything. She was so devastated by what had happened to Chloe, and I would have done anything to help her, so I volunteered at student support so I could talk to you myself. After I spoke to you about the character study, I had a brain-wave about a true-crime book. An excuse to ask you all the questions Eva wanted answers to.'

'And when you didn't find out what you wanted, you threatened me?'

'We just wanted to know the truth. When Eva realised Johanna was her half-sister, she assumed she was Chloe. She needed to find out why you'd ripped her away from her family, given her to another couple. But then it turned out that Johanna was your child, not Julie's. And once again she didn't know what had happened to Chloe. Only that you'd taken her and she hadn't been seen since. All she wants is the truth. A confession in exchange for Alice.'

'Do you know where Alice is?' Hayley said urgently.

'Alice, Alice, Alice,' her mother muttered.

'Don't worry, she's safe. For now. She's with Eva.'

'And where's Eva?'

'Eva's taken her into London. Where it will be a lot easier to make her disappear.'

Hayley sank to her knees. 'I don't believe you. Why would she keep moving her? She's here, isn't she? In this house.'

'We only came here at all because of your mother,' Ryan said. 'She wasn't supposed to be with us. Eva had put the TV on so loud she didn't think anyone would hear her taking Alice. But your mother decided she needed the toilet at the wrong time. So we had to take her with us. She'd follow Eva anywhere. They're so close. But Eva didn't want to take her all the way to London, so she dropped her here.'

Hayley shivered. There was no sound of a child in this house.

'Let's ring Eva,' Ryan said. 'You'll see.' He took up his phone and video-called her, holding up the phone for her and Johanna to see.

'Hello, Hayley,' Eva said, sneering.

'Eva.' Hayley's voice was a nervous whisper. She scanned Eva's face. Eva was Michelle, and yet not Michelle. For the first time, Hayley noticed she had Johanna's eyes, Johanna's high cheekbones. They were half-sisters. 'Where's Alice?' she asked.

'She's just here.' Eva panned the camera round and Hayley could see she was in a budget hotel room, thin beige duvets covering two single beds. A girl was sitting on the bed furthest away. Alice.

'Alice, come here. Your mum's on the phone.'

Alice bounded over to the phone, and Hayley felt a rush of relief.

'Mummy!' she said. 'Where am I? Michelle said I was going on holiday. But we've been in this room forever. We haven't even been out to do anything. I don't understand...' She paused. 'Why aren't you here?'

Hayley felt the tears sliding down her face. 'I'll be there as soon as I can,' she said. 'I love you so much.'

'I love you too, Mummy.'

Ryan hung up the phone, and tears ran down Hayley's face. Alice was alive. 'Where is she?' she asked.

'At a hotel near Liverpool Street. Eva will message you with the name once you're close by. If you contact the police it will all be over. They'll both disappear.'

Hayley swallowed. 'What about my mother?'

'Your mum stays here,' Ryan said firmly. She's collateral. You mustn't tell the police what's going on. If you do, she'll suffer.'

Hayley reached out and squeezed her mother's hand. 'Just wait here while I get Alice,' she said. Her mother looked at her vacantly, lost in her own world.

'What does Eva want from me?' Hayley asked.

'She wants to know what really happened to Chloe. That's why she's taken Alice. An eye for an eye. So you know how it feels to be without a loved one.'

'Let's go,' Hayley said to Johanna.

Ryan blocked the door. 'You need to leave your phone here. I don't want anyone to know where you are. And take the Tube. Don't drive.'

'I can't leave my phone.' She thought of Lars. She wouldn't be able to contact him. What if Ryan was just getting her out of the way, sending her across the other side of London as a distraction? 'How will Eva message me and tell me where Alice is, if I don't have my phone?'

Ryan reached into his pocket and handed her a cheap smartphone. 'Here you go. This phone isn't linked to anyone. Only Eva has the number. She'll message you on this. And don't even think about calling anyone else. I'm alerted any time calls are made.'

Hayley nodded, and reluctantly pulled her phone from her pocket. She saw she had three missed calls from Lars. She knew he'd be worried about her.

'Put it on the table,' Ryan said. 'You too, Johanna.'

They did as they were told.

'Leave your bags here too. And anything in your pockets. Wallet, house keys, purse, car keys.'

Hayley swallowed and glanced at Johanna. He was taking away anything that could identify her. What was he going to do? But she took everything from her pockets and placed it all on the table.

'How will we take the Tube without money?' she asked.

He reached into her purse and went through it quickly, pulling out two twenty-pound notes. 'Use the machine to buy Oyster cards. Pay with those.'

She nodded, feeling a growing sense of fear. They wouldn't be traceable at all. No one would know where they were.

Then Ryan came over to her. 'Excuse me,' he said, as he clumsily patted her down, looking for anything extra she might be carrying.

'OK,' he said. 'You're good to go. Take the cash and this phone. Eva will contact you on it and let you know where to go.'

SIXTY-ONE

1999

When Hayley got back to David and Julie's apartment she let herself in with the key she had meant to return. She felt sick as she turned the key in the lock, knowing she shouldn't be here, that Julie didn't want her anywhere near her. David came to the door, ashen-faced, tears rolling down his cheeks.

'Hayley.'

'David – what's wrong?' Dread gripped her.

'It's Chloe,' he said. 'She's gone.'

'Gone?' Hayley whispered.

'She's dead.'

He started pacing up and down.

'What?' Hayley said. This couldn't be true. Chloe had been screaming when she'd left. Alive and screaming.

Hayley caught sight of the back of Julie's head. She was sitting completely still on the sofa. She must be in shock.

'I'll show you,' David said, his words muffled by tears.

She followed him wordlessly to Chloe's room. She was in her cot, completely still, the blanket folded over her. Hayley could see that her chest wasn't rising or falling. She reached her hand towards her.

'Don't touch her,' David said.

Hayley swallowed the bile rising in her throat. 'I'm so sorry,' she said. But words wouldn't help now. She should never have left Chloe alone on the bed. How could she have been so alive one minute and gone the next? Once more, she remembered her hitting her head on the bedside table. Hayley felt sick with guilt. Poor, poor Chloe. Her life was over before it had begun.

'I'm so sorry,' she repeated. But David didn't answer. He was staring into the cot in disbelief.

Hayley retreated out of the room on shaky legs. The weight of it hit her. She'd killed a baby. She couldn't leave, could she? She needed to face the consequences.

She hesitated in the living room, unsure what to do. Julie rose from the sofa, finally noticing her presence. Her eyes were red-rimmed and sore.

'You killed her,' she said numbly. 'You killed my baby.'

'But she was fine when I left. She was screaming.' Hayley couldn't understand how things had changed so quickly.

'It was a head injury. They can seem fine for a while, while the damage is going on inside their brain. It killed her.'

'Oh my god,' Hayley said, pacing up and down. Julie was a doctor. She must be right. This was all Hayley's fault. But she loved Chloe. This couldn't be happening.

David came back into the room. He'd stopped crying, but his cheeks were still tear-stained.

'You need to go,' he said to Hayley.

She saw the red blanket she had bought for Chloe just the other day, folded over the back of the sofa where she'd left it. Chloe had only used it once, during a daytime nap, when the air conditioning had been on full blast. It was big and cosy. Hayley had thought that Chloe would grow into it, had hoped she'd keep it when she was older. She picked up the blanket and put it to her face, trying to absorb Chloe's smell. Tears ran down her cheeks.

'Get out of here.' David held the door open for her. She gathered up the big blanket in her arms. She couldn't leave it behind. As she turned one last time towards the house, she saw Eva in the doorway of the living room, chewing on her fingers, her eyes wide as she watched Hayley leave, carrying the bundle of Chloe's blanket.

SIXTY-TWO

NOW

As soon as they got off the train at Liverpool Street and arrived in the huge station, Hayley checked the phone they'd been given. Still nothing from Eva to tell them where to meet her. Hayley saw the CCTV camera watching them from above, and looked directly into it. If they went missing, perhaps the police would go through all the footage from the stations and find her image.

Hayley desperately wanted to call Lars and tell him that she had seen Alice, that she was alive. But she remembered Ryan saying he was tracking the calls from the phone. She thought about finding a phone box or asking a passer-by if she could borrow their phone, but it felt too risky. What if Ryan or Eva found out? She couldn't speak to Lars. She wondered if he would tell the police that she was with Johanna, that he didn't know where she was.

'What do we do now?' Johanna asked, as they stood in the middle of the station, people streaming past them.

'I don't know,' Hayley said, frowning. Once more she wondered if this had all been a ruse, to get them away from home. The hotel Eva had called from could have been anywhere, even in Ealing. Maybe Alice was still there, far away from her.

The phone buzzed in her hand and made her jump.

'Hello?'

'I'm at the Williams Hotel near Liverpool Street,' Eva said. 'Room forty-one.' Then she hung up.

Hayley looked at the map on the phone and saw they were only five minutes away. They started walking.

They got to the shabby-looking B&B, went past the bored receptionist and up the stairs. Hayley hesitated outside the door to room 41. She knew this could be a trap. She didn't have any police backup here. But she did have Johanna by her side. At least there were two of them.

'Eva?' she called out, as she knocked on the door.

The door opened a crack and there she was, her eyes darting up and down the corridor.

'Are you on your own?'

'Yes.'

'No police?'

'No.'

'Come in.'

Hayley rushed into the hotel room, looking round for Alice. 'Where is she?' she shouted.

'I'm not telling you that,' Eva said, locking the door behind her. 'Not yet. But if you don't help me, you'll never see her again. You need to tell me what you did with Chloe, whether she'd dead or alive.' Eva's voice shook with emotion.

'I don't know what happened to her,' Hayley said, repeating the lie she'd told all those years ago. 'Why are you here? Why now? And why did you pretend to be Michelle? Was it just to get closer to me?'

Eva laughed. 'You have no idea, do you? No idea what the

repercussions of your actions were. Chloe's disappearance has affected everyone I love. My father died of alcoholism because of the grief. Julie hasn't worked for years and is seriously ill. What happened changed us all forever.'

'I'm so sorry,' Hayley said, the guilt welling up inside her. She put her fingers to her temples.

Eva continued, pacing up and down the small hotel room. 'I only started thinking about it all again recently. My mother had wanted me to forget all about it and focus on my new life in England. But repressed memories aren't good for anyone. I wasn't a normal child. Then, several months ago, I saw an article online about Chloe, my sister. All I remembered was you carrying her out in a blanket that night, how I'd told the police, but you were still released. A few weeks ago I found the blanket in your bedroom.'

'You didn't see what you think you did, that night. You were so little. I was only carrying the blanket, not Chloe.' Hayley thought of the red blanket, how soft it had been.

'And why were you taking her blanket?'

'I was leaving. Julie had fired me. It was something to remember her by.'

'I don't believe you!' Eva spat.

'The police believed me. They didn't charge me.' She thought back to how afraid she'd been at the police station, how she'd had to stay in a cell overnight. She thought of Chloe and felt a surge of guilt. Maybe she should have said something back then, told the truth. But she'd been pregnant. And David had said he'd protect her.

'I remember the police station,' Eva said. 'Being taken there to give evidence. I was so scared. I remember the way the police officers looked at me, all the questions they asked, as if they thought I was making it up. They didn't believe me. It messed me up, that experience. When I moved back to England I didn't like speaking to adults. I felt I couldn't trust anyone. I wouldn't say anything at all at school. They said I had behavioural problems and I carried that label my whole life. I've just drifted along, never able to settle. Everything changed for me after what happened to Chloe.'

'None of this is Hayley's fault,' Johanna said. 'No one knows what happened that night. Chloe's been missing for over twenty years.'

'She knows,' Eva said, pointing at Hayley. 'She's always known.'

Hayley swallowed, the shame that she had carried with her for so long welling up inside her. Eva was right; she'd always known. She hadn't wanted to face the consequences, so she'd lied to the police, told them she didn't know what had happened. But she hadn't been thinking of Eva or Emily, growing up never knowing what had happened to their sister. Eva and Emily had been denied the truth of what had happened all these years. There were more consequences than she'd realised of keeping the secret.

'Look,' she said, 'you can't punish Alice for this. None of it was her fault. It was all before she was born.'

'I'm sure Alice will want to know that you took a baby. She needs to know who you really are. You got away with it at the time. But not any more. I've taken Alice in return. You took Chloe, I take Alice. It seems like a fair deal.'

'Just what is it you want from me?' Hayley said. She'd do anything to get Alice back.

'What I've always wanted. The truth. Otherwise Alice will be gone forever.'

Hayley swallowed the tears that were rising up inside her. 'I'm sorry,' she said.

'You're sorry – sorry for what?'

'Chloe's dead, Eva. She was already dead that day. There

was a terrible accident. She fell off the bed. I was supposed to be watching her...' Hayley couldn't say any more. It was too difficult. She couldn't believe she was finally telling the truth and coming clean, admitting the mistake that had haunted her all these years.

SIXTY-THREE

1999

When the sun rose in the morning, Hayley was lying on the bed in the budget hotel she'd found, staring at the ceiling, still fully clothed. She couldn't believe what had happened the night before. She'd been playing it over and over in her mind, non-stop. Poor, poor Chloe.

When she'd eventually found a hotel after wandering the streets for hours, she'd gone up to her room, put her rucksack beside the bed and lain there, waiting for the police to come and find her. Waiting for it all to be over.

She had her hand on her stomach now, thinking of the baby inside her, thinking of the future mapped out for both of them. Arrest, trial, prison. She knew nothing about the legal system, let alone the Thai legal system. Did she need a lawyer?

She wanted desperately to speak to her mother. But how could she? She couldn't imagine ever telling her what had happened. She'd be so ashamed of her. So she lay and waited for her fate.

Early in the morning there was a knock at her door. Startled by the noise, she rose and, shaking, went over to the door, expecting to see the police.

But it was David. His eyes darted from side to side.

'Can I come in?' he said.

She stood aside to let him through. There were no chairs so he sat on the edge of the bed. She sat beside him, almost too tired to stand. Her whirling thoughts had exhausted her, the guilt and the shame had consumed her.

'The police will come today,' David said softly. 'We're going to tell them Chloe's missing.'

Hayley stared at him, failing to understand. 'What happened to her?' she asked. For a second she thought that maybe Chloe had woken up again and then somehow gone missing, but that didn't make any sense.

'You know what happened,' David said. He put his head in his hands. 'She fell off the bed while you were changing her nappy. My daughter died.' He couldn't look at her.

'I'm so sorry,' she said. But words could never be enough. To say anything at all was almost offensive.

'You killed her,' he said softly, looking at his hands. 'But... I can't let you go to jail.'

'What?'

'I've buried her.' Sobs suddenly burst out of him, and he couldn't speak. When he continued his words were so quiet, she could hardly make them out. 'She was already dead. There was no saving her. So I've put her in the earth. In a pleasant place, surrounded by trees. She won't have to have a post-mortem now. Her little body won't be cut open. She's whole inside the ground, at peace.'

Hayley was still struggling to understand. 'But why?' she said.

'To protect you,' he said. 'To protect our baby.' He reached out and touched her stomach, and Hayley remembered him telling her he could arrange an abortion for her. How had his feelings changed? Or did he love her? Was that why he was protecting her?

'I don't understand,' she said.

'There's the death penalty in Thailand,' he said. 'Do you understand that, Hayley?' He reached for her shoulders, shook her slightly. 'You killed Chloe. I don't know what would happen to you. To our baby.'

Hayley felt the blood drain from her head and thought she might faint.

'Look,' David said. 'Chloe's dead. I know how much you cared for her. You'll have to live the rest of your life with this. You'll be punished enough. I can't let you face the Thai legal system.' He reached out and pushed a stray strand of hair behind her ear.

'But it was my fault,' she said. 'I need to tell the truth.'

'That's all very noble, Hayley,' he said. But you've got to stop thinking like that. You could be sentenced to death here. If you say the wrong thing, that's what could happen. Think what that would do to your family, to your parents. I can't let that happen to you.'

Hayley felt tears running down her face. She hadn't thought things could get any worse. 'But it was an accident,' she said. Surely she wouldn't get the death sentence?

David squeezed her shoulders harder, looking directly into her eyes. 'Do you really think the police will believe that? I've been here years, and believe me, the law works differently here. They won't go easy on you. They'll be looking for someone to blame.'

Hayley swallowed, terrified.

'The police will interview us all,' David continued. 'And when they do you need to say you have no idea what happened to Chloe.' He saw the fear in her eyes and his voice softened. 'Don't worry,' he said. 'I'm looking out for you, Hayley. I'll protect you.'

SIXTY-FOUR

NOW

'She's dead?' Eva collapsed onto the bed behind her. 'Chloe's dead,' she repeated, sobs wracking her body.

Johanna's face was white. Chloe was her sister too. 'You killed her and you never said? Instead you hid it?'

'I— Your father, David. He wanted to protect me. Because of you, because of my baby. We agreed not to say what had happened.'

'But where is she now?' Eva asked.

'I don't know for certain. David buried her. I suppose in Bangkok somewhere. He said it was a green place, lots of trees.'

Johanna sank onto the bed beside Eva and put her arm around her. Hayley could see the devastation written all over Johanna's face, the betrayal. 'I'm so, so sorry,' she said.

'You killed her,' Eva said. 'I was right. You killed her. You didn't allow me or Emily any closure. You let us all keep thinking she was missing, that one day we might find her and be reunited.'

'It was an accident,' Hayley said.

'You kept it secret all these years,' Eva said. 'Pretending to be a respectable wife and mother. But you didn't deserve any of that.'

'I know,' Hayley said. 'I know.' She thought about how she had planned to confess to the police, but David had told her not to. But then she'd spent a night in prison anyway, because of Eva's evidence. And how after they'd released her she had felt so guilty, but also so free, like she'd been given a second chance.

They heard a faint sound from the room next door. A knocking. A voice shouting 'Mummy!'

'Alice!' Hayley screamed. 'Alice – is that you?' It was coming from the room next door. She raced to the door, Eva behind her. It was locked. She couldn't get out. She banged on the wall. 'Alice, can you hear me?'

'Mummy!' Alice's voice was teary. 'I thought you'd left me. Michelle said she was going to look after me, that we were on holiday. But it's boring in this room. Take me home!'

'Alice, Alice… don't worry. I'm so glad I found you. We've been looking everywhere for you. Johanna's with me now. We'll take you home.' She turned to Eva. 'Open the door.'

'You're not having her back,' Eva said. 'You killed my sister.' Hayley thought of how much she had loved Emily and Eva, how she had cared for them. But she had hurt them. What she'd done had damaged Eva irreparably.

'I know,' Hayley said, despairing. She hated to hear the words, hated to think of that poor, tiny baby, hated to remember what she'd done. 'But I can't make it better now. I wish I could go back in time and change things. Watch Chloe properly, prevent the accident from happening. But I can't do that. I can only live with it. I can't fix it. I'm so sorry.'

'You're not going to get away with it. You should be in jail.'

Hayley nodded. 'Maybe you're right. But if I was arrested, Alice wouldn't have a mother. You can't do that to her.'

'You've denied me a sister,' Eva spat. 'And if you don't

confess to the police, then I'll deny you a daughter. Alice will disappear.'

Hayley saw the choice laid out, stark and clear. Her life or her daughter's. There was never any contest.

'I'll go to the police,' she said. 'Explain what happened. Hand myself in.'

'Why should I believe you?'

'I'll go with her,' Johanna said softly. 'I can record the confession. Then you'll be able to see it. Hayley won't be able to go home. I can take Alice back to Lars.'

Hayley nodded. This was the only possible plan. And perhaps now was the time to confess, to finally take the punishment she had always been due.

'OK,' Eva said. She started to pace up and down. 'But if you go to the police now, they might connect this to Alice's disappearance. You can't tell them I have Alice.'

'I won't,' Hayley said. 'I promise I won't. I won't mention Alice at all.'

Johanna spoke up. 'We're in the City of London here,' she said. 'I know because my university halls are nearby. It's a different police force. Not the Met. They probably won't draw the connection with Alice's disappearance.'

Eva nodded. 'You should use your maiden name,' she said. 'It will take them a while to join the dots. You don't have any ID with you so there'll be nothing to connect you to Alice. I'll leave here with Alice as soon as you've gone, hide somewhere else until I see your confession. If you don't confess, I'll run away with her. If you tell the police I've kidnapped Alice, then you won't see her again. When Johanna sends me your confession, I'll leave Alice where she can find her and get away from here.'

Hayley nodded. 'OK,' she said. She felt sick with what she was going to do. But it was the only way. She thought of Alice in the next room, longed to wrap her arms around her. 'I need to see Alice before I go.' She might be extradited to Thailand, might not see her daughter for years.

Eva nodded. 'I don't want to deny her the chance to say goodbye to her mother.'

She took two keys out of her pocket and unlocked their door and then opened the door to Alice's room. 'Wait here. I'll go in first, then you and Johanna.' Hayley's mind whirred, wondering if she could grab Alice and make a run for it.

Eva went inside and Hayley heard her whispering to Alice, before she came back to the door.

'She's on the bed. You can come in now.'

Hayley had imagined every awful thing that might have happened to Alice. But she looked well. She was wearing her favourite blue and orange dress with a new rainbow-coloured necklace. Hayley hadn't noticed the dress was missing when the police searched her room. Alice came running over as soon as she saw Hayley and threw her arms around her. 'Mummy!'

Hayley held her daughter tight, feeling the warmth of her body, her living, breathing daughter.

'I love you,' Hayley said. She could hardly speak through tears. She looked behind her towards the door, but Eva stood in front of it, blocking it. They were on the fourth floor. Climbing out the window wasn't an option. There was no escape.

'You have to confess,' Johanna said softly, seeing her checking out the exit routes. 'I'll come with you.'

'Confess?' Alice said, quizzically. Hayley didn't think she knew what the word meant.

She held her tight. 'I might be away some time,' she said. 'But your daddy will look after you. And Johanna. You're not to worry about me.'

'But Mum, what do you mean?'

'It's not important,' she said through tears. 'The most important thing is you know that I love you.'

SIXTY-FIVE

Hayley was shaking as they walked to the police station. She didn't know how she'd managed to let go of Alice's hand, to leave her behind. The sun shone brightly and she shaded her eyes. The people around her bustled by, ignoring her and Johanna. A family walked past with a girl of about Alice's age chatting excitedly, her mother hurrying her along. Hayley's heart tugged.

'You're doing the right thing,' Johanna said softly.

Hayley's mind spun. Was she? After all these years? Surely she should have confessed when she was younger, when she had nothing to leave behind. No Alice. Alice wouldn't have existed at all if she'd told the truth back then. But then she thought of Johanna. If she'd confessed immediately she would have gone to a local orphanage.

'I could be extradited,' Hayley said. 'I'll end up in a Thai jail.'

It wasn't until she'd got back home to England that she'd looked up Thai law and realised that she would never have faced the death penalty like David had threatened. She could have ended up in jail for years, but they wouldn't have killed her. She'd thought about going to the police back then and confessing, purging her conscience. But by then she'd restarted her life in the UK. She was about to go to university and everything that had happened in Thailand seemed like a distant memory, almost as if it had been someone else, not her. She had just put all of it to the back of her mind and pretended it never happened.

Johanna reached out and gripped her hand and Hayley took comfort from the action. She'd just found Johanna. And now Hayley was going to lose her again.

At least Lars would have Alice back, even if she wasn't there. She desperately wanted to speak to him and update him on everything that had happened, tell him she'd seen Alice, that she was OK. But she couldn't speak to him until Johanna had Alice back. And by that time Hayley might be behind bars. He'd never understand what she had done. She might never have the chance to explain.

They got to the door of the police station and Johanna pushed it open. As they went inside, Johanna got the phone out.

They walked together to the front desk, and Hayley looked into the eyes of the young policewoman standing there. The woman who would determine her fate.

She glanced at Johanna, who was holding her phone out of sight, down below the desk. She saw Johanna press the red record button.

Hayley took a deep breath.

'I'm here to confess to a crime,' she said.

When she'd finished explaining everything, the police officer looked baffled. 'I'm going to have to ask you to come inside,' she said, 'while I make some further enquiries.' Johanna started to walk inside with Hayley, but the policewoman stopped her.

'No,' she said. 'We just need Hayley. You can wait here, outside, if you like.'

Hayley felt a ball of fear harden in her stomach. She glanced back towards Johanna but the policewoman was in the way, holding the door for her, and she couldn't catch Johanna's eye. The policewoman cleared her throat and Hayley went through the door.

Two hours later, Hayley was still sitting in the same room she'd been taken to when she'd first come in. A police officer had recorded a short interview with her about what had happened and then she'd been told to wait there, and that someone would be back to see her soon. Nothing else had happened until half an hour ago, when someone had brought her a cup of coffee from the machine. She'd desperately wanted to tell them about Alice, to ask if she'd been found, but she knew she couldn't.

The police hadn't drawn the connection between her and Alice. As agreed, Hayley had given her maiden name, and she had no ID on her, so there was no reason for them to make the link. And although Hayley had been tempted to tell them, she didn't know if Eva had handed Alice back yet, and if she hadn't and she found out Hayley had told the police, then Alice could be lost forever.

Now she was just waiting, staring at the walls, every scenario running through her head. She prayed that Johanna's recording of her confession had worked, that she'd managed to send it to Eva, that Eva had handed Alice over to her. But she had no idea if any of that had happened; had no idea whether or not Alice was safe. Johanna had taken the phone with her so she couldn't look anything up online, couldn't find out if Alice had been found.

Hayley wondered if she'd be extradited to Thailand to be tried there. She remembered being in the Thai police station, spending the night at the station in a boiling hot cell. She hadn't been able to sleep at all, she'd been so terrified.

She thought of Alice, how she would have to celebrate her sixth birthday in a month's time without her mother. She wondered how much she'd remember her. Would she remember how close they were, the love between them, or would it be like it had been with Eva? Would the shadow of what she'd done obliterate all the happier memories?

The clock kept ticking as the hours passed. No one seemed to know what to do with her. She wondered if she could leave, say she'd come back another time. But when she'd asked they'd told her it wouldn't be much longer, and she just needed to wait. She thought about asking to use their phone to call Lars, but she had no idea what she could say to him if he didn't have Alice back home. It was too risky.

Just when she thought she couldn't wait any longer, that she was going to have to do something to escape these four walls, to find out what had happened to Alice, a policewoman finally came in and sat down opposite her. Hayley felt the nausea rise from her stomach. This was it. This was where she paid the price for her mistake.

'Hayley Taylor?' she said.

'Yes,' Hayley whispered, answering to her maiden name.

'I just wanted to check some details of the crime. So, just to reconfirm – it happened in Thailand?'

'Yes, in Bangkok.' She didn't know why they were asking again. She'd explained it all in the interview.

'And can you confirm when it happened?'

'In 1999.'

'Right, let me go and check something.'

Hayley was abandoned in the room again, and she put her head in her hands, wondering if it would be hours until the officer returned. But she was back five minutes later.

'I have some good news for you,' she said, as she came into the room.

'Oh?' Hayley said, holding her breath. Had they found Alice?

'We do have a repatriation agreement with Thailand, but it doesn't apply in this case.'

'Right,' Hayley said, trying to get her head round the fact this wasn't about Alice. This was about her. She felt a glimmer of hope about her future. Perhaps she could serve her sentence here. Then Alice would be able to visit her. If they had found her.

'In Thailand the statute of limitations is twenty years.'

'What does that mean?'

'It means the crimes no longer count. You wouldn't be charged.'

'What?' Hayley said. She didn't think she'd heard her correctly.

'You're free to go,' the policewoman said, smiling.

SIXTY-SIX

When Hayley left the police station it was raining, and she lifted her face to the sky to feel it touch her skin. If she'd been locked up, she wouldn't have been able to feel the rain for a long time.

She had to get home, as fast as she could. Surely Alice would be back there. Johanna must have sent Eva the recording, and Eva must have released Alice. Hayley had done everything she'd asked by confessing.

And yet she didn't know if she could trust Eva. Or even Johanna. What if they still had her daughter?

She wished she had a phone, so she could look on the internet, see if there were any updates about Alice. She looked around her as she rushed to the station. Everyone here would be carrying a phone. She just had to borrow one.

She asked the next woman walking by. 'Could I borrow your phone, please? Just for a minute.' The woman put her head down and ignored her.

She asked seven more people, until a young man said yes. She went straight to Google to search for Alice's name. Nothing new. Just the missing report. And the details of how to join the search. She looked on Facebook and saw the missing alerts in her local groups. There were no updates saying she'd been found. Her heart sank.

She handed the phone back to the man and thanked him. She had to get home, find out what had happened. Why wasn't Alice back yet? Eva had promised.

The whole journey home Hayley felt sick with fear. Where was her little girl? Why hadn't she snatched her from Eva, tried to run with her out of the hotel room when she could? She had seen her daughter, and she had left her. She felt overcome by guilt.

When she finally got home, there were police cars outside the house. They must still be looking for Alice. Hayley walked up to the door, feeling completely defeated. She'd confessed everything, but Alice still wasn't back. She didn't have her key with her, so she rang the doorbell.

It was a moment before Constable Devine came to the door.

'Oh!' she said. 'Hayley! We didn't know where you were.'

Hayley came into the house, unable to explain. She heard the clattering of footsteps on the stairs. And then a shout. 'Mummy!'

Hayley ran towards the stairs as her daughter ran down, her long hair flying behind her. She held out her arms and Alice leapt into them. Alice's fingers gripped her back as they hugged each other tightly, relief rushing through her body. Hayley never wanted to let her go.

SIXTY-SEVEN

Hayley watched the police car back slowly out of the driveway. She'd felt like hugging the police officers when she said goodbye, but had stopped herself, instead thanking them profusely. She'd only known them for just over twenty-four hours, but somehow it had felt like they'd always been there. It had been one of the most intense and traumatic days of her life.

She was grateful that they'd arrested Ryan. They'd found him by tracing her phone to Eva's house in Ealing and they had quickly rescued Susan. But they hadn't been able to track down Eva. Until they had known where she and Hayley were, they had been wary of telling the press that Alice had been found.

Hayley went into the living room and sat down on the sofa next to Alice. She'd hardly left her side since she got home. 'Do you want to play something?' she asked. 'Lego, maybe? Or we could do a jigsaw? Or colouring? Whatever you want.'

'I want to watch TV.'

'OK, then.' Alice wasn't showing any signs of stress. It seemed like Eva had treated her kindly when she'd looked after her, keeping her fed and chatting and playing with her.

Although she'd been bored in the hotel room, she hadn't been distressed until her mother had started shouting through the wall. Even when Johanna had collected Alice from the park bench where Eva had told her she could find her, Alice had been comfortable with an apple juice and a packet of sweets in her hands, in case she got hungry.

'Do you want anything to eat?' Hayley asked. 'Bread, cheese? A chocolate biscuit?'

'I'm fine, Mum.' Alice put her head down on the cushion and Hayley stroked her hair. 'I love you,' she said.

'I know, Mum.'

Lars came over. 'I think she wants to be left alone now,' he said. 'She's exhausted from going through everything with the police.'

'I know,' Hayley said. 'I just can't believe she's home. I'm so grateful.'

'What happened when you were away?' Lars asked. 'Where did you go?'

Lars had been with Alice when she'd spoken to the police and explained briefly that she'd been at the City of London police station. The police had been more concerned about where Eva might be. She still hadn't been found.

'I was in London,' she said.

'But what were you doing?'

She sighed, unsure what to say. She didn't have to tell him anything. The police had told her she wouldn't be tried, that she was free. But she owed him an explanation.

'I can't tell you in front of Alice,' she said. 'Let's go to the kitchen.'

They sat down at the kitchen table and she told him everything. How Chloe had fallen off the bed in Thailand and died, how she'd been pregnant with David's daughter at the time, and David had buried Chloe and covered it up to protect her. How Eva had always thought that she had something to do with her sister's disappearance and had kidnapped Alice to get to the truth. How Hayley had spent the afternoon in the police station, confessing, but she wouldn't be charged because it was twenty years ago.

The words tumbled out of her, and Lars let her speak without interrupting. By the time she finished she was shaking with sobs, thinking of Chloe, how tiny she'd been, how precious.

Finally, she looked up. 'I'm sorry,' she said to Lars.

He didn't say anything for a moment. But then he got up and came over to her at the other side of the table and wrapped his arms around her. He waited until she stopped sobbing in his arms and then released her.

'Do you understand?' she asked. 'Do you understand why I did what I did?' She wanted desperately for him to forgive her, to love her despite her shame and her guilt.

But he gently shook his head. 'This is a lot to take in, Hayley. It's been such a crazy day.'

'I know,' she said, her body shaking harder. He wasn't going to say it, he wasn't going to forgive her. She thought of Chloe, imagined what she'd be like today. She wondered if she'd have gone to university, if she'd have stayed in Thailand. Would she have looked like Johanna or Eva? She'd never know. Her life had been snuffed out in a careless moment, and Hayley would always have to carry the weight of that responsibility.

'We're all hungry,' Lars said. 'Let's get fish and chips. I can walk down the road and pick it up. I need some fresh air.'

'That's a good idea. Mum loves fish and chips. And Alice.' She tried to smile through her tears.

When Lars came back with the fish and chips, Hayley and Alice had already set the table. The family all sat down, each of them bone-tired from the day. Alice looked like she might fall asleep into her dinner. But as Hayley looked at them, she felt overwhelmingly grateful for her little family.

'Is Johanna upstairs?' she asked Lars. Hayley thought of how she'd been by her side, not giving up until Alice was found. She'd seen her briefly when she'd first got home, and thanked her, but then Johanna had said she needed a rest and disappeared up to her room.

'I think so,' Lars said.

'I'll just go and see if she wants to join us.' It would be good to have her at dinner with them. She wanted all her family there after such a difficult day, to eat her dinner with both her daughters.

Hayley went upstairs and knocked on the door of Johanna's room.

'Johanna?' she called out. 'We're having fish and chips. Have you eaten?'

There was no light from the crack under the door. Perhaps she was asleep.

But Hayley had a sinking feeling.

'Johanna?' she said again, knocking louder. 'I'm coming in.'

She opened the door, half expecting to see Johanna laid out on the bed in the dark, processing everything that had happened that day.

But there was no one on the bed. Hayley flicked on the light. The room was empty. No Johanna. No personal belongings either. All the photos on top of the chest of drawers were gone. Johanna had moved out all of her possessions.

She saw a note on the bed, written in Johanna's careful handwriting.

Hayley, I can't stop thinking about what you did in Thailand. I understand how accidents can happen, and how Chloe might have fallen off the bed. But I can't get over how you covered it up, how you kept it a secret for all those years. I didn't want you to be extradited to Thailand and put in prison. But Chloe was still my sister. I can't be part of your life knowing what you did. You will always be my biological mother, and I'm glad I found you and could finally answer questions about who I am. But I don't want us to be in contact any more. Johanna

SIXTY-EIGHT

A YEAR LATER

Hayley kissed her mother's head as she sat in one of the comfy armchairs at the home, a cup of tea beside her. 'I've got to go now,' she said.

'See you later, love,' Susan said, and Hayley was unsure if she knew who she was saying goodbye to. She came to visit her mother in the home twice a week and some days she was more lucid than others. Often Hayley would take in photos to show her and they'd have long conversations about Hayley's childhood. Susan remembered the red slide they'd had in the back garden that they'd run the hosepipe down each summer to turn into a water slide. She remembered the sunflowers they'd grown at the front of their house for a school competition. It was nice to talk about the happy times, to remember all the fun she'd had with her three younger brothers. Hayley had spent so long trying to forget what had happened to Chloe that she'd just focused on moving forward, never letting herself think about the past. Now it was good to remember her carefree childhood, to think about how she could make Alice's the same.

'Say hi to Alice from me,' her mother said, with a smile.

Hayley beamed. It was a day when Susan remembered she had a granddaughter. These kinds of days gave her hope.

Hayley walked back to her car through the crisp air and sat still in the driver's seat to allow herself a moment of reflection. The home had been the right decision for her mother. Without Eva, none of them had been able to cope. She thought how kind and caring Eva had been to her mother, even though she'd only taken the job to get closer to Hayley and find the truth out about Chloe. Eva was serving time in prison now. She'd been found in a remote part of Scotland a couple of days after she'd kidnapped Alice. She and Ryan had both been given four-year sentences, but they were expected to be out much sooner. Hayley had given evidence at the trial, and sat in the public gallery to watch much of the rest of it.

She was meeting Lars in town for lunch in twenty minutes, and she was running a bit ahead of schedule. Things between them were slowly improving. He had hardly spoken to her for the first week after Alice had been found, and the atmosphere had been tense, but then one evening they had had a heart-to-heart and she'd explained again how awful she'd felt about what had happened to Chloe, how she'd been young and scared, and she hadn't wanted to go to jail in Thailand. Gradually he'd begun to understand, and although he thought she should have confessed back then, their relationship was starting to get better and he was beginning to trust her again.

Hayley reached for her phone and checked Facebook, as had become her habit. It was the best way to keep up with Johanna's wedding preparations. She knew Johanna's Instagram had more photos, but that was private, and Johanna hadn't accepted her request to follow her. They'd become friends on Facebook towards the end of Johanna's time lodging with them, when they'd been starting to get closer. Although Johanna never replied to Hayley's comments, she'd never blocked her, and Hayley was grateful for that small kindness.

She'd followed avidly as Johanna had started dating Callum, a PhD student. She'd watched their love blossom, trying to stop herself commenting on every photo. She'd been delighted when they'd got engaged, and had sent Johanna a private message congratulating her. Johanna had ignored it, like she'd ignored all Hayley's other messages.

Today, Johanna had been out with her bridesmaids, choosing their dresses. There was a photo of them having afternoon tea afterwards. Karolina was with them at the head of the table, everyone smiling. Hayley felt a wave of jealousy.

She was about to click away from Facebook when she saw she had a new private message. From Emily McFarlane. She'd seen her at Eva's trial, crying when her sister was sent down. Hayley had wanted to comfort her, and to talk to her, to see how she was doing now. But she had known how inappropriate and unwelcome it would have been.

She opened the message, feeling a sense of unease. She and Emily had never spoken about what had happened to Chloe.

Hayley,

I've wanted to contact you for some time, but I couldn't find the words. There is so much I want to say to you and I've drafted this email over and over again. I wondered if we could meet in person to talk? I live in London, so perhaps we could meet for coffee here?

Emily

Hayley reread the message, unsure what to think. Did Emily feel the same way towards her as Eva did? She wondered if Emily blamed her for Eva going to jail. She wondered if she was in contact with Johanna, if she'd be able to tell her more about how she was, about the wedding preparations.

She quickly drafted a message back agreeing to meet for coffee. There was no harm in it.

SIXTY-NINE

A few days later, Hayley bought a coffee at a small café in Covent Garden and carried her tray carefully to the back where Emily had said she'd be sitting. She spotted her, sitting in the corner booth, wearing a neatly ironed green shirt and staring intently at her laptop. She glanced up as Hayley approached and stood to say hello. They looked at each other awkwardly for a moment, unsure how to greet each other. Then Emily said, 'Thanks for coming,' and sat back down.

'Were you working?' Hayley said, pointing to the laptop.

'Yeah, just catching up on a few emails. I work for a bank, in communications.'

'Ah, right. Congratulations.' She was glad Emily was doing well.

Neither of them knew what to say. The weight of the past sat between them: Eva's imprisonment, Chloe's death.

'So...' Hayley said, after she'd taken a sip of her coffee. 'I'm so sorry about Chloe.' She blurted it out.

'Me too,' Emily said, looking at the ground. 'I wish I'd known what had happened to her. We never talked about it, but I always felt her absence, even though I was just a child.'

'I was so young when it all happened. And so scared. I never meant for it to happen. It was an accident. But I should have admitted it.'

'Eva said that our father covered for you. That he was the one who buried Chloe.'

Hayley nodded. 'He knew I was carrying his baby. I suppose he wanted to protect me.'

'I felt so sorry when I heard he'd died. We didn't see him again after we left Thailand, and I missed him desperately as a child. When I got older I always thought he didn't want to see us because he couldn't get over Chloe's disappearance. I thought he was lost in his grief. But to think he knew what had happened to her. Maybe it was the guilt that made him drink himself to death.'

Hayley felt tears rising in her throat. 'I'd do anything to change what happened,' she said.

'We all would. I'm sorry about what Eva did to Alice. She just lost it.'

'You don't need to apologise,' Hayley said. 'Really.'

'You know,' Emily said, 'she was so convinced you had something to do with Chloe's disappearance. Once she saw that article about it, she talked about it all the time. I told her I didn't want to hear about it any more and we didn't speak for a while. That was when she started working for your mother. If I'd have known what she was doing, I would have stopped her.'

Hayley nodded.

Emily sighed. 'Eva and I – well, we haven't always got on. You see, we have completely different views of our childhood. I remember more about our time in Thailand than she does. She only really remembers Chloe's disappearance and going to the police. Everything else she's forgotten. But I remember what it was like in that apartment. How mean Julie was to us, how she shouted at us, didn't like us being around. And I remember how much better it was when you started looking after us, how you cared for us and Chloe more than she ever did. Our father was so distant. It was you who made our lives fun out there. All my best memories of that time are of you.'

Hayley felt a tear roll down her cheek. 'I loved you, Eva and Chloe so much,' she said. 'I only stayed in that job because of you and Eva. I didn't want to leave you with Julie.'

Emily nodded. 'You know Julie's dying?' she said.

Hayley shook her head. 'Eva said she'd been very ill for a long time.'

'She's developed breast cancer. They caught it late because she wouldn't go to the doctor. It's terminal.'

'That's so sad,' Hayley said, thinking of how much both she and David had suffered after what had happened.

'She hasn't looked after herself for years. I only know she's dying because someone my mum used to know in Thailand got in contact. I was wondering if I should go and visit her. I feel... like I need to go back to Thailand. To say my goodbyes. To Julie. To my father. And to Chloe. And I was wondering... Eva's in prison. And you're the only one who really remembers that time like I do. I was wondering if you'd come with me?'

SEVENTY

ONE MONTH LATER

Hayley and Emily were in a taxi on Sukhumvit Road, on their way to Julie's apartment. Above them, the sleek Skytrains ran through the air. Hayley remembered the engineering drawings that David had laid out on the table in his and Julie's apartment, showing how it would be built. It had been finished before she left Thailand and it was hard to believe that it had been operating for over twenty years. Beneath the trains, the road was still snarled up with traffic, bright yellow taxis filling the carriageways.

Their taxi pulled off the main road and turned down a crowded side street, full of people, motorbike taxis, street food and massage parlours. Hayley remembered when she'd first come to Bangkok, how excited she'd been by its vibrancy. She hadn't wanted to come back, but she'd felt she needed to. It was the least she could do for Emily, after what had happened to Chloe.

They pulled up outside a run-down apartment block, so different to the expensive one Julie had lived in before. Hayley felt a shiver of fear, her memories of Julie flooding back.

'I think she had to move years ago,' Emily said. 'Mum's

friend said she didn't work much after Chloe died. And after Dad died she had even less money.'

They went into the apartment block together, eyed the rickety lift and decided to take the stairs to the fifth floor.

A Thai woman answered the door in a nurse's uniform. She ushered them through into an empty living area with just a single sofa and a television. Emily explained who they were, but the nurse didn't speak any English. She bowed and pointed them towards a closed door, and then went to the small kitchen area and started washing up, humming to herself.

Hayley looked at Emily and then knocked on the door. 'Julie?' she called out. There was no answer and Emily pushed the door open.

The room was almost empty except for an old wardrobe and a bed. Hayley wondered what had happened to all Julie's things: the expensive dark-wood furniture, the cupboards of designer dresses, the shelves of books. She hadn't brought any of it with her. Perhaps she'd sold it all.

They walked into the room, saw Julie in the bed, her head resting against the pillows, staring up at the ceiling blankly. She was so thin, almost a skeleton, her face pale and drawn.

'Julie,' Emily said. 'It's Emily. Do you remember me?'

'Of course I do,' she said, her voice hoarse as she struggled to sit up. 'I'm not losing my mind.'

Emily smiled gently. 'And you remember Hayley?'

'Hayley.' Julie recoiled and Hayley realised that she should have thought things through before coming here. To Julie, she was the person who'd killed her daughter. Of course she wouldn't want her here.

'Do you want me to get you anything?' Hayley asked. It was impossible not to feel sorry for the woman in the bed. 'Some food? A biscuit?'

Julie shook her head. 'It's nice to have visitors. I haven't had many.'

'We came from England,' Emily said.

'I knew you'd come eventually.' Julie sighed. 'Is this about Chloe?'

Emily and Hayley looked at each other. 'No,' Hayley said as Emily said 'Yes.' Hayley shrank into herself. Was that why Emily had wanted her here?

She took a deep breath. She knew what she needed to say. The words she should have said years ago. 'I'm so sorry about what happened to Chloe.' She felt tears welling up in her eyes and swallowed to control them. 'I can't imagine what it was like for you. I'm sure you never got over it. None of us did.'

'It was worse for me, though... the guilt. I don't know how it happened.'

'The guilt?' Emily said. Hayley thought about how distant Julie had been from Chloe before she died. She must have felt awful about not being close to her.

'I did the one thing a mother should never do,' Julie said.

Hayley had the urge to comfort this dying woman, to put the past behind them. 'You tried your best,' she said.

'Did I?' Julie turned to her, fury in her eyes. 'I don't think that could have possibly been my best.'

'What are you talking about?' Emily asked gently.

Julie started rocking back and forth in the bed. 'I didn't mean to do it. I just lost it. She was crying and crying and crying. I think it was the head injury. She'd hit her head falling off the bed. But I'd checked her out and she seemed fine. But she wouldn't stop crying. The noise filled my brain. I couldn't think straight. And no one was there.' She looked pointedly at Hayley. 'You'd left. David wasn't back. I was on my own and she wouldn't stop crying.'

Hayley froze. What was she talking about?

'I didn't mean to do it,' Julie repeated. 'I didn't. I wasn't thinking straight. I just wanted the noise to stop. And I took the pillow. I placed it over her face. And the noise stopped.'

SEVENTY-ONE

Hayley and Emily stared at Julie, her weak body shaking with tears.

'I didn't mean to kill her,' Julie whispered. 'I would never have meant to kill her.'

Hayley thought back to that evening when she'd left the apartment, had a drink and then come back to check on Chloe. Julie had told her the head injury had killed her. But it had been Julie who'd smothered her daughter.

'I was lucky,' Julie continued. 'When I told David what had happened, he protected me. I was in pieces, but he was pragmatic, working out what to do. He was devastated but he loved me and didn't want me to go to jail. He knew I didn't mean it, that it was a mistake. He'd already lost his daughter; he didn't want to lose his wife. He said the police would work out that she'd died from suffocation, not a head injury. They'd work out it was me. It was better for Chloe to disappear, then they wouldn't be able to pin it on anyone. He buried her for us. He knew a place where she wouldn't be found. At the end of the line of the Skytrain. There was an empty patch of land there next to the final station. He put her there. He did that for me.

But sometimes I wish he hadn't, that he'd given me the chance to confess, to come clean. My life was never the same again after Chloe died. Maybe if I'd confessed back then, I would feel free of it.'

'You told me I killed her,' Hayley said angrily. She thought of all the years she'd carried the weight of her crime. 'I always believed that.'

'I wanted to blame you. I even told the press that you'd been behaving badly, and took Eva to the police station to tell them she'd seen you leaving with her wrapped in the blanket. But David told me to back off.'

Hayley's eyes flashed with anger. 'David said he was protecting me. He told me to lie to the police. But all the time it was you he was protecting.'

'We needed to keep you quiet. We'd already buried her. If you confessed and told the truth, that you thought you'd killed her, then the story would unravel as soon as you said you hadn't realised she was missing. Everything would fall apart. We needed you to tell the same story as us. And that would only happen if you believed you were lying because it was your fault.'

'I've felt guilty all my life,' Hayley said. 'I thought I was a killer.'

'Everything happened so quickly.' Julie's voice was barely audible. 'We had to decide what to do, what was for the best. I was terrified and could hardly believe what I'd done. I wasn't in my right mind. I just wish none of it had ever happened. At the time... David thought he could fix it. Chloe was already dead, we couldn't change that. It was best to bury her and try and get on with our lives. She was gone, whether I went to jail or not. But what I did destroyed David. And me too. My life hasn't been worth living since.'

.   .   .

On the street outside, Emily was still shaking. 'I can't believe that,' she said.

Hayley could hardly process what had happened. 'I didn't do it,' she said quietly.

'And Eva went to prison for nothing.'

They stood for a moment, motorbikes and people streaming around them.

'Let's go to the place where she's buried,' Emily said softly.

They took the Skytrain there, getting out at what used to be the final stop, where Julie had said Chloe was. The line had been extended years ago, and the land wasn't empty any more. There was a huge shopping mall, with lush gardens at the entrance. They went inside and bought flowers at an upmarket florist. Then they went back to gardens and laid the flowers in front of a young palm tree, next to the footpath.

'I'll always remember her,' Emily said, tears flowing down her cheeks.

'Me too,' Hayley said, her voice shaky. 'I hope she's at peace now.' It was hard to hear above the traffic on the nearby road, and people streamed past them on the way from the shopping centre to the Skytrain.

They embraced each other, each lost in their own pain, engulfed by the noise of the city.

SEVENTY-TWO

THREE MONTHS LATER

Hayley, Lars and Alice stood at the back of the church, watching as Johanna and Callum said their vows. Hayley felt a rush of joy as she heard Johanna say the words 'I do'. She squeezed Lars' hand as she watched the happy couple kiss, straining her neck for a better view.

The pianist started to play and the bride and groom walked back down the aisle towards them, everyone clapping. Johanna was smiling radiantly in a strapless, tea-length dress, greeting each of her guests as she passed by. When they got to Hayley, Johanna grinned at her. 'I'm so glad you could make it.' She leant down so she was at Alice's level. 'Make sure you get some confetti to throw,' she said.

The congregation filed out of the church behind them, led by Hans and Karolina. Karolina waved hello at Hayley as she dabbed at her eyes with a tissue.

After Johanna had left their home, Hayley had sent a letter to Karolina, explaining who Johanna was, and why she'd left the baby. Karolina had rung her when she got the letter and told her that she'd always known she was Hayley's child, and had suspected that David was the father. After Hayley had left the baby at their apartment that day, she had looked out of their window and seen her hurrying away. For the first few weeks, she'd expected her to come and demand the baby back. When she didn't, they'd gone to register her as Karolina's, claiming she'd given birth unexpectedly at home a few weeks before. Then they'd got out of the country as quickly as they could, taking Johanna with them to Sweden. They'd always worried that Hayley would want her back one day.

Hayley caught Emily's eye as she filed out behind Hans and Karolina in a bright red dress. She came over and Hayley embraced her. 'Thank you so much,' Hayley said. 'I never thought I'd get to see this.' After Emily and Hayley got back from Thailand, Emily had spoken to Johanna and Eva and explained what Julie had told them. Eva hadn't wanted to know, but Johanna had phoned the next day and they'd talked and talked. And then she'd invited them to her wedding.

Finally Lars, Hayley and Alice left the church, and stepped out into the summer sun, shielding their eyes from its glare. The bride and groom waited behind the church doors while the groomsmen handed out confetti outside. Alice filled her hands, laughing as she dropped some and it scattered around her.

'Hayley.' She heard a voice behind her and turned to see Karolina, as beautiful and elegant as ever.

'How are you?' Hayley stuttered. They hadn't spoken since that phone call over a year ago.

'I'm well. Better than well. Johanna looks beautiful, doesn't she?'

'Yes, she's gorgeous.'

'I'm so glad you could be here,' she said, warmly.

I'm just so grateful that you gave her such a wonderful childhood. She's grown into an amazing young woman.'

'I'm grateful to you too,' Karolina said. 'I thank God every day for Johanna. She made my life complete.'

'Mine too,' Hayley said, thinking about what a privilege it

was to have Johanna come into her life now. The two women hugged and then pulled away from each other as the door to the church opened.

Johanna and Callum came out, the sun shining down on them as they were covered in the pink and purple confetti. Alice threw hers high up into the air, laughing, and missing the bride and groom entirely, so it fell into her own hair and at her feet. Hayley grinned, and grasped Alice's hand, unable to take her eyes off Johanna, her beautiful, confident daughter.

A LETTER FROM RUTH

Dear Reader,

I want to say a huge thank you for choosing to read *The Nanny*. If you enjoyed it, and want to keep up to date with all my latest releases, just sign up at the following link. Your email address will never be shared and you can unsubscribe at any time.

www.bookouture.com/ruth-heald

This book was inspired by the Louise Woodward case, which was prominent in the press in the late 1990s. The case made me wonder what it would be like to be a teenager with little experience of the world, looking after a baby in a foreign country. There's a huge power imbalance between an au pair or nanny and her employers, and I wanted to write a work of fiction that explored that. At the same time, I was interested in how mistakes at a young age can have repercussions that ripple through the rest of someone's life. The course of Hayley's life changes after Chloe dies. She ends up staying in Thailand because she can't face going home. Her shame about her role in Chloe's death and her pregnancy prevents her from asking for support from friends and family and therefore she loses Johanna for many years. And yet, even when Johanna comes into her life, she is trapped, unable to form a relationship with her without reconnecting with her past and therefore her guilt.

Hayley is forever altered by what happened, and is, as a

result, an anxious mother. She has blocked out the past until it comes back to haunt her through both Johanna and Ryan. But for Hayley to redeem herself she had to nearly lose Alice, confront the past, and then lose Johanna. Only once she's truly faced up to what happened is she able to re-establish her longed-for relationship with Johanna.

I really enjoyed writing this book and exploring these themes, and I hope you have enjoyed reading it. If you have, then I would love to see your review on Amazon. Reviews really help authors to sell books and help readers discover new authors. And it's brilliant to hear what you think too!

If you want to follow me on social media, you can use the links below.

Thanks so much for reading!

Ruth

www.ruthheald.com

facebook.com/rjhealdauthor

twitter.com/RJ_Heald

ACKNOWLEDGEMENTS

Firstly, thanks to my husband, who was the first reader of this book. His support and encouragement were invaluable, as always. Thank you to my children, who bring me so much happiness and fun.

Many people have contributed to this book, in big and small ways. Thanks to my editor Laura Deacon, whose exceptional editorial instinct has helped me to wrangle the book into the final version. My beta readers, Charity Davies and Ruth Jones, have, as always, provided helpful and insightful feedback. I'm also grateful to friends in the police, who helped me with details on how the police would handle the missing persons investigation and the historic crime in Thailand. Thank you to my copy editor, Liz Hatherall, and proofreader, Jenny Page, who have helped me refine the book.

I'm very grateful to be published by the first-class team at Bookouture, who always work hard to make my books the best they can be and give them the best possible chance of reaching readers. Thanks to the publicity team, the production team, the audio team, the insights team, the finance team and the rights team and, of course, the leadership team. Thanks to my cover designer, Lisa Horton, and my audio narrator, Katie Villa.

Finally, but most importantly, thank you to my readers. It's wonderful to know you're out there, reading and enjoying my books.

Printed in Great Britain
by Amazon

86224494R00189